T0193905

STREET MONEY:

Never Trumped Over

STACKS

authorHOUSE®

AuthorHouse™
1663 Liberty Drive
Bloomington, IN 47403
www.authorhouse.com
Phone: 1 (800) 839-8640

Published by AuthorHouse 05/01/2020

ISBN: 978-1-7283-1233-0 (sc)
ISBN: 978-1-7283-1232-3 (e)

Library of Congress Control Number: 2019942688

Print information available on the last page.

Any people depicted in stock imagery provided by Getty Images are models, and such images are being used for illustrative purposes only.
Certain stock imagery © Getty Images.

This book is printed on acid-free paper.

Because of the dynamic nature of the Internet, any web addresses or links contained in this book may have changed since publication and may no longer be valid. The views expressed in this work are solely those of the author and do not necessarily reflect the views of the publisher, and the publisher hereby disclaims any responsibility for them.

CHAPTER I

"**P**ut your hands up fuck nigga!" Jay'sean yelled pointing the .40 caliber at the store owners head.

"Oh my God!" The old man screamed looking at the big gun.

"Shut the fuck up, and get yo ass over here!" He yelled, grabbing the old man by the collar pulling him away from the register.

"A brah empty that shit out." Jay yelled to Bobo.

Bobo jumped across the counter and started emptying the register.

"Don't move old man! I don't want to have to kill a senior citizen!"

"Ok t-take what you want p-please don't kill me." He said stuttering and shaking.

"Where the safe at motherfucker!"

"It's in the back y-you can have the money, just p-please don't-"

"Shut the fuck up nobody ain't bout to kill your old ass!" Jay said cutting him off and pushing him to the back of the store where the office and safe was located.

"Alright, now worry about me killing your ass! If it take you too long to open the safe and put the money in the bag, I'ma put two in your head! Jay said throwing the duffle bag at him.

"O o-k, please don't kill me I got grandkids."

"Man I don't give a fuck about your personal life, fuck all that! If you don't hurry up and open that safe and put the money in the bag, I'ma shoot your ass for moving too slow!"

Even though his old hands were shaking, he made sure he lined every number up right causing the safe to pop open. He pulled the stacks of money out the safe and placed each stack inside the duffle bag.

After he finished, Jay'sean snatched the bag out of his hands. "Give me my shit! You keep your old ass right here and don't come out for 3 minutes! If you do, I'ma shoot your ass in the face!"

Jay'sean and Bobo ran out the store and hopped in the stolen car where Kev was waiting on them. They jumped in as he sped off from the scene. When they got back to Jay's spot and split up the $14,200 between the three of them, they went their separate ways.

That was 3 years ago and Jay'sean Moss was just being released from Ridgeland Correctional Institution. How he got to this point was simple, fucking with some fake ass niggas.

Before he met Kev and Bobo he was straight, being on his own since he was 16 years old. He was renting out a single wide trailer, running a small drug operation slanging crack and weed out of the spot, him and his partner Roc in Beaufort, South Carolina.

The reason he got his own spot so young was because he felt he was already grown and kept bumping heads with his mama's boyfriends. So, he got his own spot putting the lease in his mama's name.

Despite how young he was Jay had jumped off the porch and started getting his money up early and it only made it better that he was still attending high school. He had all the young females on his dick because he had his own car, own place and his own money. The lil nigga didn't need for shit at his age, he was bossed up.

When he turned 17 and was in the 12th grade doing good still, his life changed the day he met Kev and Bobo. Knowing they were some hot boys and stayed in some shit, didn't stop him from thinking they could make his pockets fatter. They would come through buying no less than a quarter pounds, of mid-grade weed each and every time they re-ed up from him. So he knew they were about they paper.

One day they came to Jay with a lick they had been plotting on. The store had no cameras and the owner was a old man. Jay thought it was a sweet lick just as well as them. Shit with the right planning it could be done. So, Jay did all the planning trying to make sure they hit the lick right and when it was all said and done that's the same shit his co-defendants told the police.

The only thing they had on Jay, was Bobo's fingerprints and their word against Jay's. This was all because when they locked Bobo up he snitched and when they picked Kev up he did the same shit. Both telling everything they know about Jay.

STREET MONEY

Jay's first plea was armed robbery 15 years violent. (Meaning he would have to serve 85% of the entire sentence.) Jay had read his motion of discovery and knew they didn't have a gun or his fingerprints and the store owner couldn't identify him because he had on a mask at the time the robbery took place. Even though he had done something so wrong, he started reading his Bible and turned to a higher power which was in Jesus. Finding out if he laid the battles of the worldly things in the Lord's hands, after repenting for his own sins and completely believed in his heart that God's Son died for all of our sins, he would lead him through anything of this world by Him. He had gave his life to the Father, so he definitely wasn't taking that deal at all. Jay felt that wasn't in God's plan to do all the time she was trying to offer. He had a personal relationship with God and felt the District Attorney was just trying to sucker him into taking the deal, testing him trying to scare him on the fact that if he went to trail he would receive 30 years for the violent charge.

After sitting in the county jail for 7 months without a bond they offered Jay a different plea so they could get a conviction out Jay. They offered him a plea for 5 years and dropped the charge from Armed Robbery to a Strong Arm Robbery, a non-violent charge (Meaning he would only have to serve 65%) of the entire sentence.

Knowing he would be out in a little over two more years, he took the plea to put the bullshit behind him not wanting to go to trial and get 30 years for wasting the courts time. He knew if he went to trial, both Kev and Bobo would come and testify against him and make him look like a monster. So he took the small amount of time they offered him and thanked God he didn't have to do 15 or better yet 30 years, because my nigga was going to go all the way if they didn't drop that shit down. But like that shit wasn't never in God's plan and you can't change God's plans.

But that was then and now it was time for Jay to be released and get back on his grind again.

CHAPTER 2

"Jay'sean! Oh thank God my son home, thank you Lord." Brenda, said running up to hug her son while crying.

"I missed you so much." She said.

"I missed you too mama." He said squeezing her tight.

"What's the first thing you want to do?" She asked stepping back wiping the tears from her eyes.

"The first thing I want to do is get some real food. I'm so sick of powdered eggs and watered down grits." They both busted out laughing.

They hopped in her car and went to a local Denny's a couple of miles up the road from the prison.

"Dang it smell good in here."

"Will you two be dining in or ordering to go?" The cashier asked.

"We'll be dining in."

"Ok there's a table open right over here." She said walking them to the open table.

"Your waitress will be with you shortly." She said passing them both menus.

"So what's been going on with my sisters? They doing good in school?" Jay asked about his two younger sisters. Courtney was 13 and Kayla was 17 years old.

"Huuu" Brenda took a deep breath not wanting to tell Jay about Kayla's actions since he had been locked up.

"Well Courtney has been doing good and keeping her grades up, but Kayla is the complete opposite."

"What you mean, she flunking or something?"

"No she not flunking, she passing.....barely, but this girl be skipping school, stealing my money and sneaking boys in my house Jay!" The school

4

said if she miss one more day, she going to have to repeat the 12ᵗʰ grade for unexcused absences.

"What, sneaking boys in your house!? She having sex!?" Jay yelled, causing the people in the restaurant to look over at them and be nosey.

"I don't know son."

He was pissed and knew the answer to that just as well as Brenda, but would deal with Kayla later. Right now he just wanted to enjoy his first day home and breakfast with his mom. He ended up ordering cheese grits, bacon with aside of toast and a glass of iced orange juice. While his mom ordered steak, eggs, cheese grits and a glass of milk.

They enjoyed their breakfast and caught up on all the things that had been going on since he was locked up. After they finished eating, they headed home.

Since Jay had been locked up his mom had moved to Savannah, GA. Even though it wasn't a very big city, he knew he would have to adapt to the city life period. He was a, "How they say it in the chain gang, country nigga" but he had the hustle of a Nation Wide Hustler. He could take that with him anywhere. No matter where he went or where he was, he was a real hustler and a real hustler can survive anywhere.

When they pulled up to the house Jay's Uncle Buck was on the grill and a bunch of people he didn't know where in the yard chilling.

"What's up nephew!? I know you glad you home nigga!"

"Hell yea nigga!" He said, giving him a hug.

"Watch your mouth, Jay'sean." His mother said, giving him a nasty look.

"My bad mama."

"You still drinking on those Hurricanes Unc?"

"Damn right nigga and I ain't gone stop either."

"Ha, ha, ha. Where my sisters at?"

"Courtney in the backyard playing and Kayla, I don't know where her fast ass at." Buck answered him.

Even though Buck was his uncle, they acted more like brothers. Jay was only 6 years younger than him. So, they basically grew up together but over the years they became distant taking different paths in life. Jay was a hustler and Buck was a bona fide drunk.

"What's been going on with you though Unc?"

"I've been chilling nephew, working and trying to survive in these streets."

"Fasho, but what happened with that robbery situation and how you got involved in some shit like that after you seen what I went through?"

"Nigga I don't know what them folks talking about, but I didn't have shit to do with that!" Buck had let some young niggas talk him into helping them rob some regular civilians downtown Savannah, GA. (Who the fuck robs somebody downtown? All them crackers got cards. A lame would know that. The shit just didn't make sense.) Now his dumb ass was out on bond awaiting the outcome.

"Unc come on man, you ain't gotta worry about lying to me. You better worry about the judge and the DA nigga, I was just trying to build with you nigga."

"Man I'm telling you I didn't do it, them folks got me fucked up with somebody else!"

"Aight, I was just asking you don't got to get all defensive and shit, I'm still on your side."

"Jaaay!" Courtney came around the side of the house yelling running towards her brother.

"Hi, lil mama!" He picked her up giving her a tight hug. "You missed me?"

"Yes." She said behind tears.

"Stop crying lil mama, I'm home now." Mama told me you've been doing good in school too. As soon as I get some money I'ma get you something nice. Aight?"

"Ok." She smiled and gave him a hug, then ran off to go play with her friends again.

"Unc you ain't got nothing to smoke on?"

"Here." He said trying to pass him a cigarette.

"Man you know I don't smoke cigarettes. I'm talking about some weed, trees, green nigga."

"Ha, ha, ha. Yea look in the armrest of that Roadmaster, it should be a blunt in there already rolled up."

"That's what I'm talking about!" Jay went and got the blunt and came back.

"Let me hold your lighter Unc."

"Damn nigga, you want me to smoke it for you too?"

"Man come on and stop playing, you know a nigga ain't got shit, this my first day out. Now give me the lighter so I can get my mind right."

Buck passed him the lighter laughing.

"I know one thing, we can't smoke that shit right here. Yo mama gone snap. Let's go in the cut." They walked in the ally and smoked on the mid-grade weed.

Even though Jay smoked weed his whole bid this was the highest he had been in a long time, because the joints he smoked while locked up were 10x smaller than the one he was smoking now.

After they finished smoking they were walking out the cut and a red Acura pulled up bumping its music loud. Kayla jumped out the passenger side wearing some coochie cutter shorts, a belly showing top and some high heels that made her walk bowlegged.

"Brother, you finally home!" She said striding to him as fast as she could in the heels, giving him a big hug when she reached him.

"Girl what the fuck you got on? You look like a hoochie!" He said mad, looking over her outfit.

"Whatever." She rolled her eyes brushing him off like she did everybody else.

"Ain't no whatever. Mama told me how you been acting out in school and sneaking niggas in the house and shit too!"

"Jay that was over 6 months ago and it hasn't happened again since. Also, I graduate school this year. I mean I was slacking at the beginning of the year because of the pressure of me being a senior, but I got myself back on track now. Plus I pulled my grades up."

"You better have or I was going to kick your ass myself," Jay said, trying to ease up. "Who is that girl you riding with though?"

"Oh that's my home girl Brittany." Kayla said, looking back at her friend.

"She got a nigga?"

"Yea, but she be cheating on that nigga. She ain't nothing but a freak. I just be using her for rides."

"Fasho." That was the words Jay wanted to hear "cheat & freak", he was ready to get some pussy and was sick of waiting even though he hadn't been out a whole 24 hours.

"What y'all about to do?"

"We about to go to the mall. You want to ride?"

"Yea, I need to buy a outfit and some shoes. Hold on though I got to see if mama going to give me the money now or later on." He walk in the house and asked his mama for the $200 she promised him.

"Look in my purse and get my Visa card. The pin is 4727 and don't spend over $200."

"Ok ma, I got you." He walked back outside and hopped in the car with Kayla and her friend.

"Brittany this is my brother Jay. Jay this my home girl Brittany."

"What's up lil mama?"

"Heey." She said seductively smiling.

"Girl your brother is sexy as hell. I knew he was cute from the pictures, but he look even better in person."

Jay leaned back in the seat, enjoying his high and the ride to the mall, knowing he would be sliding in between Brittany's thighs soon.

When they got to the mall, Jay let them walk in front of him while he trailed behind. He didn't want the females to think one of them was his girl.

"Damn Brittany ass fat as fuck. I can't wait to hit that." Jay said to hisself watching her ass bounce as she walked in front of him.

The whole walk through the mall all the two girls did was talk about other females, how bad their hair looked and how they dressed like bums.

Jay ended up buying a pair of Levis, some Jordan's and a fresh white t-shirt. After they walked through the whole mall they left and headed back towards his mama house. On the ride back Kayla let Jay ride in the front seat with Brittany, so he could spit his game and she wouldn't not be cock blocking.

"So how old are you Brittany?"

"I'm 18."

"Fasho. You still in high school?"

"No, I graduated last year."

"Oh ok that's what's up. You from Savannah?"

"Yep, born and raised, but I'm so sick of staying here though I want to move to N.Y. or a bigger city and try to pursue my modeling career."

"That's what's up you should pursue that. You're one of the most beautiful women I've ever met." He said, lying to her face.

Jay looked Brittany over again, she wasn't ugly but she damn sure wasn't model material. She had pimples all over her face, she needed braces and the only thing she really had going on was a fat ass. So, she was disqualified.

When they pulled to his house, she wrote her number down for Jay and dropped him and Kayla off at their mother's house.

Jay went in the house and fell asleep on the couch thinking about two things, money and pussy. But the money was before everything.

CHAPTER 3

*B*eing a convicted felon Jay knew it would be hard finding a job, but it was worse than he thought. He ended up working for the labor company two miles away from his house. They mostly had crackheads and convicted felons working there, his uncle had told him about the spot.

For the last two weeks he had been working for $7.25 an hour making small money, slanging trash cans under the sun like a slave. After stacking a little money, he decided to call Brittany to take her out and try to get some pussy.

Ring, Ring, Ring. "Hello?" Brittany answered.

"What's up sexy?"

"Hi, what's up with you?"

"Nothing. I was trying to see if you wanted to go out to eat with me?"

"Of course. Where you taking me?"

"Don't worry about all, that just come pick me up in the next hour from my mama house."

"Ok." She answered smiling.

A hour and a half later she pulled up sporting a stolen skin tight Tom Ford dress, some heels and fake jewelry.

"What's up sexy? Damn you look good, turn around and let a nigga see you?" Jay said turning her around over looking at her seductive body.

"You like it?" She said turning around in a circle.

"Hell yea come show me some love." He hugged her smelling her Chanel perfume, squeezing on her plump ass.

"Um umm. Who told you, you could squeeze my ass?" She said playfully.

"Girl sooner or later that's gone be my ass."

"Whatever nigga." They both started laughing.

They hoped in the car and Jay told her to drive to Applebee's on the south side.

As they sat down enjoying themselves and talking about what they wanted out of life. Jay was actually bored by the whole conversation, he was just playing his position. All Brittany kept talking about was, model this model that, when she was nothing but a hoodrat. He couldn't wait until the dinner was over so they could go to a room, pop open a bottle and he could get some head while getting blunted.

"That's what's up lil mama, I know you going to kill the model industry once you put your foot through the door." He said rubbing on her thigh, lying.

"You think so?"

"Hell yea. Look at how beautiful you are and how your smile compliments the shape of your face baby. You're so beautiful."

"Thank you." She said smiling from ear to ear.

"You about ready to go?" Jay asked trying to get the party started.

"Yea, I'm full."

"Waitress, over here! Can I get two to go plates?"

"Sure." She responded. "A couple of minutes later she came back with the plates." They packed their plates and got on the road.

"Where to go now?" Brittany asked.

"I'm about to go get a room, you coming in?"

"Why?" She said trying to act like she didn't know what was going on.

"I don't feel like being bothered by my people, plus I can smoke inside."

"Oh ok. What side of town you getting one on?"

"Take me to the Thunder Bird on Hwy 17."

"Ok." She agreed as she drove towards the cheap hotel.

When they pulled up to the hotel Jay got out, paid for the room and came back to the car.

"The room I'm in is in the back, room 412."

They drove to the room and Brittany put the car in park, leaving it running. Jay didn't feel like chasing the pussy but he needed to fuck something A.S.A.P, so he felt he had to.

"You coming in with me?"

"For what, what we about to do?"

"What you mean what we about to do, I told you I'm about to get lifted. Just come smoke with me before you dip, you don't have to stay long. I promise."

"Ok." She said cutting the car off.

Jay grabbed the bottle of Grey Goose and orange juice out the back seat he had placed in the backseat when she had picked him up and headed for the room with Brittany right behind him. They went in the room and rolled two blunts of Loud weed and put one in the air.

"Sup, sup, sup. I'll be right back." He said hitting the blunt then passing it to her.

"Where you going?"

"I'm about to go grab some ice right quick. Smoke until I come back. I'll be right back."

"Ok." She said pulling on the blunt too hard, causing her to choke. "Damn this shit strong."

"That ain't that mid shit you be smoking on lil mama, that's loud." He said walking out the door looking back at her. Her eyes were already chinky from the high grade weed.

"When he came back to the room, Brittany was watching Friday on BET laughing extra loud from the effect of the weed.

"Damn you barely saved a nigga a piece of the blunt." He said grabbing it from between her fingers.

"I'm sorry. You told me to smoke until you came back." She said smiling chinky eyed.

"I'm just fucking with you lil mama." He said pulling out two cups, filling them with ice, liquor and orange juice.

"Here you go." He said passing her a cup.

"I don't like to drink, because last time I did I threw up."

"You probably had too much last time, you have to respect the alcohol. Just sip on it and don't try to gulp it down like kool aid."

She took the small cup of liquor and started to sip on it.

"Umm this taste good. It didn't taste like this last time."

"That's because I put more orange juice in your cup than liquor."

"I like it." She said still drinking the liquor too fast.

Jay laughed while lighting another blunt of Loud.

After watching another 20 minutes of the movie, Brittany had almost finished her cup and Jay was on his second. Jay looked over at Brittany and placed his hand on her thigh rubbing on her leg.

"You good lil mama?" He said, continuing to rub on her.

"Yea I'm good." She said with slurred words.

He took the drink out her hand and placed it on the nightstand. Her eyes were super low and he and she knew, she was feeling the drink. Jay leaned over and kissed her on the neck.

"Ummm that feels good."

"I wanted to fuck you so bad from the first day I saw you, I knew I had to have you." He whispered in her ear while rubbing in between her thick thighs.

"Sssss, I wanted you too Jay."

"I knew this bitch was a freak she just needed a little Goose to get her loose." He thought to hisself.

He moved her panties to the side and moved his index and middle finger across her clit in a circular motion, then slid them both inside her wetness causing her to part her legs the more he played inside her.

"Ssss, oooh shit!" She moaned.

Jay used his other hand to push the dress up, causing it to rise up to her waist. He leaned in and tongue kissed her while still playing in her juice box.

"Ssss shit, you about to make me cum. Oh s-shit!" She moaned out loud.

Jay slid her panties down her legs, then stripped butt naked. Brittany laid back with her legs still cocked up in the air, watching Jay roll the condom down the length of his king size pipe, glancing over his tatted cut body, making her hotter than she already was. He got on top of her and pulled her breast out the top of her dress placing one inside his mouth while squeezing on the other one.

"Ssss ummm, stick it in Jay, give me that dick daddy."

He rubbed the head of his shaft on her clit, then entered her wet pussy.

"Oooh shit this pussy wet." He said sliding inside her taking long hard strokes touching her walls.

"Oh shit I'm about to c-cum, a-again, ssss ooooh!" She said getting ready to cum again.

He pushed her legs back farther, going in her as deep as he could. Cumming with her as she gyrated under him from the hard orgasm.

"Oooh shit!" She said while shaking. After she finished shaking, she fell right to sleep. He had knocked the pussy out, literally. He slid out of her and fell asleep beside her.

For the next two weeks he had been working and fucking Brittany almost every day...

"Oooh babe I want these ones right here." She had been bugging Jay for the last week, to buy her the new Jordan's.

"Damn $160? They higher than a motherfucker."

"Please daddy, you said you would get them for me." She said pointing looking sad.

Jay knew sooner or later he was going to have to find another hustle other than working, because between fucking in hotels every other night, buying himself clothes and buying Brittany shit, he was sure he would be broke soon.

"Can I get a size 4 in these please?" Jay asked the salesman.

"Yes sir." The shoe salesman said going to get the shoes.

"Thank you baby!" She said hugging him.

After he paid for the shoes they walked out of Foot Locker hand in hand smiling.

"Brittany, Brittany! I know your ass hear me, don't make me beat your ass in this mall!"

They both turned around and faced the nigga that was disrespecting her.

"Oh my God!" Brittany said looking scared.

"Bra who the fuck you taking too!?"

"I'm talking to my bitch! Is there a problem?"

Jay looked at Brittany, she looked like she was about to piss on herself.

"Oh this your bitch? I thought this was my bitch. I just got through fucking her and buying her some shoes, but you can have her homie ain't no need to be beefing over no hoe."

Buddy stood there pissed as Jay walked off, but not wanting to check Jay because it was his bitch that said she was going to her mom's house. So, he grabbed a handful of Brittany's hair and dragged her out of the mall, slapping her up in the parking lot.

Brittany had been blowing Jay up. So, he blocked her and got back to his main goal. The money. He didn't have time to be arguing over no bitch that wasn't even his and he was only bringing in $210 a week putting in 35 hours every week busting his ass for small money by pushing trash cans. He knew the job wasn't shit, but it was all he had.......................................

STREET MONEY

Jay walked into the labor company and waited for his name to be called to go to a job site. A hour had passed and his name still had not been called, so he walked up to the desk with a slight attitude.

"Mr. Timmy, how are you doing? Um, I was wondering why my name hasn't been called yet?"

The dispatcher for workers looked at Jay like he was nothing, and went back to what he was doing, but still answering him.

"I sent someone else on your job."

"What the fuck you mean you sent someone else?"

"I mean its Friday and you already have 34 hours. If I send you out more than likely you will go into overtime."

"So what?"

Mr. Timmy looked up from what he was doing. "That means the company I work for doesn't like or want to pay overtime, when we can save money by just sending another worker with less hours on the job. That's why."

Jay was now beyond pissed off.

"Look here you little four eyed mother fucker, I know how to fucking add and subtract! I ain't one of these crackheads or drunks that come in here and work for your bull shit ass company giving you half ass work! I give y'all motherfuckers good quality work, so you can have this punk ass safety vest because if I keep this job I'ma end up beating yo ass!"

Jay threw the vest in his face and walked out the door. When he walked out he saw D smoking a cigarette.

D was from New York. Him and Jay never really talked because D was always on some, stay to hisself type shit.

D looked over at Jay. "What's good son?"

"Ain't shit good, I'm sick of these crackers making money off me working and then don't pay a nigga nothing but minimum wage a-"

"Whoa slow down, I didn't ask for your life story son. I was just seeing if you was straight, you tight as hell right now son." D said cutting him off.

"You want a port B?"

"I don't smoke cigarettes my nigga."

"Shit, what you smoke, I got that pressure too." D said referring to Loud weed.

"Well roll up then nigga, because all I smoke is pressure."

"Word I got you, let's hop in my whip."

They got in D's Dodge Intrepid with chromed out 22" inch rims. D unlocked the glove box and pulled out a small black bag. Once he unzipped it Jay knew it was some good weed.

"Damn that shit stank so good." They both busted out laughing.

"Y'all down south niggas funny son." D said out loud.

As D broke down the Loud weed and proceeded to roll up, Jay did what came best to him he started talking numbers.

"So, what's the ticket on one of them zips if you got it homie?"

D hit the blunt and passed it to Jay, as he exhaled he said, "$300."

Jay looked at him as he inhaled and said, "That's a little too high for me brah."

"I usually get one for $250 & two or better for $450 a piece." Jay said lying.

D was really testing Jay, seeing where his head was at. His connect in New York was sending him a pound of loud weed and half a brick of coke in the mail whenever he made the call and he had been trying to find someone he could trust to help him move some more weight. But from the looks of it, Jay might be the nigga he had been looking for just off their initial conversation. He got a vibe from the conversation he was having with Jay, real recognizing real. By the time they finished talking numbers, Jay went and cashed his check, grabbed some money from his house and grabbed two ounces at $450 and a third fronted to him by D for $250. D wanted to keep Jay on his team and Jay was thinking the same thing.

After that day Jay took off with the sales and started building his clientele up. Within a week Jay paid D his $250 back and within the third week he was ready to re-up again, but he realized that the sales on the Loud pack was nothing like the crack game. He had only profited $600 in a three week span, that's because he smoked some of it, sold eighths for $35-45 and quarters for $70-85. But it still added up because he continued to work at different labor companies, selling weed to the workers until he could build his clientele up and not have to work all together.

CHAPTER 4

Jay was always a hustler, through middle school he used steal his mama's food stamp card to buy candy and sold it to his classmates. When he was 14 he had to get a tooth pulled and was prescribed pain pills, he ended up selling them to some white boys.

That was when he sold his first narcotic. He was always a hustler from day one, so he knew how to adapt, he just had to readapt to the streets after being locked up for 3 years. Even though he had only been home for 3 months he wanted more for hisself.

Jay had just met with D to pick up another 4 ounces. On his way back home he stopped at BP on the East side to get some gas. After he had paid for the gas he was walking out and she caught his eyes and everybody else's that looked her way. Jay being the smooth fast acting nigga he was held the door open for her.

"Let me get that for you lil mama." He said to her.

"Thank you." The dime said smiling.

When she walked in her ass caught his dick's attention. Jay went and placed the pump in the gas tank. The same thing he was thinking about doing to this bad bitch, putting his pump in her tank. Jay looked around to see if he could see what she was driving. It was no doubt in his mind that it was the pink Honda with the 20's and Candi printed on the front glass. Bad bitches like herself always make their presence known.

When she walked back to her car and started to pump her gas Jay approached her.

"Excuse me Ms. Lady, I would like to introduce myself. My name is Jay'sean."

"My name is Candi." She said smiling.

She was 5'4, high yellow, light brown eyes, with full lips like Rihanna and a round ass that jiggled with every move she made. Her breast were B cups, but everything else made up for the lack.

"Nice to meet you Candi, how old are you?"

"I'm 21, but I can't talk to you."

"Why, do you have a man or something?"

"Yes I have a man, but that's not the reason I'm refusing to talk to you."

Jay leaned his head to the side in confusion. "So what is it?"

"I don't think you have enough money to meet my standards."

"Damn lil mama I like you already, you straight to the point like that. Well I'ma tell you like this, I'm not from Savannah, but I'm all about my money." He said laughing. "Maybe you can show me around and put me on game. So, I can see what I'm doing wrong out here. I was looking into investing some money into something else anyways."

"What do you do for a living?" Jay asked.

"I dance." Candi responded.

From her saying that Jay knew off rip that she was a stripper.

"What is that you do?" She asked.

"I work in pharmaceuticals."

Candi knew Jay was trying to be smart. "You don't look like you work at CVS or Walgreens."

Jay Laughed.

"Look lil mama just let me buy you lunch and if you think we might be useful to each other we can go from there. If not we can call it a day and go our separate ways. Is that cool?"

Candi was skeptical at first, she knew her time was like money, but ended up agreeing only because she was hungry anyways.

"Ok." She responded.

"Park your car and get in with me." Jay said.

"Hell nawl, how about I follow you, I just don't jump in niggas cars. I just meet you, you might try to kidnap me or something."

Jay didn't like, not being in control but said fuck it and agreed with her.

"Just follow behind me then." He said.

"Where are we going?" She asked.

"To eat, just follow me lil mama and stop being so overprotective."

"Whatever nigga, I'm being careful fuck overprotective." She said not caring what he was saying.

They pulled off and in the next ten minutes, they were pulling into the Long Horn parking lot off of Abercorn Street. Jay knew Candi wasn't no Burger King hoe, so he figured this was a good spot.

As they were seated to a table and proceeded to order their food Candi and Jay started to build.

"So what is it you think you can possibly help me with?" Candi asked.

Jay looked up from the appetizer nachos he was eating. "Well I'm a people's person and I read everybody I talk to. I mean I can't read minds or no shit like that, but I can read a person and deal with anybody on any kind of level."

"Oh yea, Candi said while laughing." So tell me how that's going to help me again?

"Ok, Ms. Straight to the point. From me talking to you in the 5 minutes we did talk I know you're about your paper, you dance at a club, your nigga or friend must not be holding his weight, you know you deserve more and if this conversation wasn't about money, shit your ass wouldn't even be here. Even though I am paying for lunch."

Candi was impressed, she took a long sip from her margarita and did more listening now then talking. She had underestimated Jay because of his baby face, but now wanted to pick his brain to see what he had in mind.

"Ok Mr. Pharmaceutical, go ahead then." She said attentively.

Jay's brain went to work. "Well my partner from Beaufort, South Carolina owns a small club up there and with you being as sexy as you are and a couple of other girls, with my promotions we can get this paper lil mama. Plus we can do this on your time."

"How much you talking?" Candi asked.

"I don't know, what you asking for? Plus this the country you got to think, them niggas ain't used to seeing girls as sexy as you, you going to make out good."

Candi knew Jay was right, but she wasn't slow. "I want $150 for an entry fee and I can bring two other girls at $25 a piece."

Jay thought for a minute and knew he would get his money back off the weed and door sales, only thing he had to do was call his partner Roc and put everything in motion.

"Ok lil mama, on what day you want to do this?"

"I'm free on Thursdays."

"Fasho. So, next month the first Thursday you'll be ready to start dancing then? No bull shit?"

"Yea, but like I said I won't leave Savannah without $200 in my hand."

"Ha, ha, ha, that won't be a problem lil mama."

As they ate Candi told Jay about the kind of drugs her girls liked, and how to promote the parties in different ways, so everybody could profit.

As he walked Candi to her car he couldn't help but look at her ass, with the tights cuffed under each cheek bouncing like two water balloons with each step. They exchanged numbers and they both left the parking lot with one thing on their minds, making money.

CHAPTER 5

D had just received a text from Nikki telling him that he had mail. D was smart and didn't talk over the phone about his business, just text messages and all his phones were throw away phones.

Nikki had been with D for 10 months. She worked as a manager at Publix, everybody said she looks like Megan Good, but she was much thicker. Her 5'6 thick frame double D breasts and a ass you could see by her hips, even if you were looking at her from the front.

"Hi baby I missed you so much." She said hugging and kissing D as he walked in the house.

"I missed you too baby. Where that package at?"

"That's the first thing you want to do when you come home, is check a fuckin package!? Do you even see what I got on?"

D was always cool, calm and collect but he didn't realize Nikki had on a red see through Victoria Secret bra and panty set with a matching vest. His dick got hard instantly, Nikki turned around to walk off while he looked at her ass as it swallowed the line of the thong between her cheeks making only the top of the pantie line visible.

D grabbed her arm, "Come here beautiful." He kissed on her neck and talked in her ear. "You know I miss you baby you so damn fine and you all mine. I promise just give me 5 minutes just to make sure shit right and I'ma take care of that ass. Ok?"

Nikki was now weak and her pussy was thumping.

"K, daddy." She responded.

She turned to walk in the room and D slapped her on the ass, causing her cheeks to push each other and shaking. D walked in Nikki's spare room and opened his package. He first weighed up the pound of Loud weed, not even a gram was missing. He then weighed the 2.2 pounds of

21

coke on the scale, everything weighed right. He then weighed a small bag of some shit his plug said was called Molly that was starting to hit the streets hard. Rappers like Future kept talking about it, but that didn't make him none, the only drug he did was smoke weed and he sold what he didn't smoke. If money could be made off it he was gone make it. 14 grams just like he had ordered. He placed the work in a black duffle bag and closed the door.

As D walked towards the master bedroom he could hear Trey Songz-Sex Ain't Better Than Love playing in the background. D opened the door and Nikki was laying on her back with her phone to her face scrollin' on Facebook. He took his shirt off and walked over to her.

"Put that phone down."

"No I'm mad at you." She was trying to play hard to get.

"So you mad at me?"

"Yep."

He put his hand between her thick thighs and rubbed on her inner thigh, "Come on baby don't be mad put that phone down."

"Nope." Nikki said while still looking at her iPhone.

D leaned down while still rubbing on her box, kissing her neck and then her breast.

Nikki's legs started to part, but she kept the phone up to her eyes still. D knew she was acting out because her panties were starting to get wet, so he played along with her.

"Ok, baby keep your phone."

He proceeded to do him, placing kisses on her body pulling one breast out at a time placing kisses on each nipple. Nikki's nipples were pointing at attention. He then sucked each one leaving a ring of salvia on each nipple blowing on them. He proceeded to place kisses on her belly, all the way to her juice box. To his surprise she still held the phone up. D smiled and separated Nikki's legs further apart placing his head between them, sucking on her clit through her panties squeezing her other breast.

"Sssss...Oooh baby." Nikki said while slamming the phone on the bed gripping the sheets instead.

D moved her thong to the side and placed his index finger inside her wetness while still sucking on her clit. Nikki placed her hands on the back of his head, while arching her back.

"Oooh daddy please don't stop." She said while rotating her hips in a circular motion.

He then placed another finger inside here and stopped sucking on her clit just to look at her juices roll down her butt cheeks.

"Damn baby I can't wait to slide inside of you." He said to her.

"Come on baby, I'm ready." She said looking down at him.

D kicked off his shoes and pulled down his boxers and his pants in one swift motion, revealing his erect 9 inch erect penis. Nikki still got excited every time she saw how long and fat, D's dick was as if every time was their first time. As he climbed on top of her, their lips locked. He rubbed his hard dick back and forth over her wet pussy, until she begged him to stick it in. He placed the first 4 ½ inches in and she twitched for adjustment.

"Sssss, slow baby." Nikki, said while placing her hand on his chest.

D pulled out and went back in, this time slowly placing 9 inches inside of her. When he pulled back out it looked like he spilled ice cream down the shaft of his penis. He stroked her 3 more times before placing both her legs under his forearms. As he started to take faster and longer strokes for the next 30 min.

D was now sweating.

"Oooh shit baby I can't hold it no more I'm about to cum!" D yelled out.

Nikki didn't mind she had came 3 times already and it felt like his dick was in her stomach. But it still felt good having his hot long dick inside her. D took two more long strokes, on the last one forcing his whole 9 inches inside her hard and fast holding himself inside her causing her to scream as he released hisself inside of her making her cum again.

He went limp and rolled over. Nikki laid there for a few minutes then got out of the bed and went to take a shower. When she came back she laid on him placing kisses on his chest.

"Bae why do you keep cumming inside of me? You know, I'm off the shot because it was making me too fat."

"Because I want you to have my baby."

Nikki was smiling from ear to ear. "Really I thought you was just doing it because it felt too good to pull out."

D laughed, "That too baby."

Nikki sat up. "So when was you going to ask me? How you know I want to have your baby? You don't even stay here nigga."

D laughed, "Nikki will you have our baby and will you move in with me?"

Nikki frowned, "Why I got to move in with you?"

"So I guess that a yes on the baby part and you not going to want to keep walking up and down these apartment steps, you going to be too fat."

Nikki laughed, as she hit D with a pillow.

A hour later D's phone vibrated as he received a text from Jay, "You straight on everything brah?"

He knew off top that Jay was trying to re-up.

D text him back, "Meet me at the spot." Meaning a local Chevron on the East side they had been meeting at for a couple of weeks. D put on his clothes and kissed Nikki on the forehead. She was knocked out from the lovemaking. He went in the spare room grabbed the black bag and his .45 off the table and walked out the house.

On his ride to the gas station a lot was going through D's mind. Since he had been in Savannah he had been fuckin with Nikki and the reason he fell for her is because she had her own everything, she was independent and wasn't greedy. Now that he had fell in love with her, he needed someone else that was trustworthy to hold his packages and not his girl. Last thing he wanted was his girl getting caught with all that dope. So, he knew he had some figuring out to do. He also wondered how Jay was ready for another full package after only one week.

As he pulled up in the parking lot he saw Jays blue Crown Vic parked on the side. He pulled up beside him and Jay hopped in.

"What's good, son?"

"What's up with you my nigga? Jay said smiling giving D dap."

"Shit, what you need?"

"I need 1 of them thangs." Jay responded, meaning a pound of Loud.

Before D reached in the back and grabbed the duffle bag, he had to ask Jay, "Man how you moving them zips so fast and you just jumped out here?" He didn't think he was snitching or no shit but he had to make sure.

Jay smiled, "I'm a hustler my nigga. I fuck with white people, black people, college students, bus drivers, shit wherever the money need to be made I'm there my nigga.

D looked at Jay and smiled, "Word, word." He could tell Jay wasn't lying.

STREET MONEY

It was hard for D to read Jay. Jay had spent 3 years in prison, but nobody would be able to tell if he didn't tell them, it didn't even look like he had been to the county jail before.

Jay was 5'9 160 pounds dark brown skin, with an athletic build and deep waves from brushing his hair daily while he was locked up. He also had prison tattoos that you could only see when his shirt was off. Some people say he looked like a thugged out Trey Songz. He was a pretty boy, but a gangster first with a mean hustle. His looks, talk game and swag only attracted more customers his way.

D grabbed the pound and handed it to Jay to put in his own bag.

"Yo you heard of some shit called Molly before?" D asked him.

"Yea its pure ecstasy. That's what motherfuckers on now, they don't pop pills no more. A little stripper bitch I was talking to asked me if I could get some of that shit the other day."

"Well if you think you can get it off, here then." He threw Jay the small bag. That's 14 grams just bring me back $150.

Jay did a little math in his head and figured he would make at the least $130 in profit.

"Fasho. I'll get at you later big brah."

"Be careful out here in these streets to son. These little niggas hungry and don't want to work for they food, they'll rather try and take it." D said before Jay left.

"Yea, that's why I keep this on me like a night light, even during the day. You can't see it's on me, but that bitch on me at all times." Jay lifted his shirt revealing his .40 that was on his waist.

"Word, stay safe son."

They parted ways as Jay went to get on this grind and D did likewise.

CHAPTER 6

"**R**ing, ring, ring, hello?" Candi said as her friend Coco picked up the phone.

"What bitch?" Coco said answering back.

"Girl I got something to tell you."

"If it ain't about no money, bitch you ain't talkin bout shit." Coco said in a jokingly but serious manner.

"Well damn bitch! But anyways I met this nigga the other day-"

"And he got money?" Coco said interrupting her.

"Bitch if you'll shut the fuck up and let me finish damn. Dude got a friend with a club in Beaufort, South Carolina and they looking for a couple of girls to come up there and dance on Thursdays. You down?"

"That's 45 minutes away and how much they paying?"

"Bitch they tipping, that's how much, and we got a ride there and back."

"I don't know about this Candi, how you know they got money? You been down there yet?"

"What's up with all these questions, you think I would be going if we wasn't going to get paid? Be for real now, this is me we talking about."

"You right, you right well shit I'm down."

"Don't stand me up bitch."

"Whatever bye bitch!" Coco said as she hung up happily about the new job.

Candi was happy too, if it was some bullshit she would still be getting her $200 off top just for appearing. She just had to make one more call, to Beautiful, which would be way easier than it was convincing Coco. She had to admit Beautiful was a very pretty girl, but dropping out of school in the

8th grade was her worst mistake in life. She was slow and easy to persuade at all times. She scrolled her call log and called Beautiful's number.

"Ring, ring, ring, Hey bitch!?" Candi said when she picked up.

"What's up? We work today?"

"Bitch today Wednesday. We work Fridays and Saturdays, stay off the Molly bitch!"

"Oh, ha, ha, ha, I thought it was Saturday."

Candi looked at her phone pissed. "Bitch did we work yester-, you know what I'ma leave that alone." She said cutting herself off before she got started. "I got some money for us to make though, you down or what?"

"Hell yea!"

Just like that it was a done deal. Candi went to the kitchen to fix her a victory drink, when her man walked through the front door.

"Hey baby." Candi kissed him and gave him a hug.

John shook his head, "They cut my hours again."

Candi went back in the cabinet and got a second glass for her man. "What, again? John you need to find another job."

John felt like less of a man, Candi had been paying most of the bills for the last 3 years while John went to school for law and worked a minimum wage job as a security officer bringing in $125 a week. He got refund checks from school but those went to his car payments and behind bill payments.

"I know baby but you have to look at the bright side of it. I have less than a year left in school, then I will be a police officer." John responded.

"Man John to be honest, I don't know why you didn't pick another career that offered more money, with the same amount of college time bae? When you become a police officer they don't make no real money, so you won't be making no real money."

"Because this has been my dream since I was a child. I love you and it will get better baby, once I start my career I can start getting raises and benefits." He said, kissing her shoulder.

Candi agreed with what he was saying, but felt like things would never change even after he got his job as an officer.

Candi and John had been dating since high school. In high school Candice was on the step team and a cheerleader, so dancing came natural to her. Soon as they finished high school her and John decided to move in with each other and both got jobs while attending college.

That's when they both realized paying bills wasn't as easy as their parents made it look while they went through grade school.

So it was John's idea for Candice to start dancing until he finished school, which he now hated himself for even mentioning the idea.

Candi was becoming irritated and felt everything was on her. She loved John, but was starting to feel like she was falling out of l love with him and what they had was just teenage love..............................

Jay was getting dressed to go out. He had talked to Roc about bringing the girls to his club and the percentage he would get off the door sales, everything was a go. He also had a new play, a little rich white boy that was grabbing an ounce of Loud for $500 and two grams of Molly at $25 a piece. He had already got rid of a 2 ounce throughout the day, gram for gram making a healthy profit just off selling grams. Profiting over $500 throughout just that one day and it was Friday. He felt like spending some money. He put on some Gucci cologne and headed out the door.

He stopped at a local car wash on Montgomery St. to let the best detail artist he had ever seen clean his car, "Crackhead P."

"What up P?"

"Hi, Jay! Big money Jay! J-Smooth! You got a tip for me my nigga?"

"Yea nigga hurry up, I got somewhere to be in 30 minutes."

In the next 20 minutes P had Jay's car looking brand new, in and out.

"My nigga! Boy you one cleaning motherfucker." Jay said to P.

"You paid inside yet." He said wiping the front glass.

"Man you know I paid them Indians they money, get yo dirty ass out the way nigga."

"Wait m-my tip?"

Jay gave P his usual $10 tip, and headed to Club Karma.

Before going in he rolled up five Loud blunts and bagged up ten 1/2 gram bags weed and .8 bags of Molly so he could profit some more money while he was in the club.

As he bagged up the .8 gram bags of Molly he said to his self, "Niggas be happy just to get high anyways they ain't worried about this little .2 I'm capping on." But Jay knew by him doing this it would end up putting a couple of extra $100 in his pockets. Jay was at the club early, but he knew what he was doing. Even though he came to party and spend some money, he still could make what he spent back by hustling in the club while partying.

Jay walked to the bar and ordered $100 in ones and a peach Cîroc with Red Bull. When he turned on his stool he could tell some of the stripper bitches was staring at him, but he didn't give them any eye contact to let them know he knew.

Coco tapped Candi, "I see money at the bar bitch."

Candi did a quick glance without making herself noticeable.

"I see him too, he look familiar."

"From where? I ain't never seen him in here."

"No from somewhere else. I can't remember."

"Well let's go find out bitch, that nigga Michael Kors watch got me in a trance."

"You so damn crazy come on." Candi said walking with her friend towards the bar.

As they got closer Candi started to realize who he was with his waves, dark brown eyes and handsome smile, it was Jay.

Jay saw Candi coming from the corner of his eyes. She looked better half naked then with clothes on. He could really see how fat her ass was and her dark skinned friend she was walking with was even thicker than her, but not near as pretty as Candi.

"What's up Jay?" Candi said over the music.

Jay tried to act like he didn't know her at first, "Oooh what's good with you lil mama?"

"Working, what brought you here tonight?"

"Um-uum!" Coco said clearing her throat.

"Oh my bad, this is my friend Coco. She's supposed to be coming with us next Thursday. We are still on right?"

"Fasho lil mama everything still a go. How you doing Ms. Coco?"

"Fine." Coco said smiling and blushing.

"Both of y'all two beautiful women. Y'all going to make a lot of money up in the country, no lie."

Coco liked Jay's swag just off his introduction, he was talking about money. She had to test him.

"You want a dance?" She asked while turning around revealing her fat ass with a butterfly wing tattooed on both cheeks, as she started to make them clap making it look as though the butterfly was about to fly away.

Jay smiled. "I like that, I tell you what I'ma throw some money but I need y'all to help me get off this Molly and Loud."

"Ooh you got Molly!" Coco said in excitement.

Candi looked at her girl and rolled her eyes, displeased with her reaction to the drug.

"Ok we got you nigga, so start making it rain. She could care less about the Molly she wanted the money. Jay pulled the stack of ones out his pocket and proceeded to make it rain on Coco and Candi placing some of the ones in both of their panties while they bounced their ass in front of him. He was enjoying the show and felt his dick getting hard from the ass bouncing and imaging his dick inside each one of them. Jay wasn't into dark girls, but Coco was built and looked a lot like Kalenna off Love and Hip Hop Atlanta.

After throwing about $80 dollars of the ones on them Jay pocketed the rest of the money and the girls went back to work on the their tricks for the night, but in no more than 10 minutes later Coco came back.

"Let me get $25 worth of Molly." She asked Jay.

"Fasho, meet me at the bathroom." He told her because the club still was kind of dry, it was still early for a strip club.

Jay gave Coco the small bag of Molly.

"This better be some good shit too." Coco she said giving him a twenty and five dollar bill.

"Whatever, everything I do is good." Jay said as he grabbed the money and walked off.

Jay walked back toward the corner of the club and lit some of the Loud up as the club started to get packed. While he was smoking, three people walked up asking Jay to sell them some of the weed he was smoking on. No later than the last person left Candi walked over to him.

"My people want a gram of Molly and a gram of Loud." She said over the loud music.

"Ok I got you. Tell 'em come over here though." The club was now packed enough to pull out his sack and serve in one spot, he was making a killing.

Throughout the night this was how it went. Jay had to go back to his car to bag up again, because he was booming so hard. It was 4:00 am when Jay decided to call it a night. Had had sold all of the Molly he had left, giving Coco the left over .8 bag for free because of her helping and sending money his way. He had also sold a half ounce of weed while he was there. Candi saw him walking towards the door so she made her way towards that way.

"You leaving? The club close in a little over a hour."

"Yea, I'm through for the night lil mama."

"Ok, well keep in touch, Jay." She was about to walk off and he grabbed her.

"Come here." He reached in his pocket and pulled out four $20 bills, and handed them to her.

"What's this for?" Candi asked confused.

"For you being you?" Jay smiled and walked out the club.

Candi didn't do Molly and she hadn't smoked any weed in a week, she was a sometime smoker. So what was it that was making her feel high? She then realized what it was. It was his swag, his hustle, his ambition, his looks, the way he walked, the way he moved. She was high off Jay and he hadn't even touched her.

CHAPTER 7

D woke up Sunday morning from a long Saturday night of drop offs and pickups. Nikki was sleep with the sheets over half of her naked body, revealing the top of her ass cheeks.

D slapped her ass hard.

"Ouch, what the fuck!?"

"Get yo ass up, and get ready for work." D replied.

"If you slap my ass like that again I'mma kick yo ass!"

"Yea, yea, yea, you wasn't saying all that last night nigga."

"Whatever, what time is it anyways?" Nikki asked yarning.

"Come take a shower with me and get yo lazy ass up, its 11 o'clock and do somethin bout that mouth." He said waving his has in front of his nose.

"Ok damn and nobody ain't tell you to be laying pipe all night, shit I'm tired."

They went and took a shower together and got dressed for the day. They left the house and both went to work. D looked down at his phone and had two text messages. One from Tweezy out of Yamacraw projects asking, "Had he seen his girlfriend Becky?" Meaning he wanted some white girl. The second text was from Jay saying, "He was about to run out of gas." Meaning he needed to re-up soon. He responded to Jay saying, "Give me 15 minutes on my way" and to Tweezy saying, "Give me 30 minutes, she was with me. I'm about to bring her home now."..

He met with Jay serving him 2 more pounds of Loud. Jay had also paid him for the 14 grams of Molly he had fronted him. He was impressed at how quick Jay moved whatever he grabbed or threw his way. Pretty soon he was going to have to start grabbing an extra 20 pounds a month just for Jay.

He left Jay and headed towards Yamacraw to meet Tweezy. The niggas out there were always on some bull shit. Shit they even called Yamacraw the Hell Hole. Even the people that stayed out there didn't want to stay out there. D drove towards the basketball court where he usually met Tweezy and texted him.

"Outside." D texted.

"Fasho." He texted back.

D felt like something wasn't right. A type of feeling only a hustler can feel when they feel something ain't right, but he wasn't about to let a feeling cause him to pass up on the $1,100 Tweezy was about to spend on the coke.

D backed up into a parking spot and laid his .45 on his lap. If anything went wrong he would be able to pull right out, bustin his gun.

Tweezy walked over to his car and got in.

"What's up, big brah?" Tweezy asked, already looking high out of his mind.

"What's up my nigga?" D said as he dapped him up.

"You got some of that Gorilla for me?"

"All I keep is the best B, you want to try it out?" D asked pulling out one of the ounces.

Tweezy took out a dollar bill scooped up a chunk of coke and bumped it hard.

"Suuf, suuf, damn that shit is good!" He said trying to clear out his nose.

"I told you that son. Now let's handle this business so I can dip B." He said looking over at him, as he played with his nose trying to get hisself together, not seeing the dread head approaching his driver side door.

"Tweezy started digging in every pocket he had. Damn big brah, I must have left the money in the house, hold up."

"Come on son you Od'in! I got shit to do."

As he talked shit, Tweezy hit the unlock button and D's door swung open. He reached for his strap but he was a half second too late. Tweezy already had his hand on the handle. He reached to put his hand on top of the pistol and dread head slapped him across the top of his left eye with his .9 mm.

"Augh fuck!" D screamed in pain putting both his hands over the deep bloody gash over the top of his eye.

"Shut the fuck up pussy nigga! Before I iron yo bitch ass up!"

"Man what the fuck Tweezy?"

Whap! The dread head hit him in the back of the head this time.

"Augh fuck!"

"Didn't I say shut the fuck up nigga!" The dread head yelled.

While holding his face he looked through the two hands full of blood and could see Tweezy looking in his glove compartment grabbing the stacks of money out then going in the back seat grabbing the black duffle bag containing 3 more ounces of coke and 2 pounds of Loud. When he finished raiding the car and was satisfied nothing else was in there he ran D's pockets, took the keys out the ignition, threw them across the lot and got out the car.

"Now get the fuck out my hood you ain't from here fuck nigga! You think you just goin to come to the Port and set up shop? You got us fucked up. Don't bring your ass back to the Craw or I ain't goin to spare yo lame ass next time!"

The dread head still was holding D at gunpoint until Tweezy came on the other side of the car holding D's gun. Then they both ran off.

D did his best to regroup, to regain his vision and keep from stumbling while looking for his keys. He finally spotted them, but it was two sets. His vision was blurred as fuck from the hard hits to the head and he was seeing two of everything. After trying to reach for both sets, he recovered the real ones and did his best to drive without making hisself seem like he was a drunk driver. D knew he wasn't going to be able to go to his house because he needed somebody to patch his gashes and Nikki was at work. He didn't want to go to the hospital because they would ask too many questions and call the police. So, he drove the best he could to his sister Tina's house.

Bang, bang, bang! He banged on Tina's front door hard. He knew she was home because she only worked the night shifts at the Chicken Plant and plus her car was in the front yard.

"Who the fuck banging on my shit like the pol-. Auuugh!"

"D what the fuck happened to you!?" She asked taken back about what she was about to say.

"I got robbed." D said, half passed out from losing blood.

"Oh shit, oh shit, oh shit. Sit down D!" Tina was running around the house going crazy. She came back with a towel, peroxided, oxycodone pain pills and some extra-large band aids. After she gave him the pills she guided him to the bathroom and went to work on his wounds.

"Yo, you might need stitches D." She said after working on his head the best she could.

The cuts were deep and his head was swollen. After she had finished D stripped out of his bloody shirt and laid on the couch.

Tina bring me some liquor. D couldn't believe these niggas had actually robbed him in broad day, bare faced.

After taking 6 straight shots of Patron, he started to doze off with thoughts of something other than money on his mind. He went to sleep with the thoughts of murder.……….................................

Nikki had just got off from a long day at work, she had been having a bad feeling all day. She had called D 3 times on her break and texted him 5 times. She could not figure out what was going on. Nikki knew she was his main, but also knew D was a hustler and could possibly have other bitches he fucked from time to time, she was no fool.

D was a 5'11 dark skinned, Morris Chestnut looking nigga with a big dick and muscles. But something wasn't right, he always responded to her text even if he didn't pick up the calls, he would at least text her back with "I'm working hit you right back." or "I'm busy call you right back baby." She knew her man.

Nikki didn't like D's sister Tina, but decided she would call her because of the feeling she was having.

Ring, ring, ring. "Hello?" Tina said after picking up.

"Hi how are you?" Nikki responded in a professional voice.

"That's why I can't stand this bitch, always acting like a white girl in prep school or some shit." Tina thought to herself.

"I'm good." Tina responded in a nonchalant tone.

"Have you heard from D? I haven't heard from him at all today and that's kind of wired?" Nikki said concerned.

"Yea come over to my house. He over here."

"Why, is everything ok? Why isn't he picking up my calls? What happened? Is he hurt? Is-"

"Hey, hey!" Tina said cutting her off. "He's over here and breathing, just come over damn!"

STACKS

Nikki must have did the whole dashboard because she was there in 5 minutes flat on a 15 minute drive. She worked on the South side and Tina stayed on the West side of town.

Nikki pulled up to the apartment and put her car in park before even stopping the car, then dashed to the door.

Bang, bang, bang, "It's Nikki!"

Tina opened the door and let her in. When Nikki walked through the door and saw D she didn't realize it was him at first because of the swelling of his head.

"Oh my God, D!" Nikki yelled while tears started to roll down her cheeks.

"Well hi to you too." Tina said being smart.

It wasn't the time, so Nikki brushed it off.

D woke up with the worst headache he ever had in his life.

"Hey baby." He said trying his best to smile.

"What ha-ha-happened." Nikki said trying to talk while crying.

"I got robbed, but I'm fine beautiful."

Nikki knelt down next to D and laid her head on his chest and cried until she fell asleep. She had two important things to tell D but decided to wait until another day, shit a better day than this one at least. What she had was good news that wasn't meant to be mixed with bad news...................................

Jay had been moving the pounds just as fast as he touched them, he was starting to see his money stack up and a few people had asked him for some coke. So he was ready to expand and invest into the coke game along with the rest of it. That could only mean more money. He had moved out of his mama's house and into an apartment. Putting on a front at the labor company working only 15 hours a week, catching plays while on the clock, was only helping Jay stack even more. He had about 25 stacks saved up and was going to re-up with about 8 stacks of that, but he had one problem. D hadn't been answering his text since he had seen him last Tuesday and it was now Thursday. Shit Jay was so thirsty he broke the rules and started to leave a voice mail.

He tried texting him once again. "Man what's up big brah you st raight?"...................................

D looked down at the phone. Jay had been blowing him up. He knew that he couldn't stall any longer or Jay would try to find another plug. Plus his package had arrived on Monday and he was itching to move some of the work, but he was having problems with his trust and pride from getting robbed. He knew he had to put his pride to the side and replace it with money.

"Them niggas goin to get what they deserve, let me get back on my shit." He thought to hisself.

"What's up son?" He texted Jay back.

"Man big brah, where you been at? I've been bumpin you for the last two days, you straight?" Jay texted.

"Yea B, I was out of town, I'm back now. Meet me at the spot." He texted.

"Fasho." Jay texted and headed towards the store.

When D pulled up to the gas station, Jay was already there. He parked beside him and Jay hopped in.

"What's up, big br-.......what the fuck happened to you, brah!?" Jay said, shocked looking at D's patched up eye and gash on the back of his head.

"Some niggas hit me for some Soft and Loud, but they gonna get what's coming son word is bond." D said, mad thinking about how shit went down.

"Then check this son, this shit happened in broad day no mask. Them niggas think they got nuts son!" D said hitting his hand to his fist.

"What!?" Jay said, angry.

"Man I don't know how hard you think I fuck with you, but you my nigga for real for real. I shouldn't have to tell you that. You help me eat my nigga, and I'm about my money and if a nigga fuckin with you, shit that's like a nigga fuckin with my paper."

"Word!" D said trying to gain his composer.

"So, who did this shit to you big brah?" Jay asked, waiting to see if he knew the fuck nigga they were about to ride on.

"A young boy out in Yamacraw projects son, go by Tweezy and he was with some dread head nigga." D explained.

"Tweezy? He got a chipped tooth?" Jay asked.

"Yea, you know the nigga?" D asked getting a little upset. Jay knew him.

"Yea, I know that fuck nigga brah. He got a fly ass mouth. Matter of fact I seen him at the club last Friday, acting like a million dollar nigga. Now I see why."

"Oh yea?" D asked easing up. "He be in there often?"

"I don't know, but I can find out from a lil bitch I know that work in there."

"Word, word, what club?"

"Club Karma, but for now let's handle this business. That nigga goin to get his issue and that's on me big brah."

"Tru, what you need though?"

"A 6 pounds of Loud, a ounce of Molly and what's the deal you can run me on a ounce of girl? I'm about to try to put my hands in and see what that be like." Jay said rubbing his hands together like Baby from Cash Money.

"Damn nigga you trying to take off, huh?" D asked smiling.

"I told you that when I first started this shit, nigga. What's the deal on the girl?"

"Just give me $1,300 son."

"Damn, why that bitch so high?"

"It ain't stepped on like that, it's about 78% pure coke, that's why. You can turn this 14 into 30 grams cooking up easy if you want to, no bull shit son. This ain't what they be having down here."

"Damn so what to cut it with, if I just got coke sales big brah?"

"I cut up with no dose, that's what I use." D said giving him dope knowledge.

Jay knew he wasn't lying, what for he had all the work.

"Fasho, let's do it." Jay said ready to do business.

They exchanged the drugs and money and went their separate ways. When Jay got on the road he called Candi to make sure she was still coming to the club along with the other girls..

"Ring, ring, ring, Hello?" Candi answered.

"What's up with you lil mama?"

"Nothing chilling, what's up with you?"

"I'm good I was just calling making sure we were still good for tonight?" Jay asked.

"Hell yea, as long as the money there I'm always there!"

"Ha, ha, ha, everything set for you lil mama." They both started laughing.

"Good what time we leaving then? Because those bitches don't have a car to meet up nowhere and we need to get there early to make sure they ready."

"What the fuck they do with their money, neither one of them got a car?"

"Drugs, outfits, more drugs, oh and sometimes bills and kids."

"Damn, well where you want to meet me at? I want to be gone by 10:30." Jay said, ready to get on the road sooner than later.

"Meet me at that gas station where we first met and I'll park my car out there."

"Fasho meet me there at 9:00 then." He responded.

"Ok I'll be there."

CHAPTER 8

*C*andi had just gotten out the shower and was lotioning her body when John walked through the door.

"Hi baby." Candi said, walking up kissing John.

John looked at her fat soft ass as she walked off.

"Damn baby you getting it ready for me, I need some so bad. You must have knew what I needed." John said, happily peeling off his clothes.

"Ha, ha, ha, nigga no I work tonight baby." She said still laughing.

His smile turned to a frown real quick.

"It's Thursday, you don't work on Thursdays."

"I do now since your hours got cut, we need more money coming in. So I picked up another day dancing at a club in Beaufort." Candi responded, while spraying on her Flower Bomb perfume.

When John got a whiff of the perfume it only pissed him off more. So he asked a dumb question.

"So, what the fuck you putting on perfume for?"

"John why you trying to start an argument? I'm going to work. I'm a dancer. The better I look and smell, the more money I make. What you trippin for?"

"Because I'm sick of this stripper shit that's why!" John said, getting mad.

"Well guess what motherfucker!? This so called stripper shit, is paying your bills and mine! So until you start doing that, don't tell me shit about what I have to do to make a living for your broke ass!" She said, twisting her neck and hand.

"Fuck you! I'm going to school trying t-"

"No fuck you, I'm sick of hearing that same shit! You think I like stripping, showing off my body!?" She said, behind watered eyes.

"I can't tell!" John said, not meaning it.

John had crossed the line and he knew it. He also knew it was nothing he could say or do to fix what he had said and she was right, stripping was paying the bills. She turned her back to him not giving him the satisfaction of seeing her cry, packing her Louis Vuitton bag with two different costumes for the night, putting on a Nike sweat suit to walk out the house in. When she was done she went into the bathroom and packed her makeup.

When she walked through the living room to leave, John was sitting at the kitchen table with a bottle of Gray Goose turned up to his mouth. Candi shook her head in disgust thinking about his actions and words walking out the door...

When she pulled up in front of the gas station Jay was parked off to the side. She parked beside him and got into his car.

"What's up Ms. Candi? You looking good even in a sweat suit."

She blushed, "Whatever boy, I bet you tell every bitch in a sweat suit that."

"I've seen girls wear a sweat suit before, but not like you lil mama." Jay said still trying to compliment her.

"Whatever nigga, let's go pick these bitches up before we be late." Candi said still not accepting the compliments.

"What you mean? It's only 9:05."

"Yea but you don't know these bitches, they will take all night if I don't go push they asses out the door. They ain't never had no real job so they don't have any time management skills at all."

Jay busted out laughing, while giving her the $200 he promised. They pulled off onto the highway and Candi gave him directions to Beautiful's house. Jay felt like now was a good time to pick Candi as a person, her minds well-being and learn more about her life.

"So, what you know about time management?" Jay asked testing her.

"Nigga what you mean, you think I been a stripper all my life?"

"I don't know, have you?" He asked half playing half not.

"I've only been dancing about um… a little over 3 years. But before this I worked at Wal-Mart as a cashier, and then K-mart for a year and a half. So, I know how to be on time and have good work ethics." She said matter of factly.

"Fasho, so what made you start dancing?"

"I was in school to become a pharmacist for real, not for fake like you and my boyfriend is in school for law enforcement and we both have cars and a apartment. Trying to keep up with the bills and car payments, working a minimum wage job and attending school wasn't adding up. So, I put my career on hold until he finishes school and get a better job while I take care of most of the bills now."

"Damn that's some real shit." Jay said.

"Yea, I know." Candi said while turning her head looking out the window, getting upset that her man was taking up law school to be some cheap paid, punk ass police officer.

"Turn right on the next street and park on the right." She told him while dialing Beautiful's number pulling up to the 6 bedroom boarding house. A place where multiple families stay in one big house with low income.

"Ring, ring, ring, Hello?"

"Yea we outside, I hope yo ass is packed and ready to go."

"Yea bitch!" Beautiful said back.

To her surprise Beautiful came out a couple of minutes later.

When she came out Jay had made a mental note to hisself, that she had been one of the girls in Tweezy's section that night he saw him in the club. She was acting like she would have sucked the nigga dick in front of the whole club that night, if he would have let her.

Beautiful was petite, but her face was a 10. She had long silky hair and looked like she was a mix of Puerto Rican and Black. She had on a Baby Phat sweatsuit and no shirt under it, just a bra, along with her black duffle bag across her shoulder.

"Hey girl, what's up you ready to make this money?" Candi said boosting her head up, as Jay pulled off.

"Hell yea, why you think. I'm already ready? I'm broke as a fuck and my rent was due Friday."

"Last week, why you ain't pay that shit earlier this week? We made a lot of money last weekend." Candi asked.

"Girl you know I had to get my shop on. Wait till you see my new Prada dress I got and Louis Vuitton stilettos."

"Beautiful you one of the prettiest but dum-.....You know what I'ma let this ride until later. Beautiful this is Jay, Jay this is Beautiful."

"What's up lil mama, I see how you got the name." Jay said to Beautiful.

"Thank you." She said while blushing. "You're handsome yourself but you look young. How old are you?"

"I'm 20. How about you?"

"I'm 20 too. Well not 22, with two twos. But the same age as you. Ha, ha, ha!"

"Riiiight." Jay labeled her slow just by that. He pulled open his ashtray and lit his swisher filled with Loud.

"Damn that smell good, let me hit it." Beautiful, asked with a thirsty look.

"Fasho." He replied, as he pulled the blunt some more and passed it to her.

"Candi you going to smoke with me tonight? Suup, suup, damn this some fire ass tree." Beautiful asked coughing, passing the blunt to Candi.

"Might as well, it can only take my mind off of all my stress." Sup, after just one hit Candi was already coughing and passing the blunt to Jay.

"Y'all some rookies and what's the street you said Coco stay on?"

"Zipperer Dr. off Hwy. 17 on the South side."

"Call her and make sure she ready when we pull up its 9:21" Jay said.

"Ok." Candi replied, while strolling to Coco's number and calling her.

"Hi bitch you ready? Well your ass need to be ready when we get there. We should be pulling in the next 5 min."

When they pulled up to Coco's house and blew the horn she came right out rockin some stilettos and a mini skirt that was so short you could see her ass cheeks, making the bottom of her tattooed butterfly wings visible.

Jay's dick started to get hard instantly. He didn't even care about the rest of the shit she had on, her thighs and ass were on point. They got on the highway while smoking another blunt of Loud and jamming Rich Homie Quan.

"Now tell me! What would you do for this paper?" They sang along.

"Damn that nigga be going in!" Coco yelled giving Beautiful five.

"Hell yea, he know what I'll do for some paper." Beautiful said grinding.

Everybody busted out laughing. They played his whole CD all the way to Beaufort. When they pulled up to the small club it was packed with barely nowhere to park. From how packed it was, Jay could tell that his popularity from high school and promotions had went well. So, he knew he was going to get paid.

"We the only strippers here right?" Beautiful asked.

"Hell yea lil mama every dollar, five, ten, shit even twenty or hundreds that hit the floor is all y'alls."

All she could do was smile from ear to ear.

"Damn it's a ass of people here. How they all going to fit in this club." Coco was excited to see so many cars at a club so small.

"Candi you ready bitch!? Why you ain't saying shit?"

"Cause I'm high bitch, I'm in my own zone. Bad bitch mode. So I can make these niggas and bitches came out they pockets." She said sarcastically.

"I heard that." Coco and Beautiful said at the same time giving each other five.

"Jay you got some Molly? I'm bout to turn all the way up." Coco asked.

"Ooh you got Molly? Beautiful said poking her head between the seats looking at Jay stretching her eyes wide as they could go."

"Yea, lil mama." He said laughing.

"Ahhhh shit, turn the fuck up!" Beautiful said, getting crunk.

"I got you lil mama, but if anybody ask you where the Molly, weed or coke at, or even want to buy you or they self something send them my way. Ok?" He said, as he gave Beautiful and Coco both a half gram bag of Molly free of charge.

Afterwards they all went inside the club and it was still packed more than any of them had expected.

"Jay where the bathroom?" Candi asked.

"In the back on the right side, let me show y'all." He said, leading the way.

"Tell them to play French Montana-Pop That and we'll come on the pool table and strip pole. Get them niggas to clear that shit off!" Candi ordered him.

When he walked back out he saw Roc by the DJ booth. They made eye contact and headed towards each other.

"What up my nigga?" Roc yelled over the music.

"Man ain't shit, I can't call it. But this motherfucker soo packed, I know we about to bank." Jay yelled back.

"Man you the one who did this shit. As soon as people heard yo name, everybody came out."

"Damn just like that huh?" Jay asked.

"Nigga you know you was pretty boy in high school and had all the bitches, popular and shit. Plus you brought bitches with you, so all these niggas was going to come out regardless, and a lot of the hoes came just to see you."

"Ha, ha ha, fasho my nigga whatever you say." Jay said smiling.

"Speaking of bitches. Where the strippers at?" Roc asked.

"They in the bathroom getting ready. Oh shit I almost forgot, they said tell the D.J. to make an announcement that they was coming out and to clear the strip pole and pool tables."

"The pool table?" Roc asked confused.

"I don't know what they trying my nigga, your guess is as good as mine?"

As Jay walked to the back the girls gave him their bags and he locked them in Roc's office.

The DJ cut the music, "Alright y'all niggas been asking for the dancers ever since we opened the fucking door. So, pull out yo money to throw and not show. If you a broke nigga get the fuck out the way!"

French Montana-Don't Stop blast through the speakers. "Don't stop pop that pussy, don't stop, what you twerking with!"

"All three of the girls came out doing their signature walk and stood in front of the pool table. They were standing still but there ass and thighs were shaking like dice, as they gave seductive looks. Niggas started throwing cash from everywhere.

Coco started bouncing up and down making her ass clap loud like gunshots. Plat, plat, plat! You would have thought somebody was shooting if you wasn't next to her. "Daaamn!" Was all you could hear.

Candi went to the strip pole and climbed to the top. When she reached the top of the pole she held the top of the pole with her legs and started clapping her hands to the beat. When she felt she had enough attention, she put her hands back on the pole and came twerking down into a split.

"Damn that bitch sexy!" Jay said, grabbing his dick.

Niggas was throwing all they money and the girls wasn't even naked yet.

He turned and looked at Beautiful who was laying on the pool table showing her neatly shaved pussy and from the looks of it she was blowing kisses at niggas with it. One nigga was smoking a blunt by her. She took the blunt out his mouth and started smoking it with her pussy. All you could hear was "Daaaamn!"

By the time that one song went off they all had to rake up the cash off the floor and ask Jay to put it up. Jay placed the stack of ones in each of their bags and went back to the party.

"Hi, Jay you can't speak?"

"I would if I knew who this sexy lady wa-, Erica, Erica Snow?" He said cutting his self short.

"Yes that's me." She said behind a big smile.

"Come give me a hug girl." As he was hugging her he got a whiff of her Flower Bomb perfume.

"Turn around let me see how beautiful you and your body got girl."

He made her do a circle showing her off, for his eyes. She had on some Giuseppe heels, a Michel Kors watch and earrings and a Chanel dress that hugged her every curve.

Erica had a crush on Jay when they were in high school, but when he was in the 12th grade she was only in the 9th grade. So, he wouldn't talk to her. Then he ended up going to prison. She was always a pretty girl but she was skinny back then. But everything about that young body had changed now. She had now grown into a beautiful grown woman with her smooth caramel skin, hazel eyes, curly jet black hair and perfect round ass favoring a young Stacy Dash. She was only a C cup in the breast, but her body made up for that.

"Where your man at? I know you're way too beautiful to be in here alone." Jay said digging.

"He's at home, he never wants to go out anywhere. He claims he doesn't like the club scene." Erica responded.

"Fasho. Well If I had a girl like you, we could do any and everything you wanted to do. I would never leave yo fine ass hanging. I'm just saying." Jay said shooting shots.

Erica blushed, "Whatever when I wanted you, you didn't even like me. I guess it was my braces or something, huh?"

"Ha, ha, ha, you did have braces didn't you? But nawl lil mama you got it all wrong. You was just too young then. I was talking to older girls then. I admit I was on some childish shit, that's all."

"Yea, yea, yea, tell me anything." She said smiling.

"Oh so you don't believe me huh? So let me take you out to make it up to you then?" Jay asked.

"Um no. Hello, I just told you I had a man. You think I'm one of them strippers or something?"

"Oh I'm sorry ma, I forgot about that nigga just that quick. You're so beautiful, you all I'm thinking about right now. Fuck that nigga."

"And you're a handsome man. Where is the special lady at?"

"Oh I'm single." Jay said gladly.

"Umm hum well let me have your number and I will call you if things don't work out with me and him." Erica said giving in.

"Fasho."

She keyed in his number and they went their separate ways. When he walked back to the floor 6 people asked him to buy some Loud and 3 of the six wanted Molly too and 8 other people asked him about coke. As the night went on this was an ongoing thing. He was making money and the girls were making money. When the night ended, he was out of the weed he did bring with him, coke and Molly. He only had a blunt he had left in the ashtray of his car. He sold Roc a pound, 3 other people a ounce and the rest gram for gram. Roc gave him $1,000 from the money off the door sales.

After he grabbed the girl's bags and put them in his car he was ready to dip. Candi gathered her girls up for him and they walked out the door, while niggas grabbed their asses and tried to holla. But they just kept walking ready to go count their money and sleep off the high and liquor. They pulled off from the club, no one was talking they just counted their money.

"$2,300 in one night. That's what the fuck I'm talking bout!" Candi yelled.

"I got $2,111. I ain't mad either!" Coco yelled.

"What you made Beautiful?" Coco asked.

"Hold up, y'all know I count slow."

"Nawl bitch you just slow. Let me count it for your ass." Candi snatched her money.

"Bitch you can't count $1,993 dollars, you should have stayed yo ass in school bitch."

Everybody started laughing but Beautiful.

"Fuck y'all." She said embarrassed.

"Everybody happy?" Jay asked.

"Hell yea!" All the girls echoed.

"Good." He said while lighting his blunt.

"Now give up that gas money and let's have a celebration smoke. Everybody down for next week right?"

"I'm down." They all replied.

Candi was high and tired on the way back to Savannah, but happy and feeling Jay. She ended up falling asleep with her head on Jay's chest and his hand on her ass.

CHAPTER 9

D was in a good mood it had been four weeks since he had got robbed and Jay was telling him what he wanted to hear.

"Yea brah, the lil stripper bitch I got on my team said that nigga be there almost every Friday and they be getting a room when the club close."

"Damn nigga you must be fuckin the bitch to get all that out her." D asked.

"Nawl the bitch just slow, she spilled her guts without me really asking shit."

"True, true, you ain't tell her what happened right?"

"Nigga why you even gotta ask me some crazy shit like that? I picked the bitch mind until I knew everything I needed to know." Jay said, clearing his mind.

D felt bad for testing his gangster, "My bad son, but be ready cause we strapping up tonight if he there, its Friday today my nigga."

"Fasho." Jay said and they split ways.

When D pulled back up to Nikki's apartment she was on the couch watching Scandal, in her silk Victoria Secret nightgown with nothing on under it.

"Baby we need to talk." She said while turning off the TV.

"What's up baby, what you want? A new outfit, some money for your hair?" D asked.

"No. It's more important than that." She inhaled deep and exhaled.

"Spit it out, what is it?"

"Ok, first off I'm pregnant and-"

"Baby that's great! What you acting all down and shit for!?" D yelled.

"Please let me finish Devin."

"Ok baby go ahead." He said smiling from ear to ear.

"And I want you to stop hustling and selling drugs and find a something legit. You can hustle just do it in a legal way, you're not a child Devin you're smart and we have a baby on the way. If you get locked up or even killed, I'm not having this baby. I can't do it without you. You have money and I have good credit baby, let's start a business or something." She said with tears in her eyes.

"So that's what this is all about me hustling? Come here baby." He patted on his lap for her to sit on his lap.

"You are my queen, I never thought I would ever make it this far with any woman. I love you so much you're smart, you're beautiful and my family loves you. I don't think you would ever put me in a situation to make the wrong choice. You're right baby if you're telling me something, it's not only beneficial for me but for us. So, I'm ready to be that man for you. I'm 29 years old and I'm not dead or in jail. So, I think it is time for some life changes, before anything does happen to me."

"So?" She asked waiting.

"I'm ready to retire, just give me until next month."

"You promise." She said smiling.

"I promise." He said while rubbing on her thighs causing her nipples to harden and poke through the night gown. He leaned and kissed her neck, while sliding two fingers under her gown and into her wetness.

"Ssss...god-damn...t-that...feel...soo...good." She said grinding on his hand.

He placed his thumb on her clit and rotated it in circles. He laid her down on her back. As she arched her back, he removed his hand and licked her juices off his hand.

"Suck my pussy baby please." She said almost whining.

He pulled her grown up and push both her legs back making her pussy lips part and smile at him. He leaned down and kissed both of her inner thighs.

"Baby p-please don't tease me."

"Hush and be patient, before I fuck you hard!"

"K-k, daddy." She said moaning.

He continued by sucking on and nibbling on her clit and playing with her g-spot with his fingers.

"Ssss...ooh shit right th-there daddy. I'm about to c-cuum, ssss, auugh s-shit!" She screamed out while rotating her hips on his face.

He then leaned up and removed his clothes. She was still trying to pull herself back together as he walked over rubbing the head of his dick up and down her wetness.

"Ssss damn daddy that feel soo good, stick it in."

In one swift motion he stuck his whole dick inside her pussy causing her pussy to make a skeeting noise. "Sssss, auugh!" She wiggled around trying to get some out.

"Oh fuck this pussy feel good, didn't I tell you don't rush me!?" He continued to take long deep strokes inside her, making her pussy talk to him for 30 minutes long.

"Damn baby why you fucked me so hard?" Nikki asked.

"I told you don't rush me."

"That's not fair." She said while pouting. "I told you I didn't want to be teased that was it, I didn't rush you."

"Ha, ha, ha, I'm sorry bae come let me make it up to you by giving you a bubble bath."

"And wash me off?" She said pushing it.

"Ha, ha, ha and wash you off."

After D had put Nikki to bed all kinds of thoughts ran through his mind, he had a good life going for himself. He had a woman not a rat. He had money and besides getting robbed and a few shoot outs, he was going to make it out the game debt free with just a few battle scars. He knew he was going to marry Nikki one day and he also put in his mind she wasn't picking up another package. After this month he was done. But it was good money down south and he felt like the money was going to waste if he wasn't getting it. He then came up with the best idea he could come up with, to keep the money in the family. He got up and went into the living room to call his cousin Reese.

"Yo, what's up fam?"

"What's up, son? How the south looking?"

"Sunny nigga, shit everyday a good day down here."

D knew his cousin Reese was a hot head and wasn't a hustler like hisself and he was also wanted for questioning on a murder that he swear up and down he didn't have nothing to do with. D figured this would be his perfect getaway for him to come down south.

"But listen, I want you to come down south and run my store for me." D told him talking in code.

"Word? When you want that done son, just say the word and I'm there."

"I'ma give you the word sometime next week. I'ma go ahead and book a ticket for you to come down."

"Alright son just let me know when and I'm there." Reese responded.

"Word." Then they both hung up.

D started to feel a little better about leaving the game.

"After I handle this situation, I'ma count my stash and make some investments. I'ma marry my girl too."

He was still thinking about the future when he got a text from Jay.

"It's on. He gone be there tonight, you ready?"......................................
....

Jay was in the club in his normal corner where he got off his work at. He was working but also looking at Tweezy and his partner take two bitches in the V.I.P for a private lap dance or a $100 dick suck.

He texted D, "Your bitch here."

"Word, I'm posted." D was outside sitting in a stolen black Honda.

Jay spotted Beautiful, "What's up Beautiful?"

"What's up, Jay!?" That Molly got me feeling good.

"Me too, I'm higher than a bird right now." Jay lied. "A ain't Tweezy your man? How you letting them none dancing bitches get your money, that nigga stacked up tonight too. You better go check that shit you slipping." Jay said gassing her up.

"Where he at?" She said looking around.

"I don't know but that nigga had some ugly bitches with him when I seen him."

She was already walking off while Jay was talking, looking for Tweezy and his money.

"That's one dumb ass female, all these niggas in here." He thought to hisself.

"What's up sexy?" Candi came up to Jay giving him a hug.

"What's up beautiful?"

"You tell me, she just left out of your face."

"Don't even downgrade me like that, she won't never be able to make the team and what was that just now anyways? Am I sensing a little

jealousy or some shit? Last time I checked, a nigga had your ass on lock."
Jay said being smart.

"Me jealous? I can't believe you would say such a thing and how you don't know he's not slipping?" Candi asked.

"What's that, now you flirting?"

"Whatever nigga just call me tomorrow to take me out for lunch. Bye I gotta go make this money, you acting like your girlfriend."

"Alright lil mama!" He said laughing.

He lit his Loud blunt and continued to watch the scene while catching his plays. After the club started to die down people started to leave. Just as Jay thought, Beautiful was stuck on Tweezy's arm and his dread head partner had some fat bitch with an ass bigger than life with him.

Jay knew they had both rode together, because he watched them get out the car and walk in the club together. He just hoped they didn't split up so him and D could get a two for one.

He walked ahead of the crowd and went and sat in the car with D waiting for them to come out. When they came out all four of them jumped in the red Chevy Impala. As they pulled off, D followed two car links behind them while Tweezy swerved on and off the road drunk.

"Man what the fuck that dumb ass nigga doing? Shit he going to let 12 lock his ass up, before I kill 'em."

Jay was in the passenger seat putting on gloves and wiping the guns down.

"Just chill big brah its them niggas fate to die tonight." Jay said, ready to kill something.

They followed Tweezy to where they expected him to go. A cheap hotel with some cheap ass hoes. D and Jay waited across the street parked, watching them while they paid and walked to the room.

"Look at them cheap ass niggas they only got one room." Jay said, as all four of them walked into the one room.

"Man these niggas might as well kill themselves." They both busted out laughing.

Jay handed D his gloves then gave him the murder man gun ".38 revolver" no shells will be dropped tonight. They waited 30 minutes then headed to where their ducks would be sitting.

CHAPTER 10

"**P**lat, plat, plat." Her ass was clapping on Dread's pelvis.

"Auuugh fuck, that dick feel good oooh shit, come on daddy fuck this pussy!" The oversized stripper said throwing her ass back.

Dru was fucking the fat stripper like it was his last time getting some pussy. He was fucking her so good, it was getting Beautiful wet. With his dreads swinging back and forth and his muscled ass cheeks squeezing tight every time he entered her, as she screamed.

"Plat, plat, plat, plat, ssss, s-shit, ummmm, auuugh fuck me dread!"

Tweezy on the other hand was taking a little too long to get on hard, he had popped too much Molly and couldn't get right.

"Suck on it baby I'ma get right. Here." He passed her the Molly.

While holding onto his limp dick in one hand she poured the Molly down the length of him and started to lick it making it dissolve on her tongue and his dick.

"Oooh shit that's what I'm talking about." He said, as his dick got hard as Beautiful licked and placed it in and out her mouth.

He grabbed a handful of her hair and pushed her head down the length of his now erect shaft, causing her to gag as the head of his dick entered her throat. He pulled out with a string of saliva from her mouth to the head of his dick. He slapped her bottom lip three times and entered her mouth again. This time she was ready for him, letting him fuck her throat like the pro she was.

Sluuup, sluuup, sluuup! "Ooh, shit!" He said with his eyes closed.

Boom!

"What the fuck!" Tweezy and dread head Dru said at almost the same time.

"Auuugh!" Beautiful and the fat stripper screamed.

'Y'all bitches shut the fuck up before I shoot y'all ass!" Jay yelled.

"Niggas put y'all fuckin hands up!" D yelled.

"Man what the fuck y'all doing, y'all can have these bitches!" Tweezy said.

"Yea man we didn't know these was y'all hoes." Dru said, with his dick still in the fat bitch pussy and his hands in the air.

"I'ma give y'all bitches 30 seconds to get the fuck out of here, if y'all ain't gone by then y'all bitches dying along with these niggas!" D said.

That's all the fat bitch needed to hear and she scooped up her bra, panties and clothes in one motion and almost ran Beautiful over trying to get out the door.

Beautiful was moving a little too slow for D using 20 of her seconds already.

"Bitch you want to die!?" He said pointing the gun at her.

"No please don't!" She said behind watered eyes and hands up.

"Then get the fuck out!" D said yelling at her.

And just like that she was gone. She just needed more motivation due to her condition of being slow.

"Man what is this about brah brah? We got money man, y'all can have that shit!" Tweezy said.

"Nawl you keep it." Jay said while lifting his mask.

"Damn dude I ain't did shit to you, fuck that bitch man take the money. The pussy ain't worth my life." Tweezy was talking fast.

"This shit about more than pussy, this about respect!" D said lifting his mask.

"D shit! D man it wasn't my fault it was Dru's idea man, I'm sorry."

"No it was no-

Boom! Boom! The bullets stopped dread from saying anything.

Jay had shot Dru, one catching him on the bridge of his nose and the other entering his chest. Tweezy shitted on himself and the smell was unbearable.

"Man what the fuck nigga!? You can't even hold your shit in, snitching ass nigga!" D said before firing off.

Boom! Boom! Boom!

A bullet entered Tweezy's temple, the other two went in his chest. They pulled their mask back down and ran out of the hotel.................
....

The next day, Jay was watching the news to see what they had on the murders.

"Good evening around 4:45 a.m. two black males were shot and killed in America's Best hotel on Hwy 17. At the moment officers say they have no leads but this woman, a picture of Beautiful popped up on the screen, Beautiful Johnson is wanted for questioning."

"What the fuck?" He called Candi as soon as he saw her face.

"Hello?" Candi picked up on the second ring.

"What's up lil mama, what your sexy self-doing?"

"Nothing getting dressed. I'm about to go to the mall and spend some of this money you help me make."

"Fasho, but I was just watching the news and your girl Beautiful is wanted for questioning in a double murder."

"What!!? How you figured that? Who was killed?"

"I just told you it's all over the news. They didn't give the names of who was killed they just said two black males." Jay responded.

"Oh my God, I'm about to call her, I'll call you back!"

Candi hung up and dialed Beautiful's number.............

"Ring, ring, ring, h-hello? Suuf, suuf, suuf." Beautiful picked up crying.

"Girl what the hell took you so long to pick up the phone?" Candi asked.

"T-they, k-killed, Tw-twweezy, suuf, suuf, suuf and D-Dru."

"What, who!?" Candi asked.

"I d-don't know. They k-kicked suuf, suuf, the door in a-and made me and J-Juicy leave." She said between sobs.

"Daaaamnn!" Candi said after she had verified she had really been there.

"I heard the sh-shots, suuf, when I was w-walking home."

"Damn girl where this shit happened at?" Candi asked.

"Am- America's Best."

"You walked from Hwy 17 to the East side? That's got to be like a three hour walk. Why you just ain't call a taxi or me, shit somebody with a car?"

"Cause I w-was scared they suuf, suuf, was going t-to, kill me if I u-used, my phone."

Candi looked at her phone and let what she just said run through her head.

"That's the dumbest shit I've heard in my fucking life! But I'm not even about to start with your ass, you got bigger shit to worry about, like the fucking police. You're wanted for questioning bitch and it's all over the news." Candi said to her.

"Questioning for what? I didn't do nothing."

"Duh bitch, you have to go to the police station and tell them that."

"Ok suuf, suuf. I'ma take a shower then go out there, but I'm scared."

"You will be okay, just tell them what happened and call me when you leave the station and let me know how it went."

"Ok love I you sis." Beautiful said.

"I love you too."

She called Jay back and told him what Beautiful had just told her......
....

How they figured Beautiful was there was on Jay's mind slightly. Because other than them involving only Beautiful, they didn't have shit on him. Plus he was masked up when they rode on them niggas.

"So, what's up you still letting me take you out for lunch?" Jay asked Candi.

"That is if you not too busy for me."

"I wouldn't care if I had a full scheduled I would clear it all off for you lil mama, you know I'm trying to boo you up and take you away from that lame."

"Ha, ha, ha, whatever you got too much game for me nigga." Candi said laughing.

"I only speak the truth lil mama, meet me at Outback Steakhouse at 1 p.m."

"OK." She said smiling from ear to ear.

After she left from shopping at the mall she went home and changed. She had her hair pulled back in a bun rocking a black Prada dress with a see through strips down the side of the dress making the side of her breast and the line of her thong visible on each side of her body, some Jimmy Choo stilettos and some Dolce & Gabbana shades with accessories.

She pulled up to the restaurant at 12:58 to see Jay standing in front of the door with a dozen of roses, looking good in his Robin jeans, black V-neck shirt, Gucci watch and the new red and black Jordans.

She had to admit he was a smooth ass nigga. When he sagged his pants, they didn't fall to his knees like them no swag ass nigga's do. His sag was just right. She could tell he had just left the barber shop, because his waves were making her sea sick. She liked the way his beard and mustache were lined up, she couldn't wait to ride his face one day.

Snap out of if Candice you can't fuck this nigga this your friend and business partner. She was so deep in thought she didn't realize Jay was walking up to her car. He opened her door.

"Oh! You scared me." She said.

"My bad lil mama. These are for you." He handed her the flowers.

"Thank you." She said smiling.

He leaned in and gave her a hug, she got a whiff of his Polo Black cologne.

"You smell good." He said before she could say it to him. "And damn look at you, looking all sexy. You put this on for me?"

"No boy, I put this on so I wouldn't walk out the house naked. So, I put this on for me." She said.

They both laughed.

"Whatever come on let's go eat."

After ordering their food and drinks, Candi got up to go to the bathroom. Her ass looked like it was trying to bust out from under her dress. She must have knew he was looking because she looked back at him poking her lips up.

"Damn." Jay replied while his dick started to get hard. Man I'm sick of this shit, it's time for her lil sexy ass to turn that pussy in. He dug in his pocket pulling out a small gram of Molly. He made sure nobody was looking and poured half of it in her Margarita and stirred it up placing it back in its spot. Candi came, sat in her seat and went straight for her drink taking a big sip.

"Um umm, this drink is so good. I love margaritas." She replied.

"I think I'ma have a drink with you. Waitress." He called out getting her attention.

"What can I get for you sir?" She said blinking her fake eyelashes more than needed, trying to flirt with him.

"May I have a double shot of Patron and orange juice on the rocks?" Jay ordered.

"Of course you can, you can have anything you would like. Anything else?"

"That's it." He said.

"Ok I'll be right back with your drink." She walked off switching.

"Awww somebody got a secret admirer." Candi said playfully.

"Don't even try me like that. She ain't even my type."

"Oh well, excuse me Mr. Picky. What is your type then?"

"First off she came at me, I don't like that. I like a challenge. Second she too skinny, I mean there's nothing wrong with skinny girls, but she built like a 10 year old lil girl. No ass no titties, I'm good."

"Ha, ha, ha so what is your type. What kind of women do you like?" Candi asked.

"You're my type. Beautiful, smart, sexy and ambitious. That's my type."

"Aww that's so sweet. I got to stay away from you, you got too much game."

"Yea this nigga will talk a bitch right out of her panties if she let him." Candi thought to herself.

The waitress came with their food and sat both of their plates on the table.

"If you guys need anything else just call me." They told her thanks and she left.

"So, tell me about yourself. How was it for you growing up?" Candi asked Jay, the Molly had her wanting to talk.

"Well I left mama house around the age of 16 because of her choices in men. If they would even say something I didn't like to my mama, I was kickin ass or gettin my ass kicked. So I dipped and got my own spot, but I was still doing all kinds of young nigga shit from shootouts to robbing, all kinds of dumb shit. I ended up fucking with some snitch niggas on a robbery and got locked up for 3 years of my life."

"Wow that's crazy." Candi said.

"I know right." He cut a big slice of his steak and placed it in his mouth.

"But enough about me, how were you brought up Ms. Candi?"

She wiped her mouth with her napkin. "Well my real name is Candice Frost. I was raised in a low/mid class family. My mother and father both worked hard and paid their bills, living paycheck to paycheck to make sure my brother and I had a roof over our heads. My brother resented my father for not having more to support our family and having my mama work as hard as him. When he turned 17 and decided he was tired of seeing my mother struggle he went and robbed a liquor store. When he was running out of the store with the money the owner shot him in the back two times killing him. That caused my mother to lose her mind, literally. My dad took care of her up until I finished high school. Once I graduated he left both of us for a white woman with no trace or contact. He used a lame ass excuse that I remind him so much of my brother and it was killing him to stay around. So now my mama is in a mental institution and I go see her every Sunday. I didn't ever think my father would just up and leave without saying a word. Good thing me and boyfriend had just moved in together."

Jay got up and sat next to her. Her eyes started to fill with water and a single tear rolled down her cheek. He kissed it away before it reached her chin, sending an electric wave through her body, causing her nipples to turn into rocks and poke through her dress. Jay saw her body's reaction so he hugged her and rubbed on her back.

"Damn why every time this nigga touch me it feel so good? Am I in love with him or something? Hell no! What the fuck is wrong with you Candi, you got a man pull it together. It must be the alcohol. I can't be drinking them margaritas like that, them shits too strong or some shit." She thought to herself.

"You ready to go?" Jay asked.

"We didn't finish our food." Candi said to him.

"We can get to-go plates greedy our date not over yet. I want to take you to the park."

"Ok." She said smiling.

The Molly had her emotional and the way she was feeling only the drug could affect her body in this certain way. She could feel her pussy was soaking wet and she started to think her juices had soaked through her panties and made a spot on her dress or she was just high.

"I need to go to the bathroom before we go. I'll be right back." She said, excusing herself.

"Alright lil mama."

She walked into the stall lifted her dress and pulled down her panties, looking at the small wet spot that wasn't as bad as she thought. She noticed the cool air blowing between her legs was feeling good. Cooling her off because her pussy was hot and wet. So she decided to take them off and place them in her purse. Come on Candi pull it together you not even acting like yourself right now. I need water she thought to herself. She came out of the bathroom and ordered a water to go.

Jay looked at her and smiled. He could tell she was in her feelings and had just fucked up by ordering a water. That was going to make her roll even harder. They left the restaurant and hopped in Jay's rented Navigator.

"Where the Crown Vic at?"

"It's at the house this a rental I'm thinking about trading my car in for one of these though. I wanted to see how they ride first."

"Damn these seats comfortable." Candi said sliding her back up and down the seat.

"I know right." He said knowing it felt better to her than to him because of the Molly.

She was still sipping the water as Jay turned up the music.

"Who is this? That shit going in." She said with a locked jaw.

"That's a nigga called K-Camp." His single was blasting through the speakers, "I like smoking weed, I like getting fly, I like having sex and I like girls who ride. I love that money baby, money baby, money baby!"

"I got to stop by my house real quick." Jay said.

When they pulled up to the apartments he asked her to come in real quick.

"Who house we at?"

"This my apartment silly, I left something at the house. We ain't going to be here but five minutes."

She didn't want to get out at first, but she was thirsty.

"Ok. You got some juice?" She asked.

"Yea come on."

They walked into Jay's laid one bedroom apartment. It looked as if he just walked into the furniture store and placed everything he wanted in his house. He didn't even have any pictures on the walls or tables.

"I can tell you stay by yourself nigga." Candi said.

"Why you say that?" He asked.

"Because ain't no woman's touch nowhere in here. No pictures, paintings, rugs. Just new furniture."

Jay hadn't even noticed any of that was missing until now.

"Maybe I can let you decorate in here for me one day. I'll be back, make yourself at home." He said, walking to the back.

She walked into the kitchen and fixed a glass of orange juice. Then, went into the living room and sat on his couch. It felt as though she was sinking into the sofa. Jay walked back out with a blunt in his mouth.

"I'ma smoke this before we leave because I can't smoke in the rental."

"That's fine." Candi said.

"Just like you nigga, fine as a fuck." She thought to herself.

Jay sat beside her and lit the Loud weed called Girl Scout Cookie.

"Damn that smell good. Jay let me hit it?" She asked.

"Alright, but be easy this some potent shit, you know you a lightweight."

"Ok. Suup, suup." Just like that she was on a whole nother level, her eyes turned bloodshot red and glossy as she exhaled. She started coughing as she passed the blunt back to him.

Jay passed her the glass of orange juice and she took a big gulp while he rubbed on her back.

"Thank you." She said smiling.

"You're welcome beautiful, anything for you."

"Jay why you always know the right thing to say? You make me feel so good."

Right then he knew he had her open like a book.

"Because I knew from day one I had to have you. I brought you to my house, I've never brought anybody here. That's how I know I'm feeling you."

While looking at her still rubbing on her back, with his free hand he picked up the remote and turned on his CD player. Usher-Super Star started to play softly through the speakers. He leaned over and kissed her on her neck.

"Sssss, ooh." She was so high she thought she had melted and was sliding down the couch onto the floor.

He could see her nipples poking through her dress. He leaned over and whispered in her ear.

"I need you bae." Then licked her earlobe and placed two more kisses on her neck.

"Ssss, ooh, w-what you—

"Shhh let me take care of you baby." He said rubbing up and down her inner thighs.

"Damn why I took off that thong, she thought to herself.

It didn't matter anyway her mind wasn't in control of her body. Her body had a mind of its own now.

With the hand he had on her back, he laid her back and with the other one he eased his way up her thigh parting them open. As he was leaning her back slowly he started coming towards her catching her with his lips, causing her to come back towards him and give him a lust filled tongue kiss. His dick was jumping so hard off her reactions, he thought it was going to poke a hole through his jeans.

He slid his hand down the length of her thick thighs and put his index finger and middle finger inside her juice box, placing his thumb on her clit rotating it in slow circles.

"Ssssss, oooh, r-right there, ssss, d-damn, oh my god." She arched her back up and came hard and long on his hand.

"Damn baby that nigga can't be fucking you right, you cumming like that." Jay said low.

She was trembling and trying to regroup as Jay placed his fingers in his mouth licking off her juices.

"Damn you taste good if you was my girl I'll eat you ever night." He grabbed both her legs pushing them back revealing her bald fat juice box, with her clit poking out waiting to be sucked on.

"Damn baby look at you." Jay said to hisself.

"Huuu, huu." She took deep breaths panting as he placed his tongue on her juice box licking her lips and then sucking on her clit. It was like she had forgot how to breathe.

"Ssss, ooh, huuu, huuu." She started to pant more. "Auugh s-shit daddy I'm about cuum! Ooh, ssss!" She was shaking and rotating her hips until she couldn't take no more. She laid there limp unable to move or talk.

She saw Jay undress but it was surreal to her. When he pulled down his boxers revealing his fat 9 1/2 inch dick, she wanted to get up and walk home.

"Fuck this shit, where he about to put all that? It's one thing that it's long but it's fat too, oh hell nawl." But she couldn't even move, those two orgasms took all the fight out of her. She had never cum like that before in her life. She felt him lift her dress over her head while she laid there in a daze, not able to even protest.

He placed one of her legs in the cuff of his arm and with his free hand rubbed his dick up and down between the lips of her pussy making her wetter than she already was. He placed the head in and with the juices that were on his hand he rubbed on her nipples.

"Oooh shit baby you so tight." Jay said out load.

"Huuu, sssss, ummm!" She started to try to slide back with nowhere to go but the arm of the couch. He started to slide more and more of the fat inches inside her tight hole.

"Relax baby." He could feel her trying to push him out of her.

"I'm trying to it's so big."

"Put your legs around my waist." He said, letting her legs go.

She locked her legs around his waist as he laid down and he started kissing her without going deeper inside her. But she started getting wetter from the kisses, letting him slide in deeper by the kiss.

He then started to grind inside of her touching all of her walls filling her up, something her man had never done. Causing her juices to drip down her ass and down his balls.

"Oooh, d-daddy, f-fuck me, ssss, s-shit!"

He looked down and saw how she had creamed on his dick, causing him to bust. He pulled out and put his load on her belly.

"Augh fuck!" He said, as he squeezed his dick until every drop hit her stomach. After he was done he went to the bathroom and rinsed of his stick, then ran a rag under some hot water for her.

He came back in the living room to find Candi sleep. He wiped her off, turned off the CD player, laid with her and set his alarm clock for 7 p.m. so he could wake her up for work.

CHAPTER 11

"**C**ome on baby I need you to help me get this together. Why you have to put on makeup, do your hair and all that shit? We just going to count some money." D asked looking at Nikki through the mirror.

"Because I ain't about to be caught looking all busted, D. I'm a woman this is what we do, we look pretty. Why you think you wanted to get with me?"

He walked up behind her and put his already hard dick between her ass cheeks. Even though he had on jeans, she still felt his dick through his pants.

"Don't start nothing you can't finish." She said smiling moving from left to right on his pipe.

"You lucky I want to get everything straight before my cousin come down here next week, but I'ma handle you later because you talking a lot of shit."

"Yea, yea, nigga you ain't goin to do shit." She said sucking her teeth and pushed her lips to the side.

"Ha, ha, ha, alright we going to see." He said slapping her on the ass hard.

"Ouch, I told you about slapping my ass like that!"

"Whatever, go put some clothes on so we can go?"

15 minutes later she finally came from the back. "You ready?" D asked.

"Yea I guess." Nikki put on her Seven jeans, some pink and white Air Force ones and a pink t-shirt.

20 minutes later they were pulling up to D's house in Bradley Point. They went into the house and Nikki had to throw up as soon as they entered. She had been doing this a lot lately because of the pregnancy. Plus, D smoked in the house and the smell of weed made her nauseous.

STACKS

When she came out of the bathroom, D had pulled the carpet back on the floor and pulled a few of the wood slabs out of his floor. When he opened this stash box, Nikki peeked over in amazement.

"Oh, my, God."

It looked like he owned a small bank inside the safe.

"This is my hundred dollar safe everything is rubber banded up in this one. Each rubber band is $2,000. Go ahead and count this while I go get the rest."

"Get the rest?" She thought in her head.

When he came back carrying three trash bags across his back, she was on stack 65 and still counting.

"Now this the shit that's going to take all night." He said, untying the not on one of the bags.

She looked up staring into the bag filled with money.

"All of these are 1's, 5's, 10's and 20's in here. I don't band these. I just put them in these bags. The 50's are in my fifty dollar safe. The reason why I don't band the small bills is because after I had made a certain amount of money, I couldn't fit them all in the safe. So, I bagged them up."

Nikki was at a loss for words. She had never seen so much money in her life.

"Baby you're rich. Why do you continue to keep selling drugs?"

"I don't know, this was all I was ever good at baby. I didn't go to college or pick up a trade. I was always a hustler, ever since I was in middle school and my uncle gave me my first $50 pack, this is all I ever knew. But then I met you, showing me a different side of life, that there are better things to life than material things. Telling me I can be an entrepreneur because of my cash and your credit, that's motivation. You don't know how much I love you for that. You saved my life. You and my unborn child are all I want to live for, to be there, take care and support y'all is all I want to do in life now baby."

Nikki stood there with tears in her eyes just realizing how much of an impact she had on his life. He came over and kissed her softly.

"Why you crying baby?" D asked her.

She didn't answer, she just kissed him.

"Make love to me baby." She asked while crying.

D, emptied the bag of untied money onto the couch and floor.

"What you doing?" She asked.

"Something I never did before, I know this is over $300,000. I want to fuck you on top of all this money." D pulled down his gym shorts and started to stroke his dick.

Nikki's nipples turned into rocks and her pussy started to soak. She looked back and forth from the money to him and thought she was going to cum without even fucking, as he took off the rest of his clothes. She was still standing in a daze overwhelmed from his story of her saving him, to all the money he now wanted to fuck on.

She didn't even remember him taking off her clothes, lifting her up and placing her doggy style on the couch. But when he started to eat her pussy from the back she came to her senses, squeezing a hand full of bills in both hands. He ate her pussy so good causing her to cry and cum at the same time. He entered her wet box stroking her for a hour, busting inside her. They both passed out with his dick still in her juice box and money sticking to their sweaty bodies.

They woke up two hours later showered and got back to counting the money. It took 3 hours between the both of them to count and recount the $513,000 worth of money. They both sat in the living room amazed at the stacks of money on the back wall.

"So Mr. Harris, what do you plan on investing in first?" She asked him.

"That's what I got you for, what do you have in mind?"

"Um how about a used car lot, or barber shop or even a salon? Ooh maybe a boutique clothing store?"

"Why can't we do all of them?" D asked.

"Because who's going to run all four of them at one time? And even if you find somebody to manage each one, we have to make sure the people we hire are reliable."

"You right baby, damn I'm glad you on my team." D said smiling.

"I think you should do two businesses bae. Then once we see a return on your investments and things start running good we can open another one."

"Word, word you right baby." He said agreeing.

They talked about what businesses would be the best two and went with the used car lot and a barber shop. After rubber banding the pile of money and putting it away they left and were on the way to Nikki's house but D took a detour.

"Where we going baby?" She asked.

"I want to show you something."

They pulled up to the park and D parked the car.

"Get out baby."

"D I don't feel like walking in the park tonight baby. I'm tired and my pussy hurt."

"Girl we not bout to be here long come on."

She got out the car pouting. It was 6:50 p.m. and the sun was starting to set as they walked past the pond.

"Look baby this is what I wanted to show you." He said with his hand turned out to the sun.

"Yea baby this is a beautiful sight, but we've seen and done this bef-"

"Have we ever done this?" He said getting on one knee opening a box containing a 5 carat ring.

"Baby you are all that I ever needed in my life. You make me a better man and if I don't make you mine forever I would be taking you for granted. Nikki Smith, will you marry me?"

"Yes! Yes! Yes!" She said with tears running down her cheeks.

They kissed for at least 5 minutes and went back to his house, making love until Nikki had to tap out.

CHAPTER 12

*R*ing, ring, ring.

Candi's cell phone was going off. She woke up and grabbed it off the end table. When she lifted it in the air to see who was calling, she had missed the call. The time read 7:48 p.m. and she had 18 missed calls. She sat up trying to pull her thoughts together. When she looked back and saw Jay laying behind her, she almost passed out.

"Oh shit! Jay, Jay!" She yelled while pushing him. "How you let me sleep in soo late? Wake up!"

"Ummm, what time is it?" He asked stretching.

"7:50 nigga get your ass up, you know I got to go to work tonight!" She said as she pulled her dress over her head.

"Damn, I know I set my alarm." He said, looking for his phone.

He dug in the sofa and there his phone was going off, muffled by the cushion.

"Hurry up, Jay!" Candi said, getting herself together fast as ever.

"Alright ma let me at least put on my boxers, damn! You want me to go outside naked?"

She sucked her teeth and went through her call log. She had 2 missed calls from Beautiful and 16 from John.

"Oh shit!" She said louder than she wanted.

"What happened?" Jay asked.

She ignored him and went to look at the text messages John had sent. The first one was sweet. "Where you at bae?" The second one followed. "I miss you. Where you at?" Then, it started to get bumpy from there. "Pick up the phone, what you doing?" and "Why you can't answer the phone?" The next and last two confirmed he had been sick of calling. "Why the fuck you ignoring my fucking calls!?" and "You see me fucking calling you, you probably with one of them drug dealer ass niggas from the club?"

By the time she finished reading the messages, Jay had put on some gym shorts and a tank top and was walking towards the door.

"You ready?" He asked.

"Yea let's go." She was a nervous wreck on the couch trying to think of the best lie possible. The whole ride back to her car she didn't say anything.

"You ok?" He asked.

"Yea I'm good. My boyfriend was blowing me up the whole time that's all."

"Damn my bad lil mama, I didn't mean to get you in trouble."

"You good I just got to get my lie straight because I always answer my phone through the day for him. Shit I only work Thursdays, Fridays and Saturdays and that's after hours. He knows something not right."

"Yea I see where you coming from." Jay agreed.

As soon as they pulled into the restaurant parking lot, she was already opening the door before he could put the truck in park.

"Damn, can a nigga get a hug or something?"

She turned around and gave him the light hug.

"I'll see you later if you come out." She said as she closed the door.

Just like that she was gone.

On her ride to the house she called Beautiful to see what she wanted and to also let her know she was going to use her name in her lie.

"Hello?" Beautiful answered on the first ring.

"What's up girl, what you doing?"

"Packing my bag for tonight. Girl they had me at the damn police precinct all fucking day."

"For real?" Candi had forgot she went down there.

"Hell yea and they was asking me all kinds of questions like I had something to do with that shit." Beautiful stated.

"Damn did they even say how they figured you was there?" She asked sounding more concerned than she really was.

"They said I left my I.D. there. I told them I must have dropped it when the men busted in the room and forced us out. Then, they asked me how I knew Tweezy and Dru."

"What'd you say girl?" Candi asked.

"I told them, me and him was fuck friends and we do it most Fridays after I leave the club."

"Damn that's crazy. But girrrl I need you to do me a favor." Candi said worried about herself.

"What is it? Your man want to do a three-some don't he." Beautiful said smiling.

"Bitch hell no! I need to use your name in a lie." Candi said getting upset.

"Oh Ms. Faithful lying to her man now?"

"Shut up bitch and listen. If John or me call you, I need you to say I was with you the whole day at the police precinct. Ok? Please don't fuck this up."

"You know I got you, but first you got to tell me. Who you let get in-between them thighs?"

"Bye, bitch I'll see you tonight."

"Um-" was all she got out before Candi had hung up on her.

She erased her call log to Jay and her missed and most recent call to Beautiful. Afterwards she called her man.

"Hey baby? I'm sorry I missed your ca-"

"Where the fuck you at!?" He screamed in her ear before she could finish.

"If you will let me finish I can tell you. I was with Beautiful. Her boyfriend got killed last night and they wanted her to come down to the police station for questioning. It's all over the news baby. You didn't see it?"

"That still don't explain why you didn't pick up my calls Candi! What the fuck that have to do with you!?" He said, still yelling.

"Baby they made us put our phones on silent and I fell asleep waiting on her to come out. I should be home in the next 10 minutes."

"Whatever Candi. I'll see you when you get here!"

As soon as he hung up, he was online looking at the recent crimes and to his surprise there had been a double murder and Beautiful had been wanted for questioning.

Candi was about 10 blocks away from her house replaying and rehearsing the lie she had just told her boyfriend. This was something she had to do because she never lied to him about where she was before. When she glanced in the passenger seat and saw the roses Jay had got her and the to-go plate, she almost swerved into a mailbox.

STACKS

"Oh, shit!" She grabbed the bundle of roses and to-go plate and slung them out the window like the cops where behind her and she was trying to get rid of some drugs. At that moment she realized she had on heels and a dress with no panties on. She slammed on the breaks coming to a complete stop, leaving her brakes smoking. By now she was less than 5 blocks away from her house and was feeling sick about this whole thing, but it was too late to go back and she had already said she would be home in 10 minutes, 20 minutes ago.

As she pulled up in front of her house she kept telling herself she had it, she was good and everything was going to be ok. When she opened the door John was in the kitchen cooking dinner.

"Hi baby?" He was feeling better knowing his girl hadn't lied to him, but when he saw how she was dressed he got suspicious.

"Oh now it's hi baby! You just got through cursing me out like I was nothing! Why don't you fuckin trust me John?" She said getting on the defensive side, before he could drill her with questions again.

"Baby I was worried about you, you always pick up your phone during the day and why did you put that on to go to the police precinct?" He said sliding that in.

"Ok and? You should have known I would call you back! And I put this on to surprise your ass. I was going to take you out when you came home from work, but I didn't know I was going to be at that stank ass place all day." She said, surprised at how well she had just lied.

"Damn I'm sorry baby. I'll run you a bubble bath, you want me to come wash you off." He said, walking over and giving her a kiss.

"No I'm fine, but I am hungry. I haven't ate all day. Could you fix me a plate?" She said lying.

She saw this as her chance to get away and headed towards the bathroom. She peeled off her clothes and jewelry and ran the water on hot only, then soaked in the hot water. The water felt better on her pussy than anywhere else. Jay had beat the breaks off her pussy.

When she got out the tub she could hear Miguel -Sure Thing blowing through the speakers.

"Damn I know this nigga ain't trying to make love tonight. I can't even blame him. I ain't gave him none in two weeks. Fuck, I should have gave him some yesterday my pussy hurting."

When she put on her panties and bra she went and packed her bag for work. She tried to stall as she lotioned extra slow, knowing what he was trying. When she walked into the kitchen all the lights were off and he had two candles lit on the table. He pulled her seat out for her. When she sat, he pushed her seat in and went to his seat.

"I just wanted to show you I appreciate you and love you more than anything. I apologize for cursing you out baby." John said apologizing.

"Aww baby, I love you too." She said smiling.

They said their blessing and ate the fried chicken, green beans and yellow rice he had prepared. After they finished, he cleared the table. She got up to walk to the room and he grabbed her hand.

"Fuck." She thought to herself.

He pulled her and gave her a wet kiss while squeezing and pulling on both her ass cheeks.

"Baby it's 11:00." She said coming up with an excuse.

"Yea I know we only have 20 minutes." He said while placing kisses on her neck.

She knew then the only way she was getting out the door, was to let him slide inside of her.

They took small steps back to the bedroom, while taking long deep kisses.

"Baby I love you so much." He said in-between kisses.

"I love you too bae. Woo!" She said as he lifted her into the air holding on to both her ass cheeks.

He walked her into their bedroom, placed her on the bed and started undressing himself dropping his boxers revealing his 8 inch penis. After getting naked he grabbed her leg and kissed her from her calf to her thighs. Then, sucked on her clit through her panties."

"Ssss, come on baby w-we don't have that long, ummm." She said moaning.

"K baby, sluup, sluup, sluup." He said, while still sucking on her clit through her panties.

He slid her panties down her legs. She had to admit that even though she had gotten use to his dick he still was an expert at eating pussy and she loved it.

"Ssss, ooh, shit r-right there eat that pussy daddy." She moaned.

He sucked her clit while moving his finger from left to right in her pussy hole, touching her g-spot causing her to lock her legs around his neck and arch her back.

"Auuugh fuck, I'm about to cuuuum!" She screamed rubbing her juices around his face as she came. She laid there limp shivering as he climbed on top of her. When he entered her wetness his dick wasn't phasing her at all, because Jay had stretched her hole out and she started to wonder if he felt how she was a little more open than usual. She squeezed her pussy around his dick as tight as she could and started to give the best moans she could while he did his thang on top of her.

"Ssss, auugh, damn fuck me baby, damn that dick big."

"Oooh shit this pussy good girl. I'm bout to cum already shit!"

"Fuck! Me too daddy auugh!" She screamed, faking an orgasm.

He thought in his mind he was beating the pussy up, causing hisself to cum.

"Oh shit!" He yelled taking his last stroke going in as deep as he could, busting inside of her. She didn't care because she was on the shot. She was just glad it was over.

He turned over and laid passed out on the bed. She got up holding her hand under herself trying to prevent his cum from dripping on the bed or floor. She took a quick shower before heading to the club, feeling bad for fucking two men in one day. But what was done was done, she couldn't change it. She had to focus on work so she could make some money to take care of home.

When she walked in the club she spotted Coco and Beautiful in the corner by the bar, nobody was really there seeing it was still early for the strip club.

"What y'all bitches over here gossiping about?" Candi asked.

"You the topic of the conversation bitch!" Beautiful said.

"Umm hum." Coco agreed putting her hands on her hips.

"I don't know what y'all talking about." Candi said lying.

"Bitch don't play crazy Beautiful told me how you called to use her name in a lie. I see it all in yo face, you glowing and shit, that nigga must have fucked you real good!?" Coco said.

Beautiful started laughing.

"Hoe yo ass can't hold water." She said acting mad, but knew Beautiful was going to tell Coco anyways because the three of them was close and didn't fuck with the other strippers like that.

"Soo, spit it out bitch give us the details." Coco said waiting.

"Y'all bitches nosey."

"And? Details please." Beautiful said.

"OK, ok damn. It was Jay and that nigga dick baaanging!" Candi said yelling out loud.

"Auuugh!" Beautiful and Coco screamed.

"I knew it, I knew you was going let that nigga fuck. That nigga was persistent and your nigga ain't doing shit, better yet working with shit." Coco said.

"Ummm-umm." Beautiful added.

She filled them in on how it all went down and continued their night..

Later that night Jay came through doing his normal thing, making money. Then he noticed Candi heading his way.

"What's up lil mama?" He asked.

"What's up Jay, my bad for leaving so fast, I had to make sure home was straight. I wanted to also let you know I enjoyed myself. That's the most fun I had in a long time." She said almost blushing.

"Fasho and you don't have to apologize. I just wanted to show you a good time. When you going to let me take you out again?" Jay asked.

"I don't know. I'ma have to check my schedule and see when I'm free again." She said smiling happy but turning to leave, leaving him her jiggly ass to look at.

"Damn that pussy was on point." He thought to himself.

CHAPTER 13

"Yo, nigga you ready for that trip?" D asked Reese.

"Yea son I was wondering when you was gonna call back. I thought you forgot about me or some shit." Reese said back.

"Nawl I ain't forgot bout you son. I just had some business to handle."

"Word, word. When you want me to leave?"

"Shit the ticket already booked all you have to do is call and make sure a seat is available."

"Alright, I'm bout to check on that now. Yo, where am I staying at son yo crib?"

"I got a spot for you fam. You good son." D assured him.

"Word, one."

"One." They both hung up the phone.

He had moved all of Nikki's clothes to his house and was going to let his cousin use her apartment. It had already been two weeks since he had counted up his stash and asked Nikki to marry him. Ever since that day she had made it her business to help him clean his money and become a powerhouse couple, so their child could have a brighter future than them both. She even quit her job to make everything possible for them. So she was on his ass hard about the drug game dealing, because everything was riding on this.

She handled all the paperwork and took out multiple loans, not because they needed the money, but to have a paper trail of funds. Even if the businesses were not successful at first, they could slowly pay the loans back with the dirty money claiming the funds through the businesses to clean the money.

After a week she had all the paperwork and tax I.D. numbers in order for the first building. The following week she was talking to a realtor about a second, for the car lot. D just co-signed as a silent partner on any paperwork she brought to him. He was busy trying to get everything in line for his cousin to run his drug operation, so he could take small cuts off the profits. He also made a mental note in his mind to double his order next time because Jay was running through the packages too fast.

He unwrapped the multiple layers of tape off the drugs and proceeded to weigh everything up. As usual, everything was on point. He put 3 ounces of Molly, a half brick of coke and 5 pounds of weed in his duffle bag. After he was done he texted Jay.

"Time to go to work. Meet me at the spot."

"Fasho, be there in 30 minutes." Jay texted back.

"Word." He responded. Seeing he had about 15 min to kill he rolled up some of the new batch of Hydroponic weed that just came in and relaxed.

Damn, I made it out the game. I'm 16 years deep. God must have a angel watching over a nigga or something. Matter of fact, I do have an angel with me. Damn, she is my blessing, she saved me from destruction. If it wasn't for her, I would have still been pushing work until I got caught or even killed."

He put out the roach, grabbed his duffle bag and headed out the door...

When he pulled up to the store, Jay was backing in right on time. He loved the way Jay was on his grind, it reminded him of a younger version of himself. He parked beside him and Jay hopped in.

"What's up, big brah?" Jay said giving him dap.

"I can't call it. What's good with you?" D asked.

"Shit you know it's a drought out here and niggas is starving and going crazy."

Jay's phone started going off, he hit the ignore button. But as soon as he hit it, it started ringing again.

"Word. So, what you want to do?"

"I'ma grab a quarter brick, 2 pounds of Loud and a ounce of Molly. Yea that's what I'm trying big brah, but check this out. "

He said while unzipping his MCM book bag pulling out the rubber band stacks. "I'm about to try to feed the streets and get this money while shit fucked up. These niggas got money but no work and I got work."

"Word. So what you want me to front you something extra?" He asked thinking Jay might have needed a front.

"Nawl big brah I got the bread, I just want you to be on standby." Jay answered.

"How soon you talking about?"

"Probably in the next couple of days."

"Word?" D asked surprised.

"I'ma bump you." Jay's phone was still going off constantly as he was trying to leave.

D unzipped the duffle bag and started to pass, Jay the work, while Jay answered the phone.

"I'm coming nigga give me 20 minutes." As soon as he hung up it went off again. "I'm on my way give me 20 minutes man!" Jay hung up again and placed the last of the work in his bag.

"Be careful out there son. Niggas is greasy out here and will do whatever, just to take what you work hard for. I got something to tell you too my nigg-

Jay's phone went off again and he picked it up cutting D off.

"Give me 30 minutes, I'ma swing through on you." Jay said through the receiver.

"What you was saying big brah?" Jay asked.

"Nothing go ahead and get your money up my nigga. Just keep your eyes open, what I was saying can wait. But keep your eyes open son, you might can't hear what's going on all the time, but you can see shit coming before it even happens to you. Always follow your instincts."

"Fasho that's real shit, I get the message big brah." He said giving him dap.

"Listen I know you don't go out like that but for my G-Day I'ma do it big at Club Karma my nigga and I want you to come through big homie." Jay told him.

"Oh word? Shit you know I got to come through for the lil homie 21st. Hell yea I'ma be there B."

"That's what I'm talking about, I'ma keep you posted. I know you married and got to get permission from wifey to go out and shit."

They both busted out laughing.

"That's some cold shit lil nigga, but best believe I'ma be there."

"Fasho." Jay said dapping him up.

They parted ways, D went and caught a couple of more sells then went back to the house to lay up with Nikki.

CHAPTER 14

*R*ing, ring, ring.

"Hello?" Jay picked up.

"Yes Jay'sean how are you doing? This is Mr. Timmy with the Labor Company."

"What's up Mr. Timmy?"

"I'm good, um we're running short on workers today and I was calling to see if you were available." He asked.

"Yea I'm available." Jay lied, knowing he wasn't working any more.

"Where the job at?" Jay asked.

"Waste Management in Garden City."

"Ok I'll be there. What's the pay rate?"

"$7.80 for you, since I'm calling on short notice and they're looking to hire someone so do a good job and you could potentially work for the company."

"Ok I'm on my way." Jay said almost laughing, lying to the man.

They both hung up happy.

"Sucker ass cracker. I got y'all ass this time, y'all won't make that extra $5.00 a hour off me today. He said laughing.

"Ring, ring, ring." His phone went off again.

"843, who calling me from Beaufort?" He asked hisself.

"Hello?" He answered.

"What's up Jay how have you been?"

"Who is this?" He asked.

"Erica." She replied.

"Erica?" He said acting as if he didn't know who she was.

"Erica who?" He asked.

"Damn you forgot me again, you must know at least 5 bitches named Erica and that's just in Beaufort."

"Nawl I'm fucking with you lil mama, how could I forget someone so beautiful as you. So Ms. Snow, you decided to call me?"

"Yes I did because I'm officially single. It didn't work out with me and dude, all he cared about was his job. He didn't have any kind of social life at all, it was the most depressing relationship I've ever been in in my life." She explained to him.

"Damn I'm sorry to hear that."

"Don't be because I'm happy and don't front nigga you know you're happy to hear from me."

Jay made a light laugh. "Yea you got that, I am. What you got going on though?"

"Well I was on my way to Savannah and was wondering if you could show me around. I mean I've been down there before, but I haven't learned the area and social places to go to yet."

"I can do that. You on the way down here now?" Jay asked.

"Yea I should be there in about 25 minutes."

"Ok just hit me when you get close to the bridge and I'll meet you at the El Cheapo gas station on the left, after you cross the Savannah bridge."

"Ok I'll see you soon."

"Fasho." Jay said and hung up.

Jay had some business to take care of. In that short time he had left, one of his plays had called him for a half ounce of coke and a half pound of Loud.

He pulled up in front of Dirt's house, the nigga had just called him 2 ½ hours ago for a quarter ounce of coke and a quarter pound of loud. Dirt sold crack. He would cook the coke Jay sold him. He would water whip it and make a killing off the water whipped crack. The nigga only problem was he sniffed too, sniffing up most of his profit. So that took from his money.

When he pulled in the driveway he saw Dirt peeking out the blinds with bulging eyes. Jay hated serving him while he was high, he was always on some paranoid bull shit. Jay dug in the bag and pulled out the coke, Loud and his scale. He also grabbed his .9 mm from between the seat, pulled the hammer back and placed the .9 on his waist. When he got out the car and knocked on the door Dirt peeped out the window again. Jay threw both his hands up in the air. Dirt walked to the door.

"Who is it?" He asked.

"Nigga you just saw it was me. It's Jay brah brah."

"Who with you?" Dirt asked.

"Man ain't nobody with me nigga open the door."

Dirt opened the door to let Jay in, as soon as he was inside he closed and locked it back fast. His mouth was stuck to the right side, while his lips twitched trying to adjust.

"What's up Jay?" He asked while looking out the window.

"Ain't shit nigga, but let's handle this business cause I see you skeed up and sit your ass down nigga. Damn you making me nervous and shit." Jay said, getting annoyed.

Jay put the coke and weed on the table and turned on the scale, causing Dirt to leave from the window and stare at the coke twitching his mouth.

"Weigh the white up first." Dirt said sniffing and grabbing his nose, trying to catch the drain.

"This nigga turning into a real feen." Jay thought to hisself.

"Fasho my nigga." Jay answered.

He started to sit the coke bag to the side after weighing it up but Dirt stopped him.

"Um umm let me get that my nigga!" He dug in his pocket a pulled out a stack of money peeling off Jay money fast as he could.

"Here." He said with a locked mouth giving Jay the money and grabbing the bag.

Jay weighed the weed while Dirt played with his nose.

"Here you go my nigga." He looked up to see Dirt with the white powder in his nose hair.

"Suff, suff." Dirt sniffed trying to clean his nose.

"I'm about to be out brah brah." Jay said.

They dapped up and as Jay walked to leave, his phone started ringing.

"Hello? Oh ok I'll be there when you get there."

When he got in his car to pull off, he looked up to see Dirt peeking out the window. He just shook his head.

"Boy you need to stay off that shit Dirt." He thought to hisself..

STACKS

Ten minutes later he was pulling into the El Cheapo gas station. He parked his car and didn't notice Erica in the parking lot, so he walked in the store and grabbed a soda and some chips. When he came back out he saw her red Pontiac Sunfire parked in front of the store, his phone started to ring.

"Hello?" Jay answered.

"Where you at? I'm parked outside the store, you told me to meet you at."

"I'll be there in fifteen minutes." He lied trying to test her attitude out.

He loved bad bitches, but a bad bitch with an attitude, he couldn't stand. He always ended up fucking and leaving them how he found them. He walked back in the store while still talking to her.

"Dang 15 minutes, ok. I came all this way I guess I have to wait for you then. I'm about to go in the store and get me something to drink while I wait on you, it's hot as hell today."

"Fasho, I'll be there shortly." He pulled his hat low over his eyes and walked through the store.

She walked in the store not noticing Jay. He walked up behind her and grabbed her ass. "Damn you fine miss."

"What the fuck!" She yelled while turning around trying to swing.

"Whoa, whoa, it's me it's me!"

"Boy I was about to fuck you up, I thought you said 15 minutes!" She said punching him in the arm.

"I was just playing damn. I wanted to surprise you, you look good lil mama."

Her hair was in a clip and she was rocking a name chain. She was in some gold and black coochie cutters that were made of a stretch material with the top to match, Steve Madden heels, some MK accessories and she smelled like Obsessions perfume by Beyoncé.

He opened his arms and gave her a hug and she hugged him back.

"You smell and look good yourself."

He was in a Akoo outfit, some wheat Timberlands, a gold chain and watch.

"I appreciate that." He said.

He walked behind her to the register while admiring her perfect figure, the heels made her walk bowlegged.

"Damn, I can't wait to stick my dick inside her, I know that pussy good." He thought to himself.

She placed the soda on the counter and also reached under the counter, grabbed a bag of skittles and put them up there too.

"That will be $2.68." The cashier said.

"I got it lil mama." Jay said and put a $20 bill on the counter.

"Also let me get four packs of Swisher Sweets please?" He asked the cashier.

"That will be $6.70," the cashier grabbed the $20 and gave him his change and placed the items in a bag.

"Thank you." Erica said to Jay.

"You welcome lil mama."

"So where you taking me?" She asked.

"Well first we going to hit the mall because I got to get the new Forces and from the looks of it I'm a get you a pair too."

"Why what's wrong with my heels?" She asked confused.

"Because where we going you going to wish you had on sneakers."

"And where is that?" She said curiously.

"It's a surprise, just come on you wasting time with all these questions."

He grabbed her hand and led her out the store. She locked her doors and they left.

When they pulled up at the mall he found a parking space easily seeing it was early in the day, everybody was either working or in school. When they walked into the mall, Jay's phone went off.

"Hello?"

"Jay where are you at! You were supposed to be at the job site hours ago!" Mr. Timmy said yelling through the phone.

"Oh Mr. Timmy. How are you Sir?" Jay said, trying to sound professional.

"This is what I need you to do. Take your little fagot ass out there in the sun and slang trash cans for $7.80 a hour mother fucker. Matter of fact would you work at that hourly rate or let your family member do that amount of labor for that little ass money? Do you think that would be reasonable?"

"Mothafu-

Before he could answer Jay ended the call.

"What was that all about?" Erica looked at him confused.

"I was showing someone that every black man is not ignorant."

"I heard that. I see how you got on his level and broke his ass down." They both were laughing.

They went inside the mall and stopped at Champs. Jay grabbed the new Forces, she liked them but didn't like them for herself. She decided to go with some black Pumas with gold stripes. Plus they matched what she had on. The sales associate went and grabbed their sizes and came back.

"You want to try these on sir?"

"Nawl, I'm good." Jay answered.

"What about you ma'am?"

"I'm fine." Erica answered.

They walked to the register to check out. Jay grabbed a pair of NBA socks to add to the order, he didn't need them but he knew at Champs sales reps got paid off commission and wanted to help the dude out.

"Will this be all?" The young sales rep asked.

"Yea." Jay answered.

"Your total is $177.38." The young man said while bagging up the shoes.

Jay pulled out a stack of money, peeling off two $100 dollar bills.

"You in college." Jay asked the young man.

"Yea I'm taking up business management and marketing."

"Good keep at it and you can own any kind of store you want. Hard work and determination will get you anything you want in life. Don't ever settle for being employed, become your employer as the boss. Work towards becoming the boss and you already doing that."

"Thanks man." He said handing Jay the change.

"You keep that lil brah."

"Thanks big brah. What did you go to school for that got you so paid?"

"Marketing." He lied giving the young man hope.

"I'll see you around lil nigga." He grabbed Erica's hand while walking out the store.

"Marketing huh? Nigga you was in prison for 3 years, when did you go to college?" She said with a yea right look.

"Shit I didn't even finish high school. I had to get my G.E.D in prison, but everybody need hope and motivation baby."

"Well I think that was very sweet of you and thank you for the shoes. Is this how you do all your other girls?"

"No that's how I do my girl." Jay shot back.

"Is that right?" Erica said blushing.

"That's right."

"Well I hope you're not trying to flatter me with gifts Mr. Moss, because you can't buy my heart."

"Don't get it twisted you ain't getting nothing else today. Everything else I pay for is contributed to this date."

"Whatever nigga and who said I was ready to be dating?" She ask smiling.

"Me because I'm not your last man and I'ma do everything he should have done. Now let's go to the pretzel booth." He said taking control.

"Now, I can't even argue with you on that." She said laughing.

After they left the pretzel booth Jay saw Beautiful, Coco and Candi walking towards him. It felt awkward seeing that he had been fucking Candi for a few weeks, but fuck it she had a nigga and he was single.

"What's up ladies?" He said coolly before they could come over acting ghetto.

He knew he was in the clear with Erica because she knew he brought the girls to Beaufort every Thursday from the parties, even though she had only came that one night she always heard gossip on how crunk the parties were.

"Hey Jay!" All of them yelled, giving him a hug.

"Ladies, this is my friend Erica. Erica this is Beautiful, Coco and Candi."

"Hi, how are y'all doing?" Erica said.

"We good, well we will see you Thursday Jay and have fun on your date." Candi said, sounding slightly jealous.

"Fasho y'all hold it down." He grabbed Erica by the hand and they walked off.

After sitting down, eating their pretzels and talking about their pasts, Jay was ready for the next step.

"Ok, now we going to the booth."

"What's that?" Erica asked.

"Didn't I tell you to stop asking questions and let me treat." He said while pulling her along.

They walked to the small sit down picture both to take pictures. As they took the pictures they made crazy faces and bunny ears behind each other. On the last couple Jay kissed her on the cheek while she smiled. After they were done they looked over the pictures laughing at themselves.

"That was so much fun I'm really enjoying myself." She said laughing.

"Me to lil mama." He said smiling.

They left the mall and stopping by Zaxby's, only because he wanted her to enjoy the date they could have a special dinner date another day.

"How did you know this was one of my favorite spots?" She asked pointing at the big bird as they entered the parking lot.

"Don't even try it this is one of my favorite spots, they got the best fast food hands down. Don't be trying to steal my spots."

"Ok whatever nigga. I love their salads um umm." She said thinking about the salads.

When they walked in she ordered a chicken salad with a sprite and Jay order the Wings and Things with a milkshake to go, so he could continue the date he had been planning as they went along.

"This was a good date, I haven't had this much fun in a long time." Erica said.

"It's not over yet lil mama, I got a couple of more things I want to do."

She started to ask what it was, but decided to just let him surprise her.

They pulled up to one of the biggest parks in Savannah called Lake Mayer. It was beautiful, Erica was grateful for the sight and to get away from Beaufort.

"Alright you can put the sneakers on now lil mama."

"Ok." She said reaching in the back seat and putting on her brand new Pumas.

They sat at one of the tables and enjoyed their food. Then, walked the track that was made around the Lake.

"So what do you want out of life and what are your goals?" Erica asked.

"Well you know my short term goal, which is throwing parties. My short term goal will lead me to my long term goal. Which is to own my own club one day." Jay answered with confidence.

"Oh ok that's what's up." She said impressed glad he wasn't a dumb nigga who didn't have any goals at all, that thought he could sell drugs all his life.

"What about you, what are your goals?" Jay asked.

"Well I'm already working on my short term goal by going to school for cosmetology and business. After I graduate I'm going to open my own salon."

"How is it you make it sound so easy? Where you going to get the money from to open the salon?" He asked curiously.

"Well my father started a trust fund for me when I was 3 years old, with the option to receive the funds at 18 if I went to college. I ended up doing very good through high school making valedictorian getting a full scholarship, so I left the funds in the bank so they could continue to gross. Once I finish school, then I'll use the money to start my own business. I could have went to school for something else, but I decided to go for something that I liked doing, owning my own business."

"That's what's up, that's smart as hell lil mama." He said excited for her.

"Thank you." She said smiling.

"But I got a question, where you get the cash for all the Gucci, Michael Kors, and YSL? You got a sugar daddy or something?"

"What, nigga please. I don't need a man to do nothing for me. I stay with my parents for free of charge for as long as I'm in school. So, when I work all my checks go to spoiling myself."

"Your ass still spoiled."

"Don't hate." She said smiling.

"Whatever, daddy's little girl."

They both laughed as they walked around the lake. They walked the track twice before heading back to Jay's car. When they got back in the car Jay drove towards downtown Savannah.

Jay pulled into the parking garage and found a spot to park.

When they started walking down river street, Erica figured out that the sneakers were for walking. The cobble stoned ground still had her walking sideways.

"Jay, if you would have brought me down here in heels I would have kicked your ass." She said laughing.

"Now why would I do that? Come on let's go in one of my favorite spots." He said putting his arm across her shoulder.

When they walked into the bar they had all kinds of frozen alcoholic beverages in big machines like ice cream mixers.

"Which one you want?" Jay asked her.

"Umm, I don't know it's so many to choose from. I think I'll go with the strawberry flavor."

"Fasho, bartender over here!" He said, waving his money over the counter.

"Can I get a Call-A-Cab and a Strawberry?" Jay asked the bartender.

"Coming right up." She said, grabbing his money. She fixed the drinks and came back with his change.

"Keep the change." Jay said, grabbing both drinks and walking back towards Erica to leave out of the crowded bar.

They walked down Bay Street laughing and enjoying each other's company while sightseeing. Jay stopped and bought her a handmade rose from one of the peddlers, made of palmetto leaf. They stopped at two more bars along the way. Erica was enjoying herself and feeling Jay. On the way back to the car they rode on a carriage and horse. They had been kissing for so long that they didn't even realize that they had pulled up in front of the parking garage, until the carriage driver told them they were there. He paid the driver and they headed for the car.

"This was the best date I've ever been on, ever. I don't even want it to end. Thank you so much, for showing me a good time Jay." She said a little tipsy.

"You don't have to thank me, it was my pleasure just to be with a woman as beautiful as you."

"Aww, you're so sweet." She gave him a hug and kissed him softly on the lips.

He opened the door for her and they pulled off. When they pulled off on the highway Erica was already knocked out. He was going to take her to her car but decided not to let her drive home drunk and drained from the long day of fun.

He pulled up in front of his apartment and carried her into the house.

"Damn I can get some of this pussy right now if I wanted to." He thought to hisself, but decided against it because she wasn't any regular female Erica was wifey material. He didn't want her to think he took advantage of her and only wanted to have sex, when she woke up the next morning. So he placed her in his bed tucking her in, while he slept on the couch.

CHAPTER 15

D was waiting at the airport for his cousin, Reese. He was told that at the desk the flight from New York to Savannah was running 30 minutes late, so he decided to go to Wendy's and grab something to eat while waiting. After he finished his Baconator and large Coke he walked back to the gate where his cousin would be entering the airport.

"New York to Savannah has now arrived at gate eight." He heard them say over the intercom. 10 minutes later Reese was walking through the gate with the mixed crowd of people looking around for their family members.

"Man I know I told this nigga my flight landed at 11:00 its fucking 11:28." Reese said looking at his watch.

"Yo Reese, over here you ugly motherfucker!" D said waving his hands in the air.

"Man fuck you!" Reese said smiling, walking towards his cousin giving him a hug.

"What's up son? Nigga you done put on some weight, you getting kind of chubby B." Reese said.

"Shit that's because my wife been cooking almost every night nigga. I'm eating good." D said rubbing his belly.

"Yea whatever nigga you probably can't throw them hands like you used too though you to fat. I probably can beat yo ass now son, I know them hands slow." Reese said smiling.

"Nigga my hands certified, I'll still fuck you up like I used to do when we was little." D said smiling.

'Yea you right, you did use to kick my ass. That's because your people put you in boxing and my people couldn't afford it, you spoiled motherfucker."

They both started laughing.

"Yea, yea nigga. Man so what's been going on with the fam?" D asked.

"Shit same old same old, the only thing that's changed is Victoria just had another baby." Victoria was Reese's sister.

"What? Man get the fuck out of here, that's what five." D asked.

"Add one more nigga." Reese stated.

"Six! She only 25, she Od'in for real son. She might as well get her tubes tied, burnt, or something shit." D said.

"Fuck burnt, cremate them motherfuckers." Reese said back.

They both laughed and talked about the past as they left the airport. Once they got on the road D started on a more serious conversation.

"The reason I called you down here B is because I'm getting out the dope game B, and I want you to run my operation for me."

"Oh word, why you getting all the way out the game son?" Reese said surprised.

"Yea B I got a baby on the way fam and my wife ain't having it no more."

"Damn son, she got you all open and shit. I can't believe you leaving the game."

"Yea man but this is the deal. I can introduce you to all my clientele and let them know you will be taking over my position and all I want is a 20% cut of the profits.

"True. How much money coming in every week?" Reese asked trying to figure the money out.

"Almost $20,000 a week but half of that goes to re-up." D told him.

"Damn son you been banking like that down here in the country?"

"Shit it wasn't easy and I just started to reach them numbers because of a young boy I been fuckin with. The nigga be moving weight like a bodybuilder son. He's going to be your main customer so keep him close, plus he loyal and thorough so y'all should be good."

"Word, word." Reese said taking everything in and thinking.

By the time he finished filling him in they were pulling up in front of Nikki's old apartment.

"This where you going to be staying and the red mustang is your car." D said holding the keys in the air.

"Say word son! Man you a real ass nigga, that's why I fuck with you fam. You keep it 100!" He said excited.

"I got to make sure you come in the game with everything you need my nigga. If you don't have the tools how you going to be able to work?"

"Word you right."

"But we can check the spot and the car out later. I got to make a couple of runs and introduce you to some people so we can get shit rolling."

As they rode around the city D made a few stops introducing his cousin to his plays, telling them he would be serving them from now on and the prices would stay the same.

"Damn this shit sweet all you do is pull up on niggas all day?" Reese asked.

"Yea but this shit ain't always sweet, this the South side of town this the more calm side of town. The East and West sides are where the straight up hoods are. Especially on the West niggas getting killed and robbed every other day. So don't get too comfortable and think shit sweet, because then you slippin." D warned him.

"Understood." Reese said.

When they went on the East and West sides of town, Reese saw just what D was talking about. It was the complete opposite from the South side, it was the ghetto. Niggas standing on the corners of the blocks hustling, bad ass kids running around, all the way to the busted bad looking apartments and houses. D rode down Chester Street on the West side to stop by Solo's trap. Solo cooked coke for niggas and sold crack and coke out of a abandoned house, paying the owner of the house $1000 a month just to keep the lights on and not rent the house out. The landlord knew that Solo was doing something illegal but didn't ask as long as he paid him his money he didn't want to know. If he ever got caught he knew the owner would say her never saw him in his life.

D parked a block away from the house not wanting anybody to see his car in front of the supposed to be empty house.

"Wait here right quick I'll be right back. I don't want this nigga to be acting like you the police or think we trying to rob him or some shit." D said.

D walk to the back of the house and knocked on the door.

"Who is it?" Solo yelled.

"It's me nigga open up." D yelled back.

Click clack. D heard the hammer being pulled on the pistol.

"Me who?" Solo asked.

"Man nigga it's D. What you going to shoot me?"

Solo cracked the door a little, then opened it all the way letting D in.

"Man nigga I told you about that shit I got too much work in here to get robbed or go to jail. If anybody come on that bull shit I'ma hold court right here."

"Nigga you crazy as a fuck for real, for real son. That's why I fuck with you though they don't make niggas like you no more. Niggas snitch too much these days they don't stand for shit." D said.

"Shit I been in these streets since I was 12 brah brah, they raised me so that's where I'ma die when I do." Solo stated back.

"Word, word. I got the eight ounces you texted me about but check this out, this my last trip B."

"What you mean this your last trip?" He said looking up from the stove where he was pouring baking soda into the pot."

"I'm getting out the game. She been good to me but you know she a bitch and can take everything you got. So, I'm a leave her ass alone before she take me for mines." D explained.

"No doubt, so you really done huh?" Solo asked.

"Yea B it's over."

"Damn nigga, I'm happy for you and all but shit what about me? I mean you just gone leave a nigga out here dry?"

"That's what I need to talk to you about, I'm passing everything down to my cousin. He a real nigga and I'm a let him continue everything I started. The prices and quality will remain the same from the same source." D explained.

"Fasho, but he ain't one of them young dumb niggas is he? No offense brah but everybody ain't built the same. The game ain't for everybody." Solo said knowing what he had seen and encountered in his 32 years of living.

"Nawl B, I mean he ain't me but the nigga don't make dumb moves. I'm vouching for him, he here now. I want you to chop it up with him but I wanted to get the go ahead from you before I brought somebody in your spot fam. It's all about respect."

"Well shit if you say the nigga is who you say he is, bring him in so I can meet him." Solo told him.

D walked outside and told his cousin to come on and grabbed his duffle bag containing the coke. D knocked on the door and Solo cracked it then let them both in. When Reese walked into the house and didn't see any furniture just a stove, a wooden chair, 20 ounces on a counter and boxes of baking soda lined across another. He just wondered and would ask his cousin questions later.

"Reese this Solo. Solo this my cousin Reese." D said introducing them.

"So you taking over huh? I'm sure your cousin been filling you in and everything but never call me. The first time you call me, you lost out on a customer because I'm throwing my phone away. That's how I operate, off texting just like your cousin. You see all this coke? That's my life right there. No offense, but you play with my work you playing with my life. With that said you know everything about me and we both got a understanding, this is business." Solo explained.

"Word." Reese said agreeing.

Reese didn't like the way he was talking to him like some young nigga but brushed it off. They dapped up while D put the 8 ounces on a scale weighing them up, getting Solo's approval. After he was finished Solo gave him 10 rubber band stacks. D counted the money and got back on the road to meet a couple of more people.

"Yo B what's up with your boy, he ain't have no furniture in his spot?" Reese asked.

"That's his cook up spot that's why." D explained.

"Damn that nigga got a spot just to cook in, that's why he had all them O's?" Reese asked.

"Yea son that nigga cook work for most of the niggas in his hood."

"Why you just won't supply him for the niggas he cook for, then he can serve them? I mean you could easily front the nigga the work, so he can supply the niggas he fuck with." Reese suggested.

"Because everything ain't always what it seems and all money ain't good money. He got his people he been cookin up for, he probably got a set clientele he sales to maybe. It's not my business. So, without stepping on anybody's toes and fucking up niggas money in his hood, that's how he operates. That's how problems get started and niggas start killing and robbing, because they ain't eating. He keeping everything steady in his hood. He already got a way he process and handles his business and that's the same with me. You gotta respect the game and not get too greedy. You gotta be careful in these streets and keep your eyes and ears open so you can focus on what's going on around you. Niggas is greasy and killing for petty cash. So, don't get too greedy or flashy out here B."

"Word, word, I hear you B." Reese said.

After making one more stop D drove back to Nikki's old apartment giving him the keys to the apartment and two cell phones, a throw away phone to hustle off of and a everyday use phone. While Reese checked out his used Mustang, D called Jay..

"Ummm." Erica woke up stretching.

"Where the fuck am I!?" She asked herself as she pulled the blanket back looking at her clothes. She was still fully dressed the only thing that was off was her shoes.

"Oh shit, I know I didn't fuck this man on the first date!?" She said feeling between her legs thinking the worst.

But after feeling on her body she knew her juice box hadn't been touched, so she was relieved. She got up and walked into the kitchen smelling eggs and bacon.

"Aww you making me breakfast?" She asked Jay.

"Anytime you spend the night with me, you get spoiled with a hot breakfast." He said leaning in to kiss her, she puckered her lips up but was cut off."

"Wait you brushed your teeth?" Jay asked.

"No not yet. Why?" Erica asked confused.

"Um you need to handle that then, I put you a toothbrush on the sink." He said holding his nose.

"It's not that bad." She said laughing putting her hand in front of her mouth and I don't have any clothes I'm a woman I need to shower.

"I tell you what, after you brush your teeth come eat and I'll go get you some panties, bra and clothes."

"That sounds good." She agreed.

He kissed her forehead and she went and brushed her teeth. When she came back out he had set the table with bacon, eggs, butter biscuits, cheese grits and orange juice.

"Umm that smells and looks so delicious." She told him.

"I know that's because I cooked." Jay said bragging.

"Whatever." She said laughing.

She was really feeling Jay and his personality. He really knew how to treat a lady.

"Jay I had so much fun last night and thank you for not taking advantage of me."

"Oh that's what they call it? I thought it was getting what you paid for." Jay thought to himself.

"You're welcome lil mama and I would only do to your body what you want me too." He lied, but knew it would get him one step closer to the pussy. Plus he wanted to make her his main anyways. But if she took too long to fuck he was going to go get some pussy from somebody else and come back to her later.

He grabbed her hand and bowed his head.

"God is great God is good. Let us thank Him for this food. Bow our heads we are fed. Give us Lord our daily bread. Lord I thank you for all my blessings, especially placing this beautiful woman in front of me while I enjoy my breakfast. Amen."

"Damn this nigga so smooth. Is it wrong if I want to give him some pussy now and he just got through praying?" She thought to herself.

They enjoyed their breakfast. After they were finished she helped him clear the table. He told her not to but she refused to just sit and watch him clean up after he had cooked for her. After they had washed the dishes together he got her size in panties and bra, then went to buy her some new ones. When he left, she ran her a bubble bath soaking in the water then washing her body. When she washed over her juice box she found herself thinking of Jay, she hadn't had sex in weeks. She then parted her legs and rubbed her hand across her clit going in circular motions.

"Ssssss, oooh, J-Jay." She said thinking of him, then sticking two fingers inside her juices touching her g-spot while rubbing on her clit.

"Ssss, ummm, s-shit." She moaned as she came on her hand from the excitement of what she was doing, as Jay came through the front door.

She got out of the tub and walked into the living room to see Jay on the phone texting.

"Overtime, the bar by Savannah State College?" He texted.

"Yea." D texted back.

"Alright I'll meet you there at 5 p.m." Jay texted him back.

When he looked up Erica was standing in the front of him wrapped in only a towel, with lust filled eyes, with the tips of her hair dripping wet from taking a bath.

"I got you a laced bra and panty set from Victoria Secret. You like it?" He said pulling the set out of the bag.

"Yes, I like it but I want you." She said while letting the towel fall to her feet.

Jays dick got hard as steel just looking at her perfect body. Her breast were perky sitting up right causing her nipples to point at him. When Jay looked down at her neatly shaved pussy in the shape of a triangle, he felt hisself pre-cum making his boxers stick to the tip of his dick. Shit in his mind the way her pussy was shaved made him think of a arrow pointing down to her pussy, meaning place Jay's dick here.

He grabbed her kissing on her soft lips giving her pecks, then parting her lips with his, placing his tongue on hers, then moving to her neck placing kisses.

"Ummm. That feels good papi." Erica moaned.

"Damn did she just talk Spanish to a nigga? I'm about to beat this pussy up!" He couldn't take it no more he lifted her in the air and wrapped her legs around his waist.

"I gotta fuck yo sexy ass in the bed fuck the couch. I got to lay up in this pussy." He thought to hisself while kissing on her, walking down the hall.

He laid her on the bed and sucked on her neck then on her nipples.

"Ssssss, s-shit papi that feels good." She said moaning.

He then place kisses on her belly and at the top of her love box, stopping only to take off his shirt but it still caused Erica anticipation, she wanted him bad. She looked down at him between her legs, staring over his prison tattoos.

"Damn how many tattoos this nigga got?" She thought to herself getting turned on even more.

He grabbed one of her legs lifting it straight in the air and kissed down her thigh until he got to her juice box kissing it passionately then sucking on her clit while she rotated her hips on his face.

"Ssssss, oooh papi, r-right there sssss, oooh, ummm!" This the best head

I eve-, huuu, oooh shit!" She couldn't even get all her words out he was eating the pussy so good.

Jay stopped sucking on her clit because he didn't want her to come yet. He then took off his shoes and shorts and got in the bed and laid beside her.

"Come sit on my face baby." Jay said.

"Ok daddy." She was happy because nobody had ever ate her pussy like he did.

"And I get to ride his face, I must be the luckiest bitch in the world to ride this tongue." She placed her legs across his head, he licked and sucked the juices out of her body, as she rotated on his face backwards. She could see his dick bulging in his boxers.

"Suck on it baby." Jay said as he sucked her on clit.

"Ssss, ok papi."

When she pulled his pipe out of his boxers she couldn't believe how big his dick was, but she liked it. She placed it in her mouth filling up her jaws.

"Sluup, sluup, sluup." She sucked on him as good as he was eating her out.

Damn baby that's what I'm talking about!" Jay said with his hands pushing her ass cheeks up causing him to eat her pussy even better, as she gobbled on his dick.

That made her stop sucking and look back at him from too much pleasure.

"Sssss, oooh, s-shit!" She said moaning.

"Plat, plat!" Jay slapped her ass hard, but kept licking.

"Ouch!" She yelled but kept her pussy on his face as he continued eating.

"Who told you to stop sucking? Keep sucking that dick!"

"Ok papi." She said slurping on his dick while she started to vibrate and cum in his mouth.

"Sssss, ummm, damn daddy!" She moaned as she came hard, but kept sucking on his pipe.

"That's enough but stay like that." He said sliding from under her while she stayed on her hands and knees.

He got behind her on his knees, admiring her caramel ass while pulling on his dick. He placed his hand on her back pushing her head down more, causing her to lay her head on the bed and arch her ass up.

He then spread her legs a little more causing her pussy lips to smile. Now he could see the neatly shaved arrow just like he wanted it, pointing to the pussy. He slid in her slow because he didn't want her running from him.

"Shit baby you so wet, fuck!" He said as he inched hisself inside of her.

"Huuu, huuu, huuu, huuu, ssss, s-shit, p-papi you too big." Her pussy was soaking on his dick, as her pussy made skeet and queefing noises on him.

"Sluuup, puuump, sluuup, puuump, sluuup, puuump!" Where the noises her pussy was making as he entered in and out of her.

As he continued to slide deeper in her, it was like her pussy had a grip on his dick not allowing him go in too deep. As he pulled his pipe out he could see her pussy hole stuck on his dick, trying to slide off gripping. He only had a little over half of his dick in her, but he felt he was going to come soon. Plus the way the pussy felt, looked and sounded wasn't helping. He went in deeper causing it to fart louder.

"Puuuump, sluuuup, puuuuump!"

"Sssss, oooh, auugh shit wait!" She screamed as he slid deep inside her and pumped harder and faster causing her to grip the sheets. While her ass jiggled and slipped against his pelvis.

"Sssss, oooh, s-shit, I'm about to come on this big dick papi! Sssss, oh shit!" She screamed as she came creaming on his dick causing him to pull out and bust on her ass cheeks.

"Augh fuck, damn baby!" He said slapping his dick on her ass.

She sat there stuck in the same position he put her in, with her pussy hole wide open pushing in and out trying to calm itself down.

He went and got a rag and wiped her off.

"Could you run me some water baby? My pussy hurt I need to let it soak." Erica asked drained.

"I got you lil mama." Jay said.

When Jay finished running her water she went into the bathroom sat in the tub, patting her pussy.

"Wooo Jay your dick too big. I got to get used to it before you fuck me like that again."

"I'm sorry baby I got you next time, I'll go softer." Jay said lying.

"Whatever liar." She said laughing.

After she soaked in the tub for a while, they took a shower together.

When they finished they got dressed and left the house so he could drop her off to her car and they could get their day started.

"So when you coming back to Savannah to spend time with me?" He asked Erica.

"When do you want me too?" She said smiling.

"Really I don't want you to go. I want you to stay forever but I know you got school and it's too soon for that."

"Awww, you so sweet are you getting soft for me Jay?"

"I don't know about all that, but I am feeling you lil mama and I want you to be mine."

"I'm already yours Jay you got me more than you know and you mine you think you can get the pussy and me not claim you, nigga please."

They both started laughing.

"You coming to my party though?"

"You know I'ma be there, everybody in Beaufort talking about it."

"Ok then I want you to walk in with me."

"For real?"

"Hell yea baby why not? You my girl now."

"Ok then daddy." She said smiling.

"I want you to call me and soon as you can, so I can know you made it home safe. Ok?"

"Ok."

They kissed and made plans to see each other later and parted ways.

CHAPTER 16

Jay pulled up to Overtime, a small bar by Savannah State University to meet D. He didn't see D's Intrepid parked out front, but when he walked in the bar he noticed him sitting in the far back corner conversating with somebody.

"What's up big homie?" Jay walked up showing D love.

"What's up B?" D said smiling.

"Jay this my cousin Reese. Reese this the nigga I was telling you about my homie Jay." D said introducing them.

"What's up brah brah?" Jay said giving him dap.

"So what we came here to talk about big brah." Jay asked.

"Nigga why you always straight to the point and in a hurry? Have a seat, order a drink and some wings or some shit it's on me B. The lemon pepper wings are the best ones too fam." D said happily.

"Man what the fuck is going on with this nigga. I hope he ain't bout to tell me he the police or some shit." Jay thought to hisself, but decided to sit down and order a sprite and some wings.

He didn't drink alcohol when he was out hustling, it was too risky.

"Where your car at brah and what the fuck you keep smiling and shit for big brah. You acting happier than a fagot with a bag of dicks nigga." Jay said checking him.

They all laughed.

"Nigga where the fuck you get that shit from?" He said with tears in his eyes.

"Man the 550 Mercedes out there, that's my new shit fam." D said behind tears.

"That's some flashy shit big brah but if you like it, I love it." Jay said.

"Thanks but listen up B the reason we came here is because I'm leaving

100

the game. I'm out B. Check this though, my cousin is going to be taking over for me and the prices and shit still going to be the same." He said dapping Reese up.

"Damn big homie you out, like for real, for real?" D asked.

"Yea B I'm going legit. It's over. I'm done."

"Congratulations man damn. I don't believe this shit but I'm happy for you my nigga!" He got up and gave his partner a hug.

Jay had built a relationship with D and looked up to him like a big brother. He got street knowledge from him, learning to be more observant and was happy for him but didn't like the fact he had to get his work from a new nigga. That was the only thing he was upset about. He knew that D and his cousin Reese were cut from the same sweater, but that didn't mean they were built the same, cousin or not.

"So what's your next move brah?" Jay asked.

"I'm opening a used car lot and a barber shop, everything already in motion."

"That's what's up man I got to get my shit together. I'm trying to take that legit route one day too. The streets ain't and can't be forever."

"It's ain't nothing to it B. Just find you a wife to handle all your paperwork that you don't have time for and it's done."

They both started laughing.

"Oh that's how it's so easy huh? I might have to try that." Jay said back.

Reese was sitting drinking on a Heineken not laughing anymore. He couldn't relate to anything they were saying he was broke and was ready to get in the field.

"Waitress over here, let me get another Heineken." He said passing her a five.

"Keep the change?" She asked smiling.

"Did I say keep the change?" Reese asked back.

"Broke ass nigga." She turned around to retrieve his drink while mumbling under her breath.

Reese thought he heard her say something, but didn't want to have to beat a bitch ass his first day in Georgia.

Jay and D were still laughing having a conversation about working at the Labor company, when Reese interrupted.

"So when you going to be ready to re-up again son?" He said asking Jay.

"When I'm ready I'll hit you up." Jay said to him.

Jay didn't like the way he asked that out of the blue, like he worked for him or some shit. And Jay wasn't working for nobody but Jay. He made a mental note of that to himself, how Reese might have got it twisted and thought he might be working for him. But he brushed it off and pushed it to the back of his head so he could celebrate with D.

"How many months along is the wife man?" Jay asked.

"She six months and ready to burst already. She always on her feet getting shit situated for the business. I keep telling her to sit her ass down but she said the doctor told her walking is good for the baby, shit if something happen to my seed I'ma kill her and the doctor B, word is bond."

"Nigga you a fool, ain't nothing going to happen to your baby, walking is good for the baby rookie." Jay said laughing.

"How you know? You don't have no kid's nigga."

"I got two younger sisters I helped my mama raise, that's how I know nigga."

"Oh ok so I'm kill you, her and the doctor if something happen to my seed."

They both stared laughing again.

"Hey I'm about to go have a smoke B." Reese said leaving.

"Word." D said still laughing out loud.

"So what's been going on with you, you still fucking with that stripper bitch?" D asked.

"Yea something like that." Jay said.

"What you mean "something like that? I thought the pussy was on point nigga, that lil bitch had you all open and shit. What happened?"

"Nawl it ain't nothing like that, the pussy aight."

"Oh now it's just aight, fill me in nigga." D said knowing it was something.

"Man I got this new bitch and now I know all pussy ain't the same. She got a super one my nigga. That motherfucker grab, skeet and squirt and all." Jay explained.

"Ooh shit, where you find her at?"

"Shit I didn't find her she found me. You know how I be throwing the parties in Beaufort?"

"Yea."

"This lil bitch remembered me from high school. She used to be jockin' a nigga hard, but I used to brush her off because she didn't have shit going on. Now the ugly caterpillar has turned into a butterfly. She wifey material on everything brah. Got her own money and all."

"Damn that's what up. You better lock her ass down before another nigga do and she got her own money, shiid."

"Shit who you telling. I'm working on keeping her around but let me get out of here and take my ass to work. I need to go make somethin shake." Jay said getting up to leave.

"Yea I see you in your uniform." D said.

They both knew where he was going, to hustle and the orange work vest was a front for the cops. From time to time that's how they dressed and if they got pulled over it threw the cops off track a little thinking he was either going or coming from work.

"January on the 20th brah club Karma." He yelled leaving out the bar.

"I told you I'm there nigga." D yelled back.

When Jay walked out the bar Reese was smoking a fresh lit cigarette.

"Brah brah, I'm a get with you when I'm ready. What's your number?'

They exchanged numbers, but Jay didn't like the vibe. For one, Reese had pissed him off because Jay got the impression, Reese was thinking he worked for him.

Jay left and was on his way to meet his first play when his phone rang.

"Hello."

"What's up handsome?"

"What's up sexy?" He said smiling.

"I was just calling to let you know I made it home safe." Erica said.

"Ok lil mama, but I miss you already. When I'm going to see you again?"

"Aww you do? I don't know. How about when you come to Beaufort, Thursday?"

"I can see you then if that's work. I'ma have to drive the girls back that same night. I want to chill just me and you." Jay said.

"I see what you mean, but I'm only free during the weekends. I have school and work on most weekdays. We'll have to make plans."

"Damn ok we'll figure something out baby, I'll call you later though. Ok?"

"Ok bae later." They both hung up the phone.

After Jay had sold 4 ½ ounces coke and 10 ounces of loud he figured he would call it a night.

CHAPTER 17

*C*andi had been acting funny lately. She hadn't gave John any pussy in almost a month. She always claimed she was tired or just didn't feel like it, even on the days she didn't have to work. Forcing him to jack off when he had a woman in his bed. John had called out of work earlier and had been parked around the corner from their house for the last 3 hours...

Ring, ring, ring.

"Hello?" Candi answered the phone.

"What's up?" Jay responded back.

"Nothing you act like you don't fuck with me like that since you started fucking with that lil bougie bitch." Candi shot.

"What you mean? It's only been what five, six days since the last time we fucked and two days since we talked. Plus last time I checked you had a nigga. What you sounding all jealous for?" Jay shot back.

"Jealous, nigga you got me fucked up." Candi said back.

"But anyways, I called yo ass because I wanted to see you." Jay said.

Jay knew she was jealous and it was making his dick hard. He knew she would try to fuck him better to prove her pussy was better, but he knew better than that.

"Oh yea? I want to see you too." She said back.

It was 12:15 a.m. and the only thing open was fast food and legs. They both knew what was about to go down.

"Where you at?" She asked.

"Home but I'm about to go get a room."

"Why you want to go get a room and you got a apartment?" Candi asked.

"Because I got something I want to show you, so I want to get a room. You going to come or not? You asking all these questions."

"Yea give me 45 minutes."

"Ok meet me at the Hyatt, I'll tell you which room when you get there."

"Ok." She agreed.

They both hung up the phone getting ready...............................
....

John was starting to feel bad for doubting Candi's loyalty and calling in to work sick. He was losing out on money he couldn't even afford to lose out on. In the middle of thinking how wrong he was he noticed some headlights approaching from the left. As the lights got closer he crouched down in his seat, even though his car wasn't visible he wanted to be careful not to get noticed. When he saw the pink Honda passing by, his heart started to beat 10x's faster.

"Where the fuck her ass going this late!?" He said to hisself cranking up his car to follow her..

Candi pulled up in front of the hotel and grabbed her duffle bag out the back seat. As she walked into the hotel she didn't see John following her in a distance. The only thing that was on her mind was riding Jay's dick. She went to the desk and got the key like Jay had told her and walked around the corner towards the room.

John was peeking around the corner watching to see what room she entered.

She entered into room 125 and about a minute later, a young man came to the door she had just entered with a bucket of ice opening it with a key then walking in.

"I'ma kill this bitch." He said, with hate in his heart and tears in his eyes to hisself..

As soon as Jay opened the door he walked in and turned on sports center, lighting a blunt.

Since they had been fucking Candi had been smoking more. Every time he lit up, she found herself at least hitting it a couple of times, as he smoked back to back. She was also starting not to cough as much.

"What's up lil mama?" Jay asked.

"Ain't nothing, pass the blunt though I ain't smoke all day. Suup, suup, suup." She inhaled and exhaled with ease passing it back to him.

She picked up her bag and went into the bathroom to change. When she came back out she had on a one piece red and black thong bodysuit with a slit on the pussy part, with the option to fuck with it on before taking it off. She also had on some black Manolo heels and red lipstick, giving him a fuck me face.

Jay's dick was bulging through his basketball shorts. She walked over and bent over in front of him turning off the TV, so could see her pussy lips from the back poking through the slit in the bodysuit.

"Damn baby all this for me." Jay asked surprised.

"If you want it." She said walking off, her ass bouncing with each step.

"Where you going?" Jay said holding his dick in his hand.

"Nowhere I'm just about to get my phone to turn on some music nigga, your thirsty ass."...

John was in the hallway trying to decide if he wanted to knock on the door and ask to speak to her, call her or kick the fucking door down. He found hisself pacing for too long. It had been about 20 minutes and he knew it wouldn't be long before she started fucking whoever he was. So he decided to call first...

When Candi came back she was playing Alicia Keys -Secrets.

"I won't tell your secrets, your secrets are safe with me." Alicia sang through the speaker.

Candi started rotating her hips slowly to the beat, teasing him turning around clapping her ass cheeks softly then leaning over the dresser placing her right knee on it making one cheek bounce at a time, while looking at him biting her bottom lip.

Jay walked up dropping his shorts and boxers to his feet. Then put a glob of saliva on the tip of his fingers and rubbed it on the head of his shaft walking up behind her.

"Nasty ass." She said looking at him rub his rock hard erection.

"You know you like that nasty shit." He said as he slid into her from the back.

"Ssss, oooh, shit, f-fuck, ssss, damn daddy!"

His first three strokes were slow and long, but after his whole stick was wet he started to pound deep inside her while pushing, holding her right ass cheek up with his palm of his hand.

"Damn girl this pussy good." He said smacking on her left cheek.

"Auugh, fuck, ssss, shit!" She yelled.

The music stopped playing as her phone started to ring. Jay slowed his strokes down.

"No daddy don't stop fuck this pussy, I'm about to come!" Candi begged.

Jay accelerated again.

"Shit look how wet I got this pussy. Pap!" Jay thought to hisself, slapping her ass hard.

"Auugh f-fuck daddy!"

"Pap! Who pussy this is!? Pap! I said who pussy this is!?" Jay yelled.

"Ssss, auugh f-fuck it's yours it's yours! Ooh shit daddy I'm about to cum!"

BOOM! BOOM! BOOM!

"Who the fuck is that!?" Jay slid out of Candi fast, pulling his boxers and shorts up in one swift motion and quickly grabbing his .9 from under the pillow.

She was shaking trying to regroup from the orgasm that happened at the same time as the knock on the door, causing her to come harder than expected.

Jay pulled the hammer back on his gun. While she was just removing her leg off the dresser, he grabbed her arm hard snatching her up.

"Who the fuck is that!?" He said in an angry whisper.

"Ouch why you grabbing me like that?"

"Because nobody knows I'm fuckin here! So you better start talking before I beat your ass!"

"Jay you trippin, let my arm go you're hurting me."

BOOM! BOOM! BOOM!

"Candi I know your ass in there!" John yelled from the other side of the door.

"Bitch, who the fuck is at the door!?" Jay asked.

"Oh shit, that's my boyfriend!" She said with fear on her face and tears in her eyes.

"Who? What you mean your boyfriend, you told that nigga you was here!?" Jay asked.

"Fuck no! He must have followed me here." Candi said thinking.

"Well you need to go and handle that before I do, that nigga knocking on my door like he the fuckin police! Y'all blowing up my spot making shit hot, you need to check that shit or I'm a handle it!"

"Candi bring your ass to the door, I know you in there!" John yelled from the other side of the door still.

She looked at the door, then at Jay with the pistol in his hand frowning. She knew she didn't want Jay to handle it, so she started taking slow steps to the door almost tip toeing like she was trying not to get caught but it was already done. She opened the door slowly trying to slide through the crack of the door.

"Hi." Candi said low.

"Bitch what the fuck you got on!?" He said pushing the door with force making it smack her on the forehead.

"Auugh fuck!" She yelled in pain.

She forgot she had on the bodysuit and heels, and knew he was about to do something he had never did before. Beat her ass.

She tried to slide back into the room and close the door but he grabbed her by the hair pulling her head back through the door.

"Auuugh, let my hair go John!"

"Bitch get your ass back out her!" John yelled.

He slammed her head against the door causing her to try to swing wildly trying to free herself, but he was too strong. He yanked her into the hallway, causing a couple of people to peep out their room doors.

"You fuckin around on me bitch, after I've been faithful to you all this time!?"

"Whap!" He punched her in the face causing her to stumble to the right tripping over in the heels and falling on the floor. She was crying viciously and holding her face in pain.

"A brah y'all really need to go home and talk about this or some shit, but please just leave from in front of my room!" Jay said standing in the door.

"What the fuck you say nigga!? And you fucking my bitch!" John said angrily.

"Man just take it somewhere else homie." Jay still pleaded.

John launched in the room towards him, but Jay sidestepped and punched him in his nose knocking him off balance causing his sight to go blurry.

Jay pulled him up straight by his shirt pulling the nine from behind his back pointing it at his face.

When John saw the pistol he gained his 20/20 back.

"Man I just want y'all to leave brah brah. I don't want your bitch, I'm telling you just dip!" Jay told him again.

Jay took the clip out the gun and the bullet out the chamber. He knew he couldn't kill or even shoot nobody at a hotel anyway, it was too many cameras and witnesses.

"Nigga fuck you, you ain't gone do shit!" John said dealing with his pride.

"Man listen leave brah, take your bitch and go home you making shi-"

"Fuck you!" John tried to buck at Jay again trying his hand, seeing Jay wasn't bout to shoot him.

"Whap, whap, whap, whap!" Jay started slapping the fuck out of him in the face with the pistol repeatedly.

"Jay no, please stop please!?" Candi cried.

Candi had been pulling on him trying to make him stop, but Jay had snapped and didn't hear or see her, until she jumped in between the gun and John's face almost taking one of the blows.

"You going to kill him please stop!? Please!?" She said crying uncontrollably.

"Get that nigga the fuck out of my shit!" Jay yelled.

She tried pulling him up but he was too heavy, he was dead weight to her. Johns' shirt was covered in blood, and his face looked like sandwich meat.

"Uuuh, uuuh, uuuh." All John could do was moan as she lifted his arm on her shoulder trying to walk with him. She was too weak to carry him.

Jay watched as she kept stumbling and knew the shit wasn't going to work.

"Man go take them fuckin heels off and change out that shit!" He said angrily knowing he was going to have to help her get his limp body the fuck out the room before the police came.

He knew somebody had to have called the police the way John had beat her ass in the hallway even if they didn't see what Jay had done to John. She came back in no more than 30 seconds flat ready to go.

Jay put John's arm across his shoulder pulling him up.

"Uuuh, uuuh, f-fuck you." John said as Jay dragged and walked him through the door.

"Yea I know, you blessed we wasn't in the streets because your ass would be dead fuck nigga." Jay said back.

"Candi grab that clip and bullet off the dresser and put em in my bag." Jay told her. When they walked to the elevator people were standing outside their rooms gossiping. When they saw them dragging John out down the hall covered in blood, they thought he was dead until he started moaning.

"Uuuh, uuuh, f-fuck yo-." He moaned in pain.

They walked him towards Candi's car and Jay heard the sirens wailing in the morning air and he wasn't about to stay around for the 21 questions. Jay dropped John's arm from around his shoulder putting all the weight on Candi.

"Damn, you could have at least helped me put him in the car Jay." Candi said complaining.

"Girl fuck that nigga you lucky I helped you bring his bitch ass out here, fuck that nigga! Give me my bag so I can go!" He said snatching the bag off her shoulder.

"And don't tell them folks shit about me either!" Jay ran to his car and pulled off squealing tires.

Candi struggled hard to get him in the car. His cuts were deep and wide, he was going to need stitches so she decided to take him to the hospital on the other side of town in case the police came to the close by hospital. She left out the hotel parking lot just in time, passing by the police as they were entering the hotel parking lot.

When she got to the hospital she still got questioned from the nurses and police about his well-being.

"So what happened again ma'am?" Officer Ricks asked.

"I just told you, we were walking downtown past a group of men and one of them grabbed my ass. I hit him and my boyfriend jumped in and they beat our asses." Candi lied.

"Well what did they hit him with, his face is pretty damaged?" Officer Ricks asked.

"I don't know I told you they were beating our asses. I couldn't see what it really was I think it was a pipe or something."

"And one of them grabbed your ass huh?"

"Yes that's what I said. Would you let someone grab your wife's ass?" She asked him hoping he would stop questioning her.

"Thank you that will be all for now ma'am. When they release Mr. Johnson, I will need to speak with him. If I don't get a call I will stop by you and Mr. Johnson's residence. I have the address." He handed her his card.

"Thank you." She said, grabbing the card.

After 40 stitches and patches were placed on John's head, he was prescribed 10mg Percocet pills and sent home later that day.

CHAPTER 18

Knock, knock, knock.

"Who is it?" Jay said before looking through the peephole.

"It's Chatham County Police."

"What the fuck?" Jay said to himself.

"Who are you looking for?" Jay asked.

"Mr. Jay'sean, we only have some quick questions to ask."

"Give me a minute." Jay left the pigs standing right at the door while he got a shirt to cover his tattoos. He knew they didn't have a warrant because they would have said so.

Jay opened the door walking out closing it behind him not wanting them to come in and smell the weed.

"Hi how you doing officer?"

"Ricks." He said extending his hand.

"Um. We have some questions for you, can you come down to the station? It will only take 20 minutes or so.

"Do you have a warrant?"

"No sir bu-"

"Well we can talk right here." Jay was only going to talk to the officer long enough to see what they had.

"Ok, well. Where were you last Tuesday?"

"I don't recall, where I was you got an idea?" Jay asked a question with a question, being smart.

"Well we I have received confirmation, that your I.D. was used to rent a hotel room on last Tuesday."

"Ok. Is that what you came all the way over here to tell me sir?"

"No it's not, at room 103 a crime took place a woman was pulled out of your room and beaten. Then that same man who had assaulted the woman that was pulled out of that same room, "your room" was carried out bloody by a man that looks just like you."

"Like me huh? I don't know what you're talking about, have any victims come forward?" Jay asked.

"No, but that's wh-"

"Well we don't have anything else to talk about. Are we done now?"

Officer Ricks turned red, he was hoping Jay would solve the case for him by telling on hisself. He knew Jay had beat the man but wanted Jay to fill in the puzzle for him and tell on hisself.

Jay turned and walked in the house closing the door in his face.

Ricks turned and walked to his car. He knew it was Candi, Jay and John on the video but didn't know why either one of them hadn't come forward about the incident.

It had been a week since Jay beat John's ass and they were coming at Jay like this. So he decided to lay low and make less moves than usual, because the police had questioned him about the hotel fight and he didn't know what exactly they were doing about it. He knew they had the video of parts of what happened and him helping carry John's bloody beat up body out of his hotel room. They just wanted one of them to tell on themselves, but as long as nobody said nothing they would be ok..

A couple days later Jay decided to go to Beaufort and see Erica he was stressed out and needed some special attention. They met at a ice cream shop across from Walmart parking lot.

"Yes can I get a Butter Pecan cone and a,....what kind you want baby?" Jay asked Erica.

"Chocolate." Erica responded.

"And a chocolate cone, please." He said as he peeled of a $10 bill and handed it to the lady.

"How was school today beautiful?" He asked Erica.

"It was ok, but these finals getting on my nerves. I can't wait until this school year is over."

"Yea me too so I can spend more time with you." He said grabbing the ice cream cones handing her one.

"Oh is that right?"

"Yea, you know I don't like, not being around you ma."

"What is it that you miss, is it this?" She seductively circled the tip of her ice cream with her tongue, then placing it in her mouth making a smooth point on the tip of the ice cream.

"Damn baby that's some freaky shit."

They both started laughing.

"Only for my man though."

"Oh I get to be your man now, so we official?"

"I know you didn't think you was going to be hitting all this and not have obligations? Pleeease, you might as well get rid of anybody you talking to because you're mine now."

He pulled her to him giving her a kiss taking the chocolate out her mouth.

"You the freaky one." She said smiling.

"Only for you baby." He lied knowing he had fucked Candi the other day.

They spent the rest of the day enjoying each other, walking through Walmart like little kids. Then going to get a room, suckin and fuckin each other until Erica tapped out.

"Damn baby why you do me like that, and why you keep waiting to the last minute to pull out?"

"It feel so good baby that's why." Jay said knowing what he was trying to do.

She got out the bed.

"Where you going?"

"To take a shower, then going home to study."

"What you leaving me?" Jay said acting sad.

"Jay don't play you know I'm taking my finals, and if I stay you know you not going to give me a chance to study."

"Dang baby it's like that?" Jay asked.

"Yea it's like that, you have a woman not a little girl. I have to take care of my business. Right?"

"You right baby, that's why I'm feeling you so hard. You trying to make a nigga fall in love?"

"That's one goal."

"One goal, what's the others?" Jay asked confused.

"First love, then the ring, then the kids."

"Damn you got it all planned out huh?"

"Yep, now wifey is going in the shower so she can go home and study for our future."

"Alright then baby." Jay said laughing.

When she came out the shower Jay was knocked out in the bed, she kissed him on the forehead and left the hotel happily.

When Jay woke up he went and chilled with Roc and his partner Gritz, they were shooting dice at the basketball court.

"Bet a $100 nigga!" Gritz said picking up the dice.

"Ugh! Eight my money stay straight." Gritz had rolled a 8.

You ain't sayin nothin nigga tighten up!" Roc said dropping another $100 bill down.

"Ugh!" Gritz rolled a 3.

"Yea nigga a 3, crap bring crap, it won't be long now nigga." Roc said hoping Gritz rolled a 7 and crapped out.

"So you said her nigga followed her to the room?" Roc asked Jay as they talked about what happened, while Gritz rolled the dice.

"Man I was deep in the pussy my nigga. I know he had to hear how I was dickin his bitch down brah brah. Then check this shit out she had on a one piece suit with heels. That nigga saw that shit and snapped!"

"Damn I know that nigga head fucked up my nigga." Roc said, thinking about it.

"Nigga that's just the half, this nigga tried to charge at me!"

"7 nigga don't try to pick them shits up all fast like I didn't see that shit." Roc said, stopping Gritz from continuing to roll.

"Oh you better act like you seen it then nigga. What the fuck you want me to do, just give you my money?" Gritz said, passing the dice.

"Whatever nigga. So what you do after that my brah?" Roc asked Jay.

"I pistol whipped the fuck out that nigga! Now the nigga got me under the radar and shit, because his bitch want the dick."

"That's some crazy shit, she still going to be coming to the club?" Roc asked.

"I don't know brah shit I doubt it. I ain't heard from her ass since that day and she ain't come through last night. Buddy probably got his foot in her ass now as we speak." Jay said.

They both busted out laughing.

"Damn niggas going to miss seeing her fine ass, but that's what happens when you mix business with pleasure my nigga. Of all people I thought you knew that?"

"Nigga fuck you, miss me with the bullshit. If that bitch would have threw the pussy at you, you would have caught it to."

"You ain't lying."

"Ugh 7! Hurry up and bet back nigga, you taking forever to pull that money out." Roc said rolling the dice.

"Ugh, 11! You might as well leave that motherfucker out, I'm about to get all that." Roc said picking up Gritz money for third time straight.

"Ugh! Snake eyes, damn I crapped out."

"Man let me see them shits." Jay said grabbing the dice.

He snapped his fingers twice as he let the dice go.

"Ugh, 4 Lil Joe! Both y'all niggas tighten up $100, I ain't scared of Lil Joe that's my nigga!

"Ugh, snap, snap!"

"There he go!" Jay had rolled a 1 and a 3 on the dice after just 3 rolls, picking up $400. After he finished rolling dice for a couple of hours and losing $200 dollars of his own money by the time they finished, Jay got on the road and headed back to Savannah.

When he got back home his work was low so he texted Reese to re-up.

"What's up brah? I'm running out of gas can you help me out and meet me at Overtime, the bar we first met at?"

"Who it this?" It took Reese 15 minutes to text back.

"This your people from the bar Jay."

"Aight B give me 20 minutes."

"Ok." Jay texted back.

15 minutes later Jay pulled up to Overtime parking lot. 15 minutes after that he was still waiting.

"Man where the fuck this nigga at taking forever and shit?"

10 minutes later he saw a red Mustang pulling into the parking lot, playing its music loud.

Jay hopped out the car with his duffle bag on pissed off. When he pulled the door latch on the Mustang, it was locked pissing him off even more. Reese unlocked the door and he jumped in the car with him. Jay got in and turned the radio on zero.

"What's good, B what you need?" Reese said sniffing like he had a winter cold in the summer.

"I need half a brick of soft and 2 pounds of loud." He said with a frown ready to get the fuck from around Reese hot ass.

"Damn you need 18 ounces of soft? I mean I got the 2 pounds, but I didn't know you needed that much soft. I'ma have to shoot back to the house for that B."

"What you mean, man how many you got brah?"

"Shit like 9 and a 1/2 B. I only counted you for like 8 ounces, I only brought the other one and a half in just in case you wanted it."

"Brah this some bull shit, I'll be done with them 9 and a 1/2 by the end of tomorrow night! Man fuck it, you did bring some Molly right brah?"

"Yea I got that son. Just be easy and take your time out there it ain't no rush." Reese said sounding dumb, because if he didn't waste Jay's time he wouldn't seem like he was rushing.

Jay was so mad he found hisself laughing as he dug in his bag to pull out the rubber band stacks to pay him with. He gave him the money out his bag and placed the drugs in. Jay got out the car not even acknowledging Reese.

"Be easy out there son." Reese said trying to sound bossed up.

"Yea whatever." Jay hated the way Reese said son, it was like he was trying to play him the way he said it. Like he was his child. Jay knew he needed his plug, but if Reese crossed the line he would just have to knock his ass off and explain to D later, after he killed him...

Later that next week Jay took the girls to the club without Candi again. It was live but not as much, without Candi there the girls didn't perform as well. She was their leader keeping them on point.

But the niggas wasn't mad at this though. The girls had no control over themselves without Candi there. Beautiful was soo high off the Molly, that she started letting niggas fuck for $20 at a time and that fucked up Coco's money because she wasn't bout to do it like that, not that damn cheap.

If Candi was there this would have never have happened and Jay wasn't about to cock block some pussy he wasn't hittin, or even trying to hit. It was over the pussy became cheaper than throwing money, so the good thing had come to a end. Jay thought to hisself. Jay knew the stripping hustle was over and it was time to move on to another one.

CHAPTER 19

"You still fucking that nigga ain't you!?" John yelled.

"No I'm not fucking him anymore John!" Candi said behind tears.

"So why the fuck you lied to the police, why the fuck you ain't give them that nigga name!? You probably in love with that nigga, fuck you!"

"No I'm not John I love you and nobody else! I didn't give them his name because they also wanted to know what happened to me!"

"Well you should have told them he was beating your ass and I jumped in, then he pulled a gun on me! What the fuck you mean!?"

"I wasn't thinking like that John dang, could you please forgive me please?" Candi said with tears rolling down her cheeks.

"Whatever, when I graduate in 3 months and go for training, you ain't dancing no more."

"Whatever you want baby." Candi said pleading.

"Yea I know, with yo cheating ass!"

This had been going on for the last month and it was getting worst. He had made her stop going to Beaufort on Thursday, because he knew Jay had promoted her going there from her conversations on the phone with her friends. But what he didn't know was she would still see him on Fridays and Saturdays when he came to the club to hustle. She avoided Jay though and tried not to even make eye contact with him.

John could have told the police what happened when they questioned him, but his pride had been crumbled. How could he tell anyone he followed his girl to a hotel, where she had been getting fucked at, to get his ass beat by the same man she had fucking. Then helped to the car by the man that had fucked his girl and beat his ass. All John could think about was how he could get revenge back on Jay, while he looked at his war wounds in the mirror.

CHAPTER 20

"**A**uuugh!" Coco screamed as her boyfriend got off the bus.

"What's up baby?" He hugged her lifting her off the ground.

Chuck had just been released from prison for the possession of a firearm by a convicted felon. He had a 5 year bid with 2 years to serve, if he maintained good behavior, but he ended up doing 4 years because he had got caught with 2 cell phones in the time of him being there and pissed dirty multiple times from smoking weed. While Chuck was in prison Coco made sure he had green dots and money on the books whenever he asked, he was chain gang rich.

When Chuck was out, he made sure Coco was straight though. It was only right she looked out for him. He made sure she wore nothing but the flyest shit. Chuck was always able to spend a lot of time with Coco, because his hustle was robbing dope boys. He watched them stack up, then take them for what they had grinded hard for. He would keep the money he robbed them for and sale the drugs to his partners for dirt cheap, giving them no choice but to buy everything he had. Chuck would shower his girl with gifts and diamonds making her look like a million dollar bitch.

"Damn baby your muscles got bigger." Coco said rubbing his chest.

"They did?" Chuck said looking over hisself.

"Whatever don't be flexing, you know your ass was in there working out every day."

"Yea so I can lift all this ass up." He said palming both her cheeks.

"Ooh shit daddy you making me horny, don't make me fuck you in front of all these people. You know I ain't had none since you been gone." She said lying.

"Well let's go home, because the way I'm feeling I can hit that ass in bathroom over there."

They both started laughing.

"You so freaky baby." Coco said.

"Come on let's go home bae." Chuck said walking her to the car.

When they got to the house she made him wait in the living room while she got ready for him. Chuck was tired of waiting so he got naked.

"Alright you can come back now!" Coco yelled from the room.

When he walked into the room she had on a leather two piece cowgirl bodysuit, with tassels running down the side of the pants with the pussy out, some heels and a cowgirl hat to match playing Beyoncé's -Dance For You, while a vanilla aroma lingered throughout the room.

"You ready for the ride daddy." Coco asked looking at his chocolate muscular body, getting herself hornier by the second.

He just stood there biting his lip, pulling on his erect shaft.

"Sit on the bed." She told him.

As he sat she started to dance in front of him seductively, clapping her cheeks in his face making the butterfly on her ass cheeks fly. When he grabbed her ass she slapped his hand away.

"Don't touch." She said.

She continued to sway in front of him then stopped to do a handstand, popping her pussy in front his face.

"Lick it." She said stopping.

He leaned over and licked her juices while she rotated her hips on his face.

"Ssss, ummm, I missed you so much ssss, fuck, eat it like you missed it daddy, umm it's yours daddy." She said moaning.

He slid off the bed and squatted down on his knees grabbing her waist licking. Then stood up with her still holding her waist and eating her out. Sucking her juices trying to put his whole face inside her hole.

His 10 inch pipe swung loosely in her face slapping her on the forehead. She grabbed his waist, placing him in her mouth trying to swallow his whole dick, gagging and slurping causing saliva to run down his balls and thighs.

"Damn baby that's how you do?" Chuck said coming up for a breather.

"Sluuup, sluuup, sluuup!" Coco was sucking like the pro she was.

He leaned to the side and laid her on the bed softly still licking.

"That's enough bae, come ride this dick cowgirl."

He slid up on the bed while she got up and squatted over him backwards rubbing the head of his pipe between her pussy lips.

"Damn baby that pussy wet." He said looking down.

She slid him inside of her, lowering her ass slowly.

"Ummm, ssss, f-fuck, I missed this dick, ssss, s-shit!" She moaned.

She slid slowly down his dick, then took slow bounces while rotating her hand over her clit.

"Damn baby that ass so fat, fuck girl!" He said starting to push hisself inside her as she came down, meeting her halfway, causing her to slow up from too much dick.

"Auugh, auugh!"

"What you slowing up for?" Chuck asked.

"It's too big daddy."

"Oh hell nawl you ain't about to run from this dick, turn that ass over." He said taking control.

She laid on her back and he slid inside her, going in deep as he could go, holding hisself in, knocking the breath out of her while sucking her neck.

"Oh my g-god, huuu! I'm about to c-cuuum!" She screamed as she wet the bed, causing him to let loose inside of her cumming with her.

After another round of intense pleasure they laid in the bed pillow talking about what she had been doing to maintain lately and he told her some prison stories. When she fell asleep he grabbed his .45 out of the closet and took her car to ride through his hood and holler at his people.............................

"Who the fuck that is creeping all slow and shit?" Black said feeling his waist to assure his .9 was in place.

"Oh shit my nigga, when they let your ass out brah brah!? You almost got your ass popped creeping up and shit!"

"Nigga what the fuck you worried about it for, you ain't send a nigga no Green Dot. And last time I checked, you shoot with your eyes closed." Chuck said fucking with Black.

Everybody on his block was laughing and clowning Black about the 4 year old joke, from when he was shooting at a nigga with his eyes closed.

"Whatever nigga I was 15 then. I done been in 5 shootouts since then." Black said trying to defend hisself.

"Yea and what you hit?" Chuck said still fucking with him.

"Shit one nigga in a shit bag." Black said.

"Damn 5 shootouts and you only hit one nigga? I was just fucking with you, but yo ass really can't shoot." Chuck said laughing.

Everybody started laughing again.

"A but where Mook at?" Chuck asked.

"He at Asia house."

"Fasho I'll be back I'm about to go check him out right quick." Chuck said giving everybody love.

Chuck headed towards Mook's baby mama's house. Mook ran Frazier Homes Apartments supplying all the little niggas with drugs keeping his projects pumping money.

Knock, knock, knock...

"Who is it?"

"Chuck."

"Who?"

"Chuck nigga!"

Mook opened the door.

"Oh shit look what the wind blew in! What's up my nigga, when your ass got out?" He said letting him in the house.

"This morning brah it feels good as hell to be home." Chuck said, giving him a hug.

"Why you over here nigga? I would have been in some pussy all day."

"You think I ain't get no pussy before I came to see your ugly ass nigga? I got to get back to the money pussy don't pay me."

They both started laughing.

"Fuck you nigga." Mook said walking down the hall and came back with three rubber banded stacks and 2 ounces of Loud.

"Here you go brah." Mook said passing it to him.

"I appreciate that brah, I'm broke as a fuck."

"You good nigga, if it wasn't for yo ass I wouldn't be in the position I'm in now."

"Fasho, that's some real shit. But you ain't get no work from me? You know I like to go out and get my own."

Mook stood there rubbing his chin and thinking.

"Boy you know what I just might have something for you. You gotta lay on him though and not kill the nigga, because I'm a still need the nigga to supply me with the work after you lick him."

"Fasho what side of town he off? The East, South side?"

"Nawl this nigga from New York. My original plug had got out the game, leaving his lame stuntin ass cousin to run everything, but don't kill the nigga brah please because I'm a still need this nigga brah for real."

"I got you my nigga. I won't kill the nigga damn, just hit me up when you ready to re-up with the nigga and I'll follow him and lay on his ass until he get comfortable."

"Word. What's your number brah?"

They exchanged numbers and Chuck went back home to get some more pussy and smoke some of the Loud with his girl.

CHAPTER 21

"It's your boy, Yo Jeezy with E93 Jamz, Savannah's Hip Hop and R&B leader. I want to give a shout out to my boy Jay. Happy G Day big dog! It's going down at Club Karma tonight ladies get in free, fellas pay what you weigh. Ha, ha and we got a guest appearance from Lil Boosie. It's going to be packed so you better get there early or you might not get in."

It was the day of Jay's party and everything was set up like he wanted. He had rented a 2018 Mercedes Coupe CL550, drop top all white and double parked it out front of the club. Then he went and hit the mall up with D and Reese.

"So how does it feel to be a real nigga with a lot of money?" D asked.

"Ain't shit big brah just another day, but it is my day so I'ma celebrate."

"Shit it feels damn good to me." Reese said trying to make hisself a part of the conversation.

He felt he could relate to what they were talking about since he had started making money.

As they walked through the mall all the bitches were jockin them. They talked to some of them giving them free V.I.P passes for the party. They bought a couple of pair of shoes and outfits and once they finished shopping they went to D's house to get ready for the night.

"Damn big sis it look like you about to burst." Jay said looking at Nikki's stomach as she let them in.

"Boy I can't wait until I get this baby out of me." She said giving Jay a hug.

"Don't be trying to sneak a feel on my wife either nigga." D said.

"Damn my bad, I didn't know I couldn't hug her." Jay said laughing.

"Shut up Devin." She said slapping his shoulder.

"You're all mine. I don't want nobody touching you." D grabbed her by the waist and gave her a kiss.

"What's up?" Reese said to Nikki walking towards the back with his bags.

"Hi Reese." She said back.

"So how many months are you now sis?"

"Eight months, I'm due any day now."

"You ain't lying." Jay said looking at her stomach.

"Come on nigga let's go get right." D said walking Jay towards his man cave.

D had his man cave laid for a king, a pool table, a 60 inch flat screen T.V., a sofa, two recliners and a weight set.

"Reese!" He yelled for his cousin while going to the fridge pulling out a gold bottle of Ace of Spades.

"We going to do it big tonight son." He said twisting the cork out.

"What's up fam.?" Reese came in fresh wearing a Jesus piece on his chain, the new mid top Kevin Durant's, a Gold Audemar, Polo pants and a matching shirt.

Pop! "Let's make a toast to my nigga Jay." He passed them both glasses, filling them up until the fuss touched the rim.

"To my nigga making it to see 21 without being locked up or killed." They touched glasses and threw the drinks back.

"Damn that shit good." Jay said.

"Hell yea B pour me up again my nigga."

They all refilled their glasses.

"That was the buzz, now for the flight." D said grabbing the blunt off the pool table.

"This some White Rhino. This some of the best weed I've smoked, on everything fam. Everybody talking about Train Wreck and Girl Scout Cookies, but this shit right here is that one son." D said admiring the weed.

"No doubt B, that shit will put you to sleep, if you sit down too long it's over." Reese said.

"Damn light that shit up then." Jay said ready to smoke.

"Here you go, you light it." D said passing him the blunt.

"Suup, suup, suuup, damn that shit potent." Jay said coughing. He usually didn't cough when he smoked but this was some A1.

D and Reese followed suit after hitting the weed, coughing their lungs out too.

After they finished smoking Jay took a minute and called Erica.

Ring-

"Hello?"

"Damn baby you must have been waiting for me to call you." Jay asked.

"Yes daddy I miss you, and I'm ready to see you. When do you want me to leave?"

"You can leave now we should be there at the same time. You got the dress on I got you?" Jay asked her.

"Yes it fits me soo good, wait until you see me, you going to want to fuck on the spot."

"Damn don't tempt me, because I won't even show up to my own party."

They both started laughing.

"Boy you crazy, but let me finish doing my makeup and I'll call you when I'm close."

"Ok."

They both hung up the phone and Jay went to get dressed. He had picked out a pair of blue Stacy Adams, a all-white Armani silk shirt and pants, a Gold Audemar, a Jesus piece chain and some gold Gucci frames with see through lenses. Shit he even had on all white polo boxers. He had went to the barber shop earlier that day leaving his hair thick making his waves look like speed bumps. He sprayed on some Polo Black Cologne and was ready to show niggas how to fuck the city up.

When he walked out D was in a red Versace silk shirt, black silk pants, some black and red gators matching his shirt, along with a gold flooded out Audemar.

"My nigga we bout to shut the club down tonight, we cleaner than three whistles."

Before they left they smoked another blunt, not wanting to smoke in D's Mercedes. Reese drove his own car, because when the club closed they had plans on leaving with females and Reese had plans to take some pussy home tonight too.

Ring, ring,...

"Hello?" Erica answered.

"Where you at baby?" Jay asked.

"I should be there in the next 5 minutes. You there already?"

"Yea we about to park. You park across from the white Mercedes." He had reserved a spot for her too.

"Ok don't get out I want you to walk in with me." Erica said.

D drove through the parking lot and parked his Mercedes besides Jay's backing in. Jay and D jumped out and they could see all the hoes eyes glued to them and their jewels. D went in the trunk and got his Gucci duffle bag out while Jay walked over to get Erica out the car. The club was already packed and it was still early.

Reese walked over to join them.

Erica got out the car rocking the all-white Vera Wang dress with the back cut out that he had picked out, some white and gold louis Vuitton heels, a gold female Audemar matching his, gold earrings and some Mac lip gloss, with her hair hanging in long curls.

"Damn baby you look like you came out a magazine." Jay said.

"Thank you handsome." She said kissing him, then wiping the gloss of his lips.

They looked like stars walking past the line. They could hear people with mixed emotions, "They must be the owners of the club. Damn that bitch bad. Them niggas paid."

And the haters saying stuff like, "That shit fake. Them tracks in her head. How they skipped the V.I.P. line?"

Jay didn't know most of the people who were there. The club was packed with different people from different cities only because of Boosie, but Jay's presence was still known because of his appearance.

When they got up to the club door security knew who Jay was, barely frisking him and his crew and not even checking Erica at all. When they walked into the club it was so crowded you could barely move.

"Move! Make a hole! Get the fuck out the way!" The big security guard yelled walking Jay and his crew towards his V.I.P booth. They all overlooked the club in amazement once they were situated.

"Damn B this shit too live, I didn't know y'all got it in like this down south!" Reese said yelling over the music.

"Yea this shit super packed and it's only what 11:30." Jay said.

Erica was bouncing slowly to the beat. They were playing Yella Beast -That's On Me.

A waitress was walking by and D grabbed her by the arm and whispered in her ear over the music. A little while later three sparkled bottles of Ace of Spades came heading there way.

"Happy Birthday baby boy, I told you we were doing it big tonight." D yelled.

"Fasho my nigga." Jay gave D dap smiling.

They each grabbed a bottle while the groupies and money hungry strippers headed to stand in front of their section. Beautiful and Coco were amongst the crowd that came too.

"Jay! Jay! Damn you don't know me no more!?" Coco said out yelling at him.

He looked and saw them yelling and motioned for security to let them come to his section.

The large man helped them both up the few steps.

"Happy Birthday!" They said giving him hugs.

"Where y'all girl at?" Jay asked.

"I don't know, that bitch been acting stank all night." Beautiful said.

"Oh fasho. Y'all want some of this Ace though?"

"Hell yea!" They echoed together.

"Y'all a trip." Jay said laughing.

After he poured them up a glass he lit some of the loud he got from D and had every weed smoker's nose was on radar in the club for the A1 Loud.

I like smoking weed, I like getting high, I like having sex, I like girls who ride, I like that money baby, money baby, money baby, that's the shit I like. Jay was rapping with the song vibing and relating to one of his favorite songs. D pulled the duffle bag from under the table and tapped Jay and Reese.

"I ain't bring this shit to show, we about to throw this shit B!"

They each dug in pulling out the rubber banded $1's and $5 dollar bills. They peeled the rubber bands off and started making it rain on whoever was by their section. Jay gave a stack to Erica letting her make it rain on Coco and Beautiful, while they clapped their ass for the crowd.

Lil Boosie hadn't even hit the stage yet and they had the club jumping.

By the time he hit the stage they had already threw at least 15 stacks, but when he came to the stage that made them throw another 15, just 30 minutes he was up there. Jay looked over to his left and could see Candi looking sick. She wasn't collecting like her girls because of resentment.

The whole time they were balling out throwing money they didn't notice the nigga at the bar watching them, hating.

"I'ma get that nigga." The man said to hisself.

After Lil Boosie performed he came over to Jays V.I.P where the crowd was and took pictures with a couple of people, including Jay and his crew. After that he left. By that time the club was dying down.

"What's up with you Red, you want to chill with me for the night?" Reese said whispering in Beautiful's ear.

"As long as the money right, we can do whatever you want." Beautiful said back.

"That's what's up. Let me tell my people I'm out, don't go nowhere."

"Ok." Beautiful said.

Reese heading for D.

"Yo family, I'm out. Y'all good?" Reese asked.

"Yea why you leaving though?" D asked.

"Because I'm about to go get a room and dick one of these bitches down it's about to shut down in a little while anyways."

"Fasho we probably bout to dip in a minute too." D said and dapping his cousin up.

"Alright B get at me." He said and dapped Jay and left.

"You ready baby?" Jay said squeezing on Erica's soft ass.

"Yes I'm soo fucked up, I can't wait to ride that dick daddy, umm um." Erica said tipsy.

"Yo, D you ready to ride big brah?" Jay asked D.

"Yea man let's go before I end up leaving with one of these girls and getting killed tomorrow." D said looking at the asses as they passed him by.

"Well let's go then, because I don't feel like helping Nikki hide your body with that baby on the way and all."

They both started laughing.

"Whatever nigga." D said.

It was harder to get out the club then it was getting in with everybody trying to leave at one time. After 10 minutes of pushing, through the crowd of niggas that where ass grabbing on the females, trying to get one of the freaks to go home with them. They had finally made it outside.

"You got what you need out your car and locked the doors bae?" He asked Erica.

"Yea bae let's go." Erica said leaning on Jay tipsy.

"Alright fam. I'm out." D said.

"Alright brah brah."

They gave each other dap and D hopped in his car to leave.

Jay had to stunt one more time before leaving letting the hard top back on the car and turning up his music. The new single by NBA Young Boy -Outside Today blasted through the speakers. Everybody watched as the all white Mercedes exited the parking lot with the top off.

CHAPTER 22

"**O**oh shit, you just going to swallow a nigga dick like that fuck!"
"Sluup, sluup, sluup." Beautiful's mouth made noises as she swallowed him.

Reese had brought Beautiful back to his house and she was on her knees giving her signature head. Reese's dick was down her throat and when he would reach the bottom of her throat she would extend her tongue out licking on his balls. She was a pro at dick sucking.

"Damn you so pretty ma, look at me while you do that shit." Reese said grabbing a hand full of her hair, pushing hisself deeper inside her mouth.

She looked up at him with her big light brown eyes, with his dick in her mouth.

"Damn you sexy Red, shit. That's enough before I cum."

She took his dick out her throat, leaving saliva dripping down his 8 ½ shaft.

"Come here." He said as he picked her up off the floor laying her slim body on the bed. He grabbed both of her legs by the ankle with one hand holding her legs in the air, then pushed them back admiring her shaved juice box. He made her pussy wetter than ever. Reese put his face in and started eating her like a tornado.

"Oooh shit, d-damn nigga, oooh ssss, f-fuck, eat that pussy nigga ssss!" She moaned as he ate her out.

Reese pushed her legs back even further and liked her booty too.

"Huuu, oooh shit, ssss ummm you so, ssss n-nast, ssss ummm, I'm about to cuuum auugh fuuuck!"

Beautiful had never had anybody lick her booty hole, causing her to cum hard in his mouth as he continued to lick from her ass to her juice box.

After she stopped shaking Reese went to the dresser and did a line of coke, causing him to get rock hard and beast up.

"Wooo!" Beautiful yelled as Reese caught her off guard, grabbing Beautiful by her thighs pulling her to the edge of the bed.

"You got a rubber?" She asked him.

"Girl shut the fuck up we don't need no condom!"

"No I'm not about t-, auugh fuck!" She screamed.

He had slid into her wet pussy fast touching the bottom and placing the weight of his body on the top of her not allowing her to run from the pressure.

Beautiful tried to wiggle from under him but couldn't get away. Reese kept his chest on hers and rotated his hips pumping inside her fast and hard as her juices ran down her ass cheeks. She didn't want to do it without a condom at first, but it started to turn her on the way he was taking her pussy.

"Ssss ummm, ssss oooh fuck!" She bit down on his shoulder as her pussy skeeted on his dick.

"Fuck lil mama!" He yelled slowing up his motion.

He couldn't cum he was too high off the coke. So when she finished coming he got off the top of her releasing her legs sliding out of her wetness and went to the dresser and took another bump of the coke.

"Suuuf, suuuf."

"Let me hit some of that." Beautiful said needing something to take the edge off.

"You did raw before ma?" Reese asked.

"Yea nigga." Beautiful lied, knowing the most she had done was Molly.

"Alright this some potent shit, it's barely cut." Reese warned her, but walking up to her with a bump of coke on a dollar bill for her to hit.

"Ok. Suuuuuf." As soon as she held her head back up from the hit, she knew she had fucked up.

Am I spinning or is the room spinning she thought to herself. She felt Reese's freaky ass getting turned on again.

He turned her around from the back pushing her head down to the bed and rubbed his dick between her ass cheeks. He just didn't know if he let her go she would fall over. She was super high.

He bent her over more licking her butt cheeks. Then between them placing his finger inside her booty hole fingering her.

She knew what was next but couldn't move or talk she was stuck, but still could feel what he was doing to her.

"Twa!" He spit in his hand rubbing it on the head of his penis.

"You a freaky ass nigga." She thought to herself as he entered between her butt cheeks. She wanted to scream but couldn't talk, she wanted to run but couldn't move. The only thing she could do was take deep breaths and pant every time he went deep inside her tight booty hole.

"Huuu, huuu, huuu, huuu!" She panted as he drilled her from behind.

He rotated his hand on her clit for 15 minutes as he pounded a place nobody had ever entered.

She came again shaking and dripping her juices down his balls, causing him cum also. Her hole held on to his penis, as he came inside of her causing her to pass out as the hot nut entered her.........................

"Damn baby be easy." Jay said trying to control the wheel, he was almost home.

Every since they had pulled out of the parking lot of the club, Erica had been trying to suck the brown off his dick. Jay still had the top back on the car and the wind was feeling good as it blew on the wet saliva that slid down his shaft and balls. Erica was drunk and being extra freaky.

When he pulled up to his apartment, Jay damn near had pry his dick out of her mouth.

"Ummm daddy give me my dick. I can't take it no more I want it now!" She said behind slurred words.

"Hold on bae. We at the house now. You need me to help you out the car?'

"Yea I can't walk in these heels no more, I'm fucked up."

Jay started laughing.

"Ok stay right there I'll carry you in."

"Ok daddy."

He went and unlocked and opened the apartment door. He came back and helped her out the car. Then carried her in the house.

"Bae I'm so in love with you." She said kissing on his neck.

"You drunk lil mama you don't mean it." He said walking her through the door.

"Don't tell me I don't mean it, I know when I'm in love with somebody." Erica said getting mad, letting the alcohol control her attitude.

"Ok lil mama I'm sorry. Well if you really in love with me, I need to tell you that I've been in love with you. I was just waiting for the right time to tell you."

"You are?"

"Yes baby I've been in love with you for a while now."

"Aww that's so sweet. I want you to make love to me bae. I need you inside of me soo bad right now, I need to feel you."

"Ok baby." He said, walking with her in his arms.

Jay carried her to his room, laid her on the bed and stripped out of all his clothes. Erica laid on the bed watching getting hornier by the second.

Jay walked over and kissed her softly on her lips then sucked on her neck.

"Ssss umm, that feels so good daddy."

He unzipped her dress pulling it over her body, revealing her naked perfectly curved body. Her nipples were like rocks. Jay sucked on one and squeezed on the other. Then rotated back and forth between them.

"Ummm, damn daddy you know what my body needs, sssss that feels so good." She said moaning.

"Your body is my body, of course I know what to do to it." He said still kissing and sucking on her.

He then placed kisses down her belly stopping at her juice box, squeezing her clit between his lips nibbling on it.

"Sssss, god damn oooh!" Erica moaned.

He stopped and continued placing kisses down one of her legs to her feet, sucking on her toes. After he finished sucking her toes he allowed her leg to rest on his chest and shoulder. Then grabbing the other one kissing in between her inner thigh first then down her leg to her toes sucking them, the same way as he had done other. Then he placed her other leg on his other shoulder.

"Baby why you teasing me like, this you driving me crazy!?" Erica asked.

"Be patient."

Erica's juice box was so wet, when he put his tongue inside of her box his tongue got wetter.

"Ssss ummm, ssss y-yes papi, put your finger in it while you lick it. Ssss ummm I'm about to cum already s-shit!" She screamed gyrating on his hand and face.

Jay didn't even give her time to recover with her legs still on his shoulders, he slid up and entered her creamy juice box.

"Huuu, ssss shit!" She screamed as he grind in her slowly.

"Damn baby you feel so good." Jay said talking to her as he grinded inside her.

"Skuuut puuup, skuuut puuup, skuuut puuup." Erica's pussy responded for her, she couldn't talk because he was touching her soul.

Jay grinded inside her for 45 minutes causing her to cum three more times before he came inside of her leaving it in.

CHAPTER 23

*C*oco had just woke up at 12:30 in the afternoon from a long night of partying and dancing at Jay's party. Even though she was tired and her love box was swollen from having sex with Chuck constantly since he had been home, that didn't stop her from getting up and cooking for her man. She swayed around the kitchen listening to Drake and Nicki's song Moment for Life.

"Damn bae what your fine ass in here cooking." Chuck said walking up rubbing on her ass.

"Good morning baby." Coco said, giving him a kiss.

"I'm cooking steak, hash browns, cheese eggs and grits."

"Umm-um that shit smell good. How much longer until you finished?"

"Nigga go sit yo greedy ass down and don't go in my pan either."

"Whatever if you take too long I'ma come back in here and eat you for breakfast. Pop!" He slapped her ass hard.

"Oh well I might take longer just because." Coco said, being freaky.

They both started laughing.

Chuck walked into the living room and turned on the T.V. looking at Sports Center highlights.

After Coco finished cooking she sat their plates on the table.

"Come eat bae the food is done." She said placing two glasses of orange juice on the table.

As soon as Chuck sat down he started killing his plate.

"Damn girl you put your foot in this shit." He said with a mouth full of food.

"You like it?"

"Hell yea, umm-um pass me the ketchup bae." He said.

"I had so much fun last night. What about you bae?" Coco asked him.

"It was aight. That shit was too packed though. I don't like when the club be over packed like that."

"I asked you did you want me to reserve a V.I.P. section for you."

"Yea I know, I just didn't know it was going to be that packed in there or I would have done that." He said.

"Hell yea, that shit always be packed when rappers come through, but that shit was extra packed for my baby daddy Lil Booosie! Sssss Ooooh ooh!" Coco said putting emphasis on the rapper's name.

"Aight now don't make me beat that ass and kill that lil rap nigga." Chuck said, playing but serious.

"Bae you know I love you. I'm just playing with yo crazy ass." Coco lied knowing if Boosie let her, she would ride his dick from Georgia to Louisiana.

"Whatever big head but a, who them niggas was that was throwing all that money and popping bottles of Ace of Spades last night?" Chuck asked.

"Who you talking about? A lot of niggas was throwing money bae." She knew who he was talking about but didn't want to say. Coco knew what he was thinking about, she knew him like a book.

"I'm talking about the niggas that had the suits on, you know who I'm talking about. One of the niggas pulled you and that skinny bitch in their V.I.P section. That nigga and his people was throwing money like they was million dollar niggas. You know who the fuck I'm talking about. Let me find out you fucking one of them niggas." He said to her looking her in the eyes to see if she would lie.

"Oh you talking about Jay? Boy please ain't nobody fucking nobody, but you. That's one of Candi's old niggas and I don't know the other two niggas he was with. I just know Jay." She said trying to put herself in the clear, but she knew the 21 questions were still coming.

"Oh fasho. What side of town he off of?" He asked.

"I think he stay somewhere on the South. I don't know exactly where at though. He used to promote parties in South Carolina for us. Me, Candi and Beautiful would go up there and dance at a small club on Thursdays."

"Why y'all stop going?"

"Because Candi dumbass got caught fucking him at a hotel, by her boyfriend and he just stopped taking us." She lied again not wanting to tell him how it was really Beautiful's fault fuckin niggas for $20 a nut. Coco knew she couldn't tell him that part because he would have thought she was selling pussy to, so she passed on telling him that part.

"So that's all the nigga do promote parties?"

"No he sell drugs too. He be hustling out the club on Fridays and Saturdays."

"Oh yea, you got his number?" He asked.

"No but I can get it from Candi." She lied again knowing she had Jay's number.

"Fasho well you need to do that A.S.A.P."

"Damn I hate when this nigga be involving me in his bullshit. Why he just won't sell dope or get a job or some shit? I can do without all the flashy shit he gives me, shit I make my own money. He gone end up getting hisself killed, or even me killed. This is my last time doing this shit I don't give a fuck what he say or threaten to do to me. I have a little girl to take care of, shit his little girl. If I die who going to take care of her? I know she barely with me, but a bitch still ain't ready to die fuck that. If he can't understand that after this time we don't need to be together." Coco thought to herself.

Ring, ring, ring-

Chucks phone went off interrupting her thoughts.

"Hello?" He answered.

"What's up homie? Oh yea. Aight. Fasho." He said in the receiver then ended the call.

"Who was that one of your lil bitches?" Coco said with a attitude.

"Girl shut the fuck up that was my people, I gotta go and handle some business. I need the car for a couple of hours, I'll be back."

"Why can't I ride?" She asked.

"Because it ain't going to be nothing but niggas around that's why. Now where the keys at?"

"Whatever they on the dresser. Let somebody tell me they saw you with a bitch in my car, I'm a fuck you and that bitch up." She said with a attitude.

"You trippin." He said going to get the keys.

"No you trippin, yo ass just came home and going to chill with them fuck ass niggas! Fuck them niggas they ain't do shit for you when you was locked up!" She yelled telling him the truth.

Chuck ignored her getting dressed to leave. When he came back out she was watching reruns of Martin. He kissed her on the cheek and headed out the door.

"Call Candi and get that nigga number." He told her before leaving out the door.

15 minutes later he was parked across the street from Mook's baby mama's house waiting for a red Mustang to pull up..........................

"What's up, brah brah? Damn what took you so long?" Mook asked Reese.

"I've been getting to this money as usual B. I had to make a couple of bigger stops before I came out this way." Reese lied knowing he hadn't been doing shit but fucking Beautiful all day.

"How many you need though?" Reese asked him.

"7 of 'em brah." Mook said, with a slight attitude.

"That's all? You got all the cash right?" Reese asked.

"Yea nigga I don't do credit." Reese said pulling out the bands of cash, counting out $8,400.

"Word son." Reese took out 7 ounces and placed them on the table taking the money.

"You can weigh them up but I got to dip, just hit me if something short and I'll drop what was short off and a lil extra, but everything goin to weigh up right, because I weighed 'em up before I came."

"Alright brah brah, I'll get back with you later on." Mook said dapping him up walking him to the door.

"Fronting ass nigga you gone get yours." Mook said to hisself watching Reese leave.

Reese got back in his car and pulled off making his runs showing off for Beautiful, flashing letting her count the money he made on his stops.

Beautiful was thinking of how to squeeze more money out of Reese since he had it like this. She had only charged him $200 for the pussy last night and knew now that she could have charged more.

"Baby can I have $150 to get my hair done." She asked.

"Yea go ahead and take in out sexy." Reese said to her.

They stopped at a Burger King then headed back to his apartment. After a long day of pull ups and drop offs, it was time to fuck and get high.

The whole time they drove around doing their thing, they didn't see the car following them through the city.

They got back on the highway and every time Beautiful saw a white car she would duck down, thinking it was the police because of how high she was off of the cocaine.

"Red you good, why the fuck you keep ducking down? Don't start tripping and shit I told you that shit was strong. Stop acting all paranoid and shit you making me nervous. Here smoke on a cigarette, it will mellow you out."

Beautiful lit the cigarette and pulled it. It felt as though cold air was being blown through her body causing her to loosen up.

20 minutes later they were pulling back up to his apartment.

Reese went in the bathroom to brush his teeth. As he brushed his teeth and tapped the toothbrush on the sink and turned the water on to the faucet. Everything was extra loud in her ear. The four taps on the sink seemed like they dragged on for minutes at a time. She wanted to tell him to stop but just twitched her lips to one side. She was higher than she had ever been in her life.

Reese walked out and opened the closet, while she watched him with bulging eyes.

"You see this? This is how we get all the money we was throwing in the club last night." He said pulling out one of the bricks and pounds that filled up the duffle bag.

"That was my money we was throwing last night, I brought that out just to show my lil niggas how we do it up North." He said lying zipping the bag back up.

CHAPTER 24

*C*huck had followed the red Mustang back to the apartments and was laying low monitoring Reese at the apartment watching them get out the car and enter the apartment with a duffle that he was sure was filled with money the way they was moving.

"Where the fuck I know that bitch from? She look familiar as a fuck." Chuck thought to hisself.

"Oh shit that's the little bitch that dance at the club with my girl and that's one of them same niggas that was in the V.I.P throwing all that money. A nigga hit the jackpot with this one."

He waited in the car for 3 hours hoping they didn't leave again. After smoking four blunts of Loud he went in the trunk and grabbed his ski mask, gloves, zip ties and .40 caliber. He rolled the ski mask up on the top of his head, to not look suspicious while walking up to the apartment. He walked up the stairs to the door of the apartment he seen them enter.

Knock, knock, knock.

Knock, knock, knock.

"Who is it?" Reese said from the other side of the door.

"Jehovah witness." Chuck said back.

"I don't want to talk I'm a Christian." Reese said on the other side of the door.

Knock, knock, knock.

"Do you know the true story sir, I only need about 5 minutes of your time." Chuck said lowering his mask, knowing he would piss him off enough to open the door by continuing to knock and not leaving.

Knock, knock,

Chuck's knocks were cut short by Reese swinging the door open angrily.

"I said I don't want to fucking talk now get your ass-"

Chuck put the big pistol up to Reese's lips cutting his mouth off.

"Nigga shut the fuck up and back up slow. If you scream I'm a feed yo bitch ass a bullet!" Chuck said low but with force.

Reese's eyes got extra big as he stared shocked, holding his hands in the air and backing up into the apartment.

"Where the lil bitch at?" Chuck asked.

"She in the room B." Reese said terrified.

"If I find anybody else here I'm a kill everybody! Lay your bitch ass down and put your hands behind your back!" Chuck said pushing him on the couch.

He pulled out the zip ties and strapped both of his hands and sat him on the ground.

"Ouch, fuck man these shits super tight B."

"Whop!" Chuck hit him with the gun.

"Augh fuck!" Reese yelled as blood ran down the back of his head.

"Now you ain't thinking about your wrist no more nigga. Shut the fuck up and show me where that bitch at! I tell you when to talk!" Chuck said grabbing him by the arm pointing the pistol at the side of his head letting him lead the way.

"What was taking you so long to come back, I was about to come get your ass." Beautiful said.

Chuck heard the girl talking from behind the door they were headed towards. When he opened the door Beautiful was naked, as her head slid down a line of coke. "Suuf, suuf." When she looked up she saw the masked man standing over her.

Chuck put the gun to her temple.

"Bitch you scream you die! Go lay your ass down on the bed and put your hands behind your back! Chuck told her.

You, sit your bitch ass on the floor." He said pushing Reese down on the floor.

"Man please don't kill me I-I don't want t-to die." Reese said behind tears.

Seeing him cry caused Beautiful start to crying to. Her heart was beating extra fast from the coke plus being held at gunpoint wasn't helping.

"P-please let us live." Beautiful said.

"Both of y'all shut the fuck up, before I shut y'all up!" Chuck said, zip tying her hands behind her back.

"Pop! Turnover and sit beside him." He said slapping her on the ass.

Once she was beside him he started talking again.

"Now that we're all settled in this can be a good night for everybody. One, y'all can give me what I want and I just leave. Or 2, everybody can try to play superman or woman and think these bullets don't kill and everybody die and I still get what I want. It's y'all choice y'all got 30 seconds to decide before I pull the trigger on one of y'all and I just used 10 of 'em. Now where's the money and the dope?" Chuck said getting to the point.

He walked over and pointed the gun at Reese nose.

"Times up brah."

"Wait please! It's in the closet, the money and the dope!" Reese said with tears running down his cheeks.

Chuck walked over to the closet and looked around spotting two duffle bags. The one he kept getting out of the car with which contained money and another one. He looked inside the first bag, then unzipped the other one looking at the slew of drugs it contained inside.

"Bingo!" He zipped the bags back up and placed them on his back.

"Well you didn't lie to me and I appreciate that. Now before I leave I need both of y'all cell phones and I'll be out y'all love bird's way. So where the phones at?"

"Mine is on the bed." Beautiful said crying.

"Mine is on the nightstand." Reese said still crying like a little bitch.

He grabbed both of their cell phones and took the batteries out and placed them in one of the duffle bags, he then zip tied their legs together and wrapped socks around their mouths in case they tried to scream for help after he left.

"I appreciate not having to make this a murder scene. I'm happy I didn't have to turn a robbery into a drug related homicide and stop crying like a lil bitch homie that shit ain't cool. Grow some nuts nigga damn!" Chuck said, walking off.

He left out the house and ran to his car pulling out the apartments slow, then smoking a blunt of Loud once he got on the road good. He pulled over on the side of the road placing the mask, gun and gloves inside a trash bag putting the bag in the trunk of his car. He got back on the road and headed home to see what he had came up on.

When he made it home Coco was sleep. After he finished going through the bags he had made 25,000 in cash, came up on a 2 bricks, 17 ounces of coke and 6 pounds of Loud.

"I knew that nigga had money, I can't wait until I get them other two niggas." Chuck thought to hisself.

CHAPTER 25

*A*fter being in the zip ties for 20 minutes, Reese hopped to the kitchen and turned backwards pulling the silverware drawer open. He dropped three knives before getting control of one of them. Once he tried and realized he wasn't going to be able to cut hisself loose he hopped back to the room.

"Get up!" He said in a muffled voice behind the sock.

Beautiful struggled to get up still crying. After she figured the only way to stand up was to slide up the wall, she maneuvered and hopped towards him.

He turned showing her the knife. She turned around and tried her best to place the knife in between the zip ties without cutting herself or him.

"Ouch! You poking me." He said.

"Stop moving!" She said muffled.

After 5 minutes of sawing she had cut through his zip ties. After he was loose he snatched the knife out her hands, cutting his legs loose then throwing the knife on the floor, running to the closet to check for what he knew was already gone.

"Fuck! Damn this shit fucked up! Bitch you set me up didn't you?" He said trying to blame somebody.

He went under the mattress and pulled his .9 from under it. He then walked up to her and snatched the sock out of her mouth.

"You better start talking bitch, what the fuck is going on!" He yelled at her.

"What the fuck? How the hell I set you up and the nigga tied me up too? Nigga you tripping cut me a loose and take me home!" She said starting to cry again.

"Bitch let me find out you set me up and you ain't going nowhere! Who said you could leave!? You ain't going nowhere until I figure out what the fuck is going on!" He said yelling.

"Damn my gun was so fucking close! I started to buck and try to run back to the room and grab my shit, but that nigga hit me when I opened the front door!" He said trying to justify his bitchness.

"Nigga you wasn't going to do shit, crying like a lil bitch and shit." She thought to herself.

"I don't want to be here no more. I just met you and it's already been too much. I just want to go home. Can you please just cut me a loose? I'll walk home."

"Bitch didn't I just say you wasn't going nowhere!" He grabbed the knife and cut her legs a loose.

"Now come do a line!" His ego was crushed. He had cried in front of a bitch he was fucking and got robbed. He looked around in amazement that the nigga was so fucking dirty that he left the eight ball of coke on the dresser, that he sniffing on.

"No!" Beautiful yelled.

"Click, clack!" He pulled the hammer back on the pistol and wrapped his hand in her hair. He was feeling played already getting robbed in front of her and crying, now to get yelled at or told no by a bitch wasn't making it better.

"Bitch get your ass over here!"

"Ouch, ok, ok! I'm coming, let go of my hair!" She yelled as he pulled her by her hair.

"Suuuf, suuuf, suuuf, suuuf." He did two lines back to back.

Do one he said pushing her head down to the dresser.

"Suuuf, suuuf!" After she had sniffed the line he snatched her head up and threw her on the bed.

Beautiful felt like she was on a upside down roller coaster from the line she had just done and him throwing her on the bed right after.

"Lay your ass down!" He yelled.

Reese was trying to do everything in his power to make hisself feel like he was in control of something. So he ate her juice box, with the pistol still in his hand.

"W-why do we got to do this?" Beautiful said not wanting to have sex anymore.

"Shut the fuck up!" He yelled to her.

Beautiful didn't know this nigga and she didn't like what had happened, but Reese's controlling ways were still exciting her and it turned her on. Or maybe it was the coke.

"Ssss fuuuuck!" She moaned.

He stopped before she came and dropped his shorts and entering her hard and fast, sexing her for 2 hours straight with her arms still tied behind her back.

Every now and then he would stop sexing her to look out the window because he had become paranoid. After he was done, she fell asleep as Reese cried silent tears of anger and shame.

"Man why the fuck every time I try to come up, a nigga take me back down!? Why me, why not the next nigga!? Man fuck everybody from now on. I'm playing for keeps. Fuck everybody. I gotta get mine son! Now I gotta deal with D punk ass. Man fuck that nigga!" He cried hisself to sleep gripping on his .9.

The next day he woke up sniffing a line and sexed on Beautiful again. He then took her home not wanting to share what little of the coke he had left. He would have told her to take a cab so he wouldn't have to waste his gas, but he drove her home so he could see where she stayed at. In his mind she was now his bitch, she had seen too much.

After he dropped her off he scraped up a couple of dollars out of the arm rest in his car and got a bottle of gin going back home to try to drink and sniff his problems away.

CHAPTER 26

D had been calling Reese all day he hadn't heard from him since Jay's party, he knew something wasn't wright.

"Bae did my cousin call your phone?" He asked Nikki.

"No why?" She said, rubbing on her stomach.

"Because I haven't heard from that nigga since Jay's party and that's unlike him, usually the nigga be blowing me up or will pop up on me or some shit."

"Hum, go by his apartment when you leave the dealership and check on him. I'm sure he's okay." She said to him.

After a long day of work selling two used cars, D still hadn't heard from his cousin. So after closing up a little early he headed to his cousins spot.

"Damn that nigga car here why the fuck he ain't picking up the phone." D said to hisself getting out of his car heading up the stairs.

Knock, knock, knock...

Reese didn't come to the door so D used his spare key and opened the door.

"Reese, Reese, you in here!?" D yelled turning on the living room light.

"Yea I'm coming fam!" Reese said trying to put the small bag of coke up and fix hisself up.

He walked out into the living room sniffing and pulling on his nose because of the drain.

"What's up B I've been calling you all day, why you ain't been picking up the phone!?"

"Man suuuf, you ain't going to believe this shit son. I got robbed B, these county niggas got me!"

"What! You got robbed by who!?" D said mad.

"Suuuf, I don't know man. Them niggas had on masks and caught me when I was walking in the door." Reese lied making it seem like it was more than one person trying to catch the drain.

"They were standing outside and when I opened the door they hit me in the back of the head and forced me in the house."

"What they get!?" D asked.

"They got everything B! One held me at gunpoint while the other one zip tied me up, suuuf." He said sniffing from the drain.

D held his head slightly to the side, ducking to look in his cousin's eyes.

"Nigga you high!? You fucking with your nose B and we just got robbed for everything but you got time to play with your nose! Yo ass didn't pick of the phone to call me not one time to tell me what the fuck happened!? All the fuckin product I gave you to move is gone, but you got time to get high right!" D yelled pissed at his cousin's actions.

D swung a right hook and hit Reese in his jaw causing him to stumble.

Reese caught hisself on the entertainment center. When he got his balance he came back up swinging a quick three piece.

D dodged the first two, but the last one caught him in the mouth pissing him off.

"You still hit like a lil bitch nigga!" D said eating the punch.

Reese knew that D was a better fighter than him, but wasn't going out bad again. Reese rushed at him hard and fast swinging wild. D blocked the first punch and the second one he counter blocked it, catching him with a right hook then two quick left jabs backing up resetting again. When Reese swung again, D ducked and punched him in the stomach causing him to ball up and fall to the floor.

"Get your punk ass up you think that coke hit hard!? Nigga I hit harder!" D yelled.

He kicked Reese in the stomach.

"Fuck wrong with yo dumb ass nigga! Look at the fucking lick we took and you fuckin with yo nose! My cousin!? You got me fucked up!" He kicked Reese again causing him to cough up blood.

"Where the fuck that shit at!? I know you got some more, your ass was already high when I got here!" D said walking towards the room leaving Reese on the floor.

D was on a rampage tearing up the room, flipping the mattress and opening all the drawers. Once he got hold of the coke, he heard a familiar noise.

"Click, clack!"

"What the fuck you going to do shoot me nigga, your family? I'm your fuckin cousin B!" D said turning around facing him.

"Nigga fuck you!" Reese said.

D charged at him.

Boom! Boom! Boom!

D fell to his knees holding his chest with blood seeping through his shirt.

"Y-y y-you shot me cou-." D laid down going into shock.

"Yea nigga I run shit! A nigga ever try me I'm a kill 'em family or not!" Reese said, with cold eyes.

He dragged D's body in the bathroom and headed out the door.

CHAPTER 27

Jay hadn't heard from D and Nikki kept calling Jay like he was lying to her.

"Jay I know you know where he at that nigga better have his ass home by midnight or I'm throwing all his shit out." She said to Jay.

"Nikki I promise I haven't heard from him. You tried calling his sister?" Jay asked.

"Yea she hasn't seen him, but I think her ass probably lying. That bitch don't like me."

"Well if I hear from him I'ma tell him you said bring his ass home big sis." Jay said.

"Whatever, bye Jay cause I know you know where he's at."

Click the line went dead as she hung up in his face.

"Damn where the fuck that nigga at, better yet where that nigga cousin at with the work? That nigga ain't never on point I'm a have to let D know he going to have to come up with some other than this shit. This nigga making me miss all kinds of money.

He called Erica.

"What you doing bae?"

"Nothing waiting on you to come back." Erica said.

"What you got on?" Jay asked.

"Nothing just one of your t-shirts."

"Nothing else? No bra no panties?" He asked excited.

"Nope."

"Damn I'll be back in a little while lil mama. I gotta have you." He said.

"Ok baby, I'm waiting on you." She said.

When he got back to his apartment Erica was looking better in one of his t-shirts, then he would ever look in it.

"Damn you sexy in everything you put on girl." Jay said.

"Whatever nigga you don't like what I be wearing you like what's under it."

They both started laughing.

"You ain't lying." He said.

She threw one of the pillows at him.

"Oh shit it's on now!" Jay yelled.

He threw one of the pillows back at her and they started to pillow fight, slapping each other in the head with the pillows.

Ring, ring, ring...

"Hold up, time out my phone ringing." He said laughing.

"You lucky cause you was about to get beat down."

"Hello?"

"Hey Jay. What's up, this Coco."

"I know, what's up sis?"

"Umm, my cousin in town for a couple of days and wanted to know, hold up. What you wanted cuz? Oh how much you would sell him a Mike Vic for?"

"Of girl, Loud, Molly, what?" Jay asked.

"Of Loud." She asked.

"Oh I'm out of loud hit me later."

"Ok." She hung up.

A couple of minutes later Coco called back.

"My bad Jay this me again, he wanted to know how much for a four way of girl?" Meaning four ounces.

"Um since it's your people just tell 'em all I want is $5,000."

"Ok. He said that's cool, can you come through?" Coco asked.

"Give me about 25-30 minutes." Jay said.

"Ok."

They hung up with each other.

"Where you going bae. I thought you was in for the night?" Erica asked pouting.

"I was but Coco just called me and said her people in town, and she needed something real quick."

"Why she waited so late?" Erica asked.

"I don't know, but I'm not about to leave her hanging. She made me a lot of money when we used to go to take them to the club in South Carolina."

"Well you need to hurry up and come back because you supposed to be spending time with me." Erica said.

"Ok bae after this I'ma come home and lay up with you for the rest of the night." Jay said trying to convince her.

He kissed her on the lips and headed out the door....................... ....

"Bae after this time I promise this is the last time." Chuck said to Coco lying.

"You say that shit every time we do this shit Chuck. When does it stop? You going to end up getting me killed. Then who going to take care of our daughter? I know not you."

Chuck was getting sick of her mouth and was ready to hit the lick and move to Atlanta like they had planned.

"Bae just chill out we got money. We just need a little more to be comfortable and this nigga got it. The shit will all be over before you know it. Now call that nigga back and see what the fuck takin him so long." Chuck said.

He was extra thirsty to hit the lick, he was going to pull the .40 out on Jay and hit him across the head a couple of times. Once Jay understood he wasn't playing, he was going zip tie him and make Jay tell him where his apartment or stash house was at. After he got what he wanted he was going to kill him.

Chuck knew Jay was a small built nigga but he wasn't going to underestimate no man. "Once I hit that nigga with this .40 I know he going to break down, they all do." Chuck thought to hisself, while Coco called him again.

"Hello?" Jay answered.

"Yea, where you at?" Coco asked.

"I'm on my way it's only been 20 minutes."

"Oh cause he thought you wasn't coming or something. Aight then."

"Fasho."

They hung up with each other...........................

STREET MONEY

Jay was on the highway heading towards Coco's house and he was having that hustler's intuition. The one you get before you get locked up knowing it was coming. Or the one they get right before something bad happens.

In a rush to get back to Erica he left his pistol at home, but he dismissed the thought of going back to get it. Not going with his mind because he was less than 10 minutes away from Coco's house.

Ring..

"Hello?" Jay picked up on the first ring.

"Damn that nigga too ready to get high, he told you to call me again?" Jay asked.

"Yea, he said how much longer you going to be?" Coco asked.

"I'm about to pull up now, tell him to come outside." Jay said.

"Ok."

Two minutes later Jay pulled up to see Coco was standing outside with a big black muscle head nigga. When Jay looked at the nigga he was getting that feeling again, but he had came this far and wasn't about to turn around now. Plus he knew Coco was good people.

Jay pulled up and lowered his window halfway to do a hand and hand transaction, because it was late and he didn't have his banger and knew even though Coco was good people, the goons were still out.

"What's up Jay, what you been up too?" Coco said talking through the window causing him to lower it a little more.

"Shit chillin, but I gotta go make another run. Your people ready?" Jay asked.

"Yea."

He let the window back up halfway as Coco walked towards her house to let them conversate.

"What's up brah? My name Brandon." Chuck said giving him a fake name.

Chuck stuck his hand in and gave Jay dap.

"You got the girl?" Chuck asked.

"Yea here you go, you can check it out." Jay said passing him one of the ounces, then looking in his rear view mirror.

"Damn this look like some good shit brah brah. Let's go in the house so I can try it out." Chuck said trying to get Jay out of the car.

"Nawl I'm good my nigga. If you want to test it out go ahead, I know it's some good shit and weight right."

"Aight hold on, I'll be right back." Chuck said, going to the house.

Jay was getting pissed off he hated dealing with petty niggas. The coke was good and the weight was on point.

Chuck was even madder than Jay, because Jay didn't get out of the car.

"Man why the fuck this nigga taking so long?" Jay said to hisself still in the car.

Jay was getting paranoid. He started to count the one ounce as a loss and go back to his house and come back with his chopper and wet Coco's house up.

Five minutes later Chuck came back out.

"Damn brah you wasn't lying that's some A1 shit." He said.

"I told you everything was good big brah." Jay said.

"Let me go ahead and pay you. I appreciate that too man." Chuck said feeling on his back pocket then digging in the other, coming back up with a big .40 pointing it through the crack of the window at Jay's head.

"Don't move fuck nigga, get yo bitch ass out the car!" Chuck yelled.

"Man what the fuck, you gone rob me brah?" Jay said putting his hands in the air.

Jay could see the bullet through the barrel of the gun, telling him the gun was already cocked.

Chuck pulled at the door handle, but it was locked. So he put his arm through the cracked window to unlock the door while holding the gun steady. He was sliding his hand down the side of the door searching for the lock as Jay stared at the pistol aimed at his head.

Chuck looked down for no more than a half a second to hit the unlock button. But when he looked down Jay ducked his head and pulled the gear stick down and mashed the gas all in one fast swift motion, squeezing his eyes closed.

Boom! Boom! Boom! Boom! Boom! Boom! Boom!

Jay's heart was beating super fast. Everything that was happening caused his life to flash before his eyes. His mother, jail, God and other life lessons flashed through his head quick like a flashes but he still saw them all.

"Damn that nigga must have killed me." Jay thought to hisself.

Jay looked up swerving trying to gain control of the wheel. Once he did, he got on the highway doing 90. When he saw a Shell gas station, he pulled over looking hisself over, feeling over his body lifting his shirt up and down.

He didn't have any bullets in his body, but his ears were ringing and his hands wouldn't stop shaking but he was ok.

"Fuck! That bitch set me up, I knew something wasn't right bout that shit. I'ma kill that bitch and that nigga!" He yelled.

He looked his car over, the rear view window and the passenger window were shot out. The front glass was cracked from a bullet bouncing off of the dashboard and getting stuck in the glass. The trunk had multiple bullet holes in it. Jay went back inside the car and a bullet hole was in the armrest and C.D. player also.

He got back on the highway still in shock from nearly being killed, with murder on his mind..

"Man I can't believe this little nigga bucked on me like that. I know I hit his ass at least twice though. If he ain't dead I know he in a shit bag, his dumb ass put his life in my hands trying me like that. I don't believe this lil nigga bucked, shit!" Chuck yelled to hisself.

Coco was looking out the window after she heard the gunshots.

"What the fuck is going on!? This shit wasn't supposed to take place at my house." She thought to herself.

When she saw Chuck cursing she thought he had been shot and her stomach started to turn and her eyes filled with tears.

When she saw him walking towards the front door realizing he was ok she wanted answers and her feeling went from sad to mad.

"What happened, are you ok?" She asked.

"Yea, that lil bitch ass nigga bucked on getting out the car and tried to pull off, so I lit his ass up!" Chuck said.

"What in front of our house, why the fuck would you do that shit outside the house? Are you crazy!? Somebody is going to call the police on your dumb ass. You're going back to jail!" Coco yelled at him.

"Nobody ain't see shit girl, so chill the fuck out!"

"What you think this is, a game or a movie or some shit? You just can't shoot a nigga and nobody tell on you stupid ass! Plus that nigga know where the fuck we stay and where I work! What fuck was you thinking!? I thought you had this shit planned out!? That was some dumb ass shit the whole plan you came up with was dumb as a fuck! The money you hit that lick for is not going to be enough for us to just up and move! I work for my money, I don't have to fuckin rob people this shit is crazy!"

"Bitch didn't I tell you to shut the fuck up! Wop!" He slapped her causing her to fall to the ground.

Coco got up and ran into the bathroom, locking the door and crying on the floor.

She was so done with Chuck already and he hadn't even been home 6 months. She was doing fine dancing at the club and paying all her bills. She didn't even need Chuck to spoil her she could spoil herself she didn't need him or his life threatening ways. She could hear the sirens wailing in the background and then her car cranking up.

When he slapped her, she realized he would never change or be the man she wanted him to be. A lot of different things ran through her mind but most importantly was her daughter. She hopped Jay didn't think she had something to do with this, if he was still alive, because she didn't want to go to jail she just wanted to raise and take care of her child from now on out.............................

Jay pulled back up to his apartment parking his car in the back and placing the car cover over it to keep people from being nosey and asking questions. He was still a little shook and didn't know if Coco told anybody where he stayed.

"Dang baby what took you so long to come back, I missed you." Erica said as Jay walked through the door.

When she looked in his eyes she realize something wasn't right.

"What's wrong?" She asked.

"That bitch tried to set me up, I can't believe this shit!" Jay yelled.

"She tried to set you up?"

"Yea, when I got there the nigga she said was her cousin, was trying to get me to get out the car. But when I told him I didn't want to come in, the nigga pulled out on me trying to force me out the car. I pulled off and the nigga tried to light my ass up. I got bullet holes all in my shit!" He stressed.

"Oh my God! He was shooting at you when you tried to pull off!? He was trying to kill you!" Erica said.

"Bae, if you would have seen how the shit went down and how my car look. I'm supposed to be dead right now!"

Erica started crying.

"Why you crying bae?" He asked.

"B-because I don't want to lose you."

"Girl you not going to lose me, I'm here and fine. I'm not going nowhere, ok?" He said as he hugged and kissed her softly.

"Ok." She said.

Jay continued kissing on her and ended up making love to her. They both fell asleep in each other's arms.

Jay woke up through the night having multiple nightmares replaying the event over in his dreams, but he died in his dream every time. This was his third time having the dream, and each time he woke up in a cold sweats.

"I'm a kill that bitch and she going to tell me where that nigga at too." Jay said to hisself.

CHAPTER 28

Reese needed some money to get back up North fast. He was on the last of the coke he had left and that made him realize killing his cousin was a bad idea. Nikki had been blowing him up, she had called him at least 30 times leaving him voicemails, saying she knew him and D were out fucking bitches and others crying saying please tell D to come home. His cousin's body was still on his bathroom floor he couldn't bring hisself to move him.

"Man fuck you D, if it wasn't for you shit wouldn't be like this! Bitch ass nigga, suuuf, suuuf!" He said looking in his mirrors paranoid and making sure his nine was still in his lap.

All the plays had been blowing him up with text to re-up, but he didn't have shit. A text from Solo popped on his screen.

"You straight brah?" Solo texted him.

A plan formed in his head fast.

"I'm on my way B." He text back.

The coke and nine had him feeling like Deebo, he figured he could take what he wanted. Especially since he caught his first body yesterday, he felt real gangster.

When he pulled up in front of Solo's trap he pulled the hammer back on his nine and placed it on his waist line. He knew Solo might try to buck the jack so he wanted to prepare hisself for whatever he had to do, to take what he wanted.

He grabbed the blue book bag he stole from Walmart and headed the back door.

Knock, knock, knock...

"Who is it?" Solo asked.

"Reese."

STREET MONEY

The door cracked enough for Solo to peek out to make sure Reese was by hisself. When he saw that Reese was alone, Solo opened the door letting him in with his .45 in his hand.

"What's up B? I see you at it as always." Reese said.

"You know I got to make sure the streets eat nigga. What's up with you lil brah?" Solo said as he walked over to the pot placing his pistol on the counter, continuing to cook up the dope.

"Go ahead and-

"Nigga don't fucking move!" Reese said cutting him off with his gun in his face.

"Bra what the fuck you trying!?" He said holding his hands up.

"Shut the fuck up B! Yo bitch ass think you run shit!? I run shit!" Reese yelled.

"Whap!" He hit Solo in the back of the head, but Solo was anticipating the hit and tried to scramble and reach for his gun after the hit.

"Boom!" Reese let off when he moved.

The bullet entered through the back of his head and came out of his eye causing Solo's head to swell up like a pumpkin as he hit the floor.

Reese grabbed the 14 ounces of coke off the counter and stuffed them in his book bag and walked out the back door.

When he got in the car he unzipped the book bag, took out one of the ounces and stuck his nose in the bag.

"Suuuf, suuuf, I told these fuck niggas I run shit. Now all I gotta do is get D body out my spot, and move these ounces then I'm out." He thought to hisself driving back to his apartment..................................

"I'm too pregnant for this shit. His ass didn't come home last night, must have gotten drunk and fell asleep over some bitch house." Nikki thought driving around looking for D's car.

She had already been by his sister's house, so she pulled up in front of Jay's house and banged on the door causing Jay to jump up.

Jay was shell shocked from being robbed. He grabbed the pistol from under his pillow and went to the door.

"Who is that Jay?" Erica said whispering, getting scared because of his actions.

"I don't know." He said putting on his gym shorts, walking lightly to

the front door and looking through the peephole. Erica was damn near on his back.

"Who is it?" He asked.

"It's Nikki."

"Who the fuck is Nikki!" She said getting mad and not whispering anymore.

"Girl hush. That's D wife, remember?" He said unlocking the door.

"Oh yea I remember her."

When he opened the door, Nikki's eyes were filled with tears and hope.

"Hi Jay, how are you doing? I didn't mean to bother you and your company this early. But I haven't heard from D since yesterday and this is unlike him he would have at least texted me. Have you seen him?" She said with watered eyes.

"Nawl big sis I haven't seen him since my party. He called me yesterday but that's about it. Are you ok? You look tired as hell sis, come in and have some water or something." He offered.

"No I'm ok. I'm fine really, but if you hear from him tell him to please come home."

"Ok sis. You know I will. But on me, I haven't seen that nigga."

"Ok." Nikki turned around, wobbled back to her car and pulled off, heading towards Reese's apartment.

CHAPTER 29

*E*ven though Jay was still shell shocked from the past events he still had to keep his business up and running. When he woke up he went in his stash and took out $18,000. Then walked Erica to the door to leave for school.

"Be careful please baby. I don't want you to do anything crazy." She said.

"I'm not bae, I'm good." Jay said lying.

"Ok, I love you daddy."

"I love you too lil mama." He said, then kissed her on the lips while rubbing on her ass.

"Alright now don't start nothing you can't finish." She said biting her bottom lip.

"Girl stop trying to tease me, you know you ain't bout to give a nigga none. Yo ass already pushing for time to make it to class now."

They both started laughing.

"You know I like to play with your mind so you can think about me when I'm not around." Erica said.

"You ain't even gotta worry about doing that, you got everything a nigga need baby."

"Good I'm glad you and him know who y'all belong to." She said, grabbing his stiff penis then turning and walking out the door.

"Now you know, you wrong for that." Jay said as she walked off.

"I love you too baby. I'll call you as soon as I get out of class." She said laughing.

Jay went back in the house and called Glass Masters to come and replace the windows on his car. It was bad enough he had bullet holes in the inside and on the outside of his car. So he at least wanted to replace the windows before driving it to the paint and body shop. He then called a car rental car company and reserved a rental, by 12:00 p.m. all his windows had been replaced and he was headed to Ralph's auto body and repair shop on the West side to get his car repainted and interior worked on.

"What's up, Ralph?"

"Hi, what's up with you young blood you trying to get it painted again?"

"Yea but I need it painted by next week, not the next couple of weeks like the last time. It took you three weeks to get my car back to me last time."

"Yea but I can't help that, you got people in front of you I just can't stop painting they car and start working on yours." Ralph explained.

"Man look here big brah I understand all that, but we both know money talk and bullshit walk a thousand miles. My shit got shot up and I got the money up front plus a bonus for your troubles if you can get my car back to me by next week."

Ralph was rubbing on his chin thinking about the profit.

"Ok let's see what we talking about."

Jay pointed out the bullet holes inside his car and on the outside.

"Damn young blood you lucky you ain't get hit, all these holes in this car shit and shit. I see you went ahead and got new glass put in the front and the back already. That was shot out too ain't it?"

"Yea but I ain't lucky I'm blessed, it wasn't time for me to go." Jay told him.

"I hear that."

"So how much you talking about Ralph?"

"You trying to get it wet?"

"Yea 4 coats of clear Candy Apple Red."

"For everything give me $5,500, I'm going to do the inside too."

"Word." Jay grabbed his book bag out the back seat and gave him 6 rubber banded stacks of money.

"That's $6,000, I'll be back next Monday. I need my shit back by then Ralph. You've been paid already, so let's get to it."

"Ok." Ralph said thumbing through the 100's.

Jay hopped in the taxi he had called and headed to pick up the rental. After he picked up the rental a 2018 Chevy Impala, he thought about D.

"Damn big brah, what the hell you got going on, not going home and shit?" Jay thought to hisself as he called D's phone but got the voicemail again. He then he texted Reese to re-up and figured he would ask him if he seen D.

"Yo you straight?" Jay asked him talking about the drugs.

"Yea, I'm straight, meet me at Over Time." Reese texted.

"Word I'll be there in 15 minutes." Jay texted back.

When he pulled up into the parking lot to his surprise Reese was already parked in the parking lot.

"Damn that's a first." Jay thought to hisself.

Jay parked beside him and grabbed his duffle bag making sure his pistol was on his waist. Ever since he got robbed and shot at, he made a vow that he would rather get caught with his gun than without it. Jay wasn't trusting nobody.

"What's up brah?" He said dapping Reese up.

"What's good B?"

When he looked in Reese eyes he recognized a familiar look, but couldn't put his finger on it.

"What's up brah you ain't heard from D lately, and what the fuck happened to your head?"

Reese kept checking the mirrors and twitching his mouth from side to side. He was high as a kite, and Jay could see it all in his eyes.

"Some niggas jumped me in the club last night, I'm good though B. Nawl I ain't seen that nigga D. He been actin weird."

"Damn, Nikki came to my house early this morning looking for him she said he ain't been home since Saturday."

"I ain't seen him either B, he ain't answering my calls or text. That nigga been on some other shit lately." Reese said lying.

"Damn I wonder what the fuck that nigga got going on, this ain't like D brah." Jay said.

"Shit I don't know, but I gotta keep it moving regardless of what that nigga doing. You ready to do this business or what fam?"

Reese was getting sick of all the questions and would have killed Jay and just took the money if they weren't in public.

"Damn that nigga D trippin, but let me get 9 ounces of girl, 2 pounds of-"

"I ain't got no weed or Molly all I got is coke!" Reese said getting frustrated, like Jay was supposed to know he only had coke.

"Damn brah brah you got a nigga missing a lot of money out here, how you don't have Molly or weed?"

"Look B either you want the coke or not? Shit fucked up out here it's a drought on weed and Molly." Reese said lying.

"Well let me get 11 ounces of girl then brah, damn. When you gone be straight again on everything else?" Jay asked.

"Everything will be good in a couple of days fam. Just hit me up." Reese said thumbing through the money.

"Fasho."

Reese gave him the ounces and Jay put them in his bag. They dapped up, and Jay got in his rental and left.

"Man I'ma have to holler at D about that nigga, he fucking up his business. If shit keep going like this I'ma have to find another plug. I wonder where yo ass at anyways though." Jay thought to hisself.

"Man then I got my own problems to handle. I ain't got time to be worried about somebody else shit." Jay said pulling off and going to catch a couple of plays before going back home to get ready for the night...

When Nikki got close to Reese's apartment and saw D's Mercedes parked out front she got happy, then angry at him for not calling her. She then knew for a fact he probably had a bitch in the house, so she was ready to kick somebody ass.

"Reese ass knew he was over here too that's why his ass hasn't been picking up the phone, with his bitch ass nigga!" She thought to herself.

She pulled up and parked her car behind D's blocking him in, just in case he tried to run out the apartment and leave in his car. She opened the glove compartment and grabbed her old apartment keys out and a box cutter, then headed for the front door.

She unlocked the front door slowly, not to be heard. When she saw nobody was in the living room she headed for the spare room, pushing the door open with force. To her surprise nobody was there.

"I know you in here D! So you might as well bring your ass out, you and that bitch!" She yelled.

She walked out the room pulling the hall door open, to find nobody there.

"Ok nigga I'm a fuck you and that bitch up now! You should have came out and talked with me like a man, instead of running and hiding like a little bitch!" She said heading to the master bedroom.

She pushed the door open and looked around and saw what looked like a wine stain on the floor. She then dismissed the thought of it being wine, when she saw how it puddled and the thickness of it. It was trailed across the floor to the bathroom. Her heart started to beat 30 times a second, as her body moved towards the bathroom door but her brain was saying don't go. She twisted the nob and pushed the door open. When she saw the suit she had picked out on the body laying limp in a puddle of blood, she almost fainted.

"Auuuugh!" She screamed at the top of her lungs and fell to her knew causing her water to break. She was a wreck now laying on her side squeezing and opening her eyes hoping her vision would be different when she opened her eyes.

"My baby, she thought to herself." She reached for her cell phone in her pocket. Her hands were shaking so hard she couldn't put her code in to unlock her phone causing it to safe lock giving her an option to only make an emergency 911 call.

"Hello 911, state your emergency."

"I-I-my-m-m he-"

"Ma'am I can't understand what you're saying could you speak in the phone."

"M-my b-baby." She said still crying stuttering.

"I can't understand you ma'am, but I have pinpointed your location just stay on the phone until help arrives. Are you hurt, do you need an ambulance?"

"Y-yes."

"Alright just stay on the line, help is on the way."

Nikki didn't hear her anymore, she had passed out..................
....

As Reese was approaching his apartment he could see the police lights flashing, from blocks away. His heart sunk in his stomach, but he still decided to drive past to make sure they were not at his house. When he saw they were his heart sunk in his ass.

"What the fuck!? Damn I got to get the fuck out of here!" He said looking at the body bag on one stretcher and Nikki on another being placed in a ambulance. He ducked down and cruised past the scene.

He called Beautiful to let her know he was on his way over to his house. He wanted to fuck her a couple of more times, before he headed back up North.

CHAPTER 30

*C*huck didn't go home after the shooting he felt Coco might be right, so he stayed at his mama's house a couple of days. Coco had called him and told him the police had asked questions but nobody knew who the gunman was or what had happened so he felt he was in the clear to come back home.

He had took the work he had robbed Reese for and the ounce he robbed Jay for, to his partner Solo and sold him everything for $50,000 a price he couldn't argue with. Now that everything was clear, Chuck was headed back home, but first he stopped by Zale's and bought Coco a $9,500 dollar engagement ring.

"Chuck why the fuck did you take my car and leave me stranded at this house like that!?" Coco yelled as he walked through the door.

"I'm sorry bae I thought they was about to take me to jail."

"Give me my damn keys! I have had to get a ride from my fucking mama and I got a car. What kind of shit is that?!"

"Daddy!" Alexis said running and jumping in his arms.

"Hi baby girl what's up, what you been up to?"

"Nothing I was at grandma's house. You see my baby?" She said holding up the doll.

"Oh that's a pretty baby just like you." He said tickling her making her giggle.

Coco was mad but she could only smile when she saw him playing with their daughter.

"Bae I have to tell you something." Chuck said.

"What?" She said trying to put her attitude back on.

He put Alexis down and got on one knee and pulled out the small box.

"Bae I know I'm not perfect by a long shot and I've made a lot of mistakes in my life, but the best thing I've ever done in my life was placing you in it. You gave me the world by having our child and I don't want you to think I take y'all for granted and I love you and I want to become a better father. Will you marry me?" He said opening the box.

Coco wasn't expecting this at all and had tears rolling down her face.

"Daddy, daddy, why you making mommy cry? Don't cry mommy." Alexis said.

"Yes, yes, yes!" She said wiping the tears from her eyes jumping on his neck kissing him.

"But please promise, if not for me for our daughter that you're done with the illegal life you was living? We can't take losing you again."

"I promise bae, I'll open a small corner store or even get a job if I have too. When I was at my mama's house, all I thought about was you and my baby."

He got up and placed the ring on her finger and kissed her softly on the lips.

"It's okay mama don't cry." Alexis said.

"I'm not crying because I'm sad silly, mama is crying because she's happy."

"You cry when your happy mama?" Alexis asked.

Chuck picked Alexis up and swung her around causing her to laugh.

"Yes, me and mama getting married baby girl she isn't sad!"

He said swinging her around as the little girl laughed.

Coco went to finish cooking dinner. She was making fried chicken, green beans and macaroni and cheese. As she flipped the chicken in the grease she admired her ring smiling.

"I hope he really is changing for us." She thought to herself.

Coco set the table and they started to enjoy their dinner.

"Bae I want to move and start a new life, a fresh start. I don't care how much money we have let's just leave. We can make more money let's start over fresh." She said looking at him.

He drank some of the juice to wash down the food.

"Yea let's do that bae I'm sick of Savannah. What about Jacksonville Florida. It's only 2 hours away, shit that way we would still be close to our families."

"Yea that sounds good bae. How about next weekend, what we waiting for?" She wanted to get out the house she was in as soon as possible, because she hadn't heard shit from or about Jay and he hadn't been picking up her calls.

"Ok bae, whatever you want wifey." Chuck said smiling.

She was glad he said that. On the other end, he was glad she said she was ready to move because he had a feeling the police were coming to pick him up for the shooting any day now.

They finished eating and put Alexis to bed. The got her clothes ready for school the next day and afterwards they went in their room to celebrate their engagement.

"Baby did you mean everything you said tonight?" Coco asked.

"Yes baby I wouldn't have put a ring on your finger and proposed to you like that if I didn't. Come here and let me show you how much, I love you."

He pulled her close kissing her and rubbing his hands across her juicy ass, then sucking on her neck.

"Ummm that feels soo good bae, I love you so much. Please don't leave us again." She said rubbing her hands on his muscled back.

"I won't baby I promise." He lifted her shirt over her head revealing her big chocolate breast then sucking on her nipples.

"Ssss, I like it when you do that. Ssss, ummm that feels so good."

He picked her up and laid her on the bed pulling off her booty shorts, they had a small wet spot in the middle. When he looked at her juice box he knew why.

He separated her pussy lips with both his hands causing her clit to stand at attention. He sucked at her clit causing her juices drip on the bed.

"Ssss, d-damn daddy." She said grabbing the back of his head.

"F-fuck, oooh, oh my god." She came on his face rotating her hips giving him a milk mustache.

"You want me to do you daddy?" She asked.

"No baby tonight is all yours." He slid out of his shorts and boxers, then grabbed two pillows and stacked them beside her.

"What you doing bae?"

"Lay on these." He instructed.

She got up and laid on her back over the pillows.

"Like this." Coco asked.

"Yea."

STACKS

The pillows caused her back to arch up and her pelvis to go in a downward position. He climbed on top of her parting her legs and sliding the head of his shaft between her wetness entering her slowly.

"Ssss ooooh, ssss um ummm." She moaned.

He then pushed her legs up causing her juice box to angle on his shaft. Every time he entered her he touched the back of her wall.

"Oooh s-shit daddy, w-what you doing to me, ssss f-fuck!" She creamed cumming hard on his dick again.

They made love in that position for 20 minutes, causing her to come three times...

Jay had parked the rental car 3 blocks up the street and was in Coco's backyard for 4 hours waiting for all the lights to go off. He had been in her house before so he knew where the different rooms were at. He watched as her daughters room light flicked off. He had seen when her cousin pulled up so he knew he was there too.

After all the lights were out he waited another 15 minutes and went to the master bedroom and listened for sounds of conversation or movement. When he heard her moaning, he didn't know if his dick got hard because he imagined her naked or because he was about to kill her and that fuck nigga that tried to rob him she called her cousin.

He walked to her daughter's room window and took the screen off the window. When he tried to lift the window it was locked, but he figured he could easily crack one of the squares of the glass window and push it out, without making too much noise. He grabbed a small rock off the ground and tapped one of the squares hard cracking it, then pushing it out.

Cling! Cling!

"Damn." Jay thought to hisself.

He looked through the blinds to make sure he didn't wake the little girl up. She was still sleeping. He stuck his hand in the small hole and unlocked the window. He then walked back around the house to the master bedroom to make sure they hadn't heard the noises he had made. When he heard them still fucking, he went back to the little girl's window lifting it up and climbed in.

"Oh shit!" He said almost slipping on the clothes that were on the dresser.

Alexis moved around, but didn't get up.

Jay slid one of her pillows off the bed and headed for the door, closing it back after he exited walking slowly down the hall towards the living room. He wanted to make sure he was right, that nobody else was there. After seeing nobody else was there he headed back down the hall to the noises.

"Auuugh fuck daddy, ssss shit you fucking me good oooh." He heard Coco moan.

Jay put his hand on the knob turning it slowly, then pushed it open fast turning on the light.

They looked up at him like two deer's caught in the path of some oncoming headlights.

"What the fuck!" Chuck yelled.

"Pussy nigga you scream again, I'm a shoot your dick off!" Jay warned him.

"Man what you doing?" Chuck asked like he didn't know what he had done.

"Jay please, please don't do this I have a daughter to take care of." Coco said crying.

"Well since you know who it is, I might as well let both of y'all see the nigga that y'all tried to kill." Jay said lifting his mask.

"Jay it wasn't me I promise, it was his idea." Coco said with tears rolling down her face, pointing at Chuck with her ring hand.

"Who your cousin, the dude you fucking right now!? The one that that must have put that rock on your finger!? Bitch you got me fucked up!" Jay yelled.

"Coco shut the fuck up that lil nigga ain't-"

Boom!

The pillow muffled the sound but the shot was still loud.

"Auuugh fuck! My dick! Auuuuuugh!" Chuck screamed as loud as Jay had heard anybody scream in their life.

Coco was screaming too, but Chuck was screaming soo loud that Jay couldn't take it. So he shot Chuck in the face, causing the blood splatter in her Cocos' face.

"Oh my God! Oh my God!"

"Bitch shut the fuck up!" Jay yelled.

She was shaking with fright and pissed on herself.

"Why Coco, why!? That's all I want to know before I kill your ass!"

"I-it was C-Chuck's idea." She said shaking and crying uncontrollably.

"Well guess what bitch until death do you part!"

Boom! Boom! Boom!

He lowered his mask back down, leaving them lying beside each other. When he walked out the room Alexis was standing in the hallway with her doll in her hand. Jay had to think fast he knew the police would be on the way soon and he didn't want the little girl to be traumatized seeing two dead body's especially not her mothers.

Jay scooped the little girl up and ran to the back door and locked it. Locking Alexis outside then running to his car. Jay jumped in the car and pulled off the mask and headed back to his house cursing on the highway doing the speed limit.

CHAPTER 31

*B*eautiful woke up the next afternoon from a long night of sucking and fucking. Candi had called her and told her to ride to the mall with her and to be ready by 1:30.

When she came out the shower Reese was still in her bed knocked out. She walked over to his pants and took out $800 to spend at the mall.

"This nigga got money he ain't going to miss this little shit. She said to herself. She got dressed putting on an YSL dress, coach heels and her MCM purse she had just bought last week.

15 minutes later, Candi was pulling up calling and blowing the horn.

"I'm coming bitch damn!" Beautiful said looking herself over in the mirror.

She walked outside switching like she had the fattest ass.

"Bitch bring your bony ass on!" Candi yelled.

"Bitch don't be hatin." She said opening the car door.

"Y'all hoes ain't never ready. I've been calling Coco ass all day. It's supposed to be a girl's day out. She must be in the house laid up under Chuck ass. I don't give a fuck if I have to go in there and pull her ass off his dick. Y'all bitches going to chill with me today.

They both started laughing.

"I can tell who do need some dick. If John was fuckin you right you wouldn't be worried about pulling nobody off they man dick." Beautiful said laughing.

"Whatever bitch me and my man are good." Candi lied knowing Beautiful was right this one time, out of many.

They drove to Coco's house smoking on a joint Candi had in the ashtray. When they pulled up to Coco's house it was circled in yellow tape.

"What the fuck is going on?" Candi said driving slowly up to the house.

"I don't know and why they got yellow tape around her shit?" Beautiful said.

Candi saw a neighbor two houses down on the porch and decided to ask them what was going on. She pulled up at the house and got out the car.

"Hello. How are you doing?" Candi asked.

"I'm fine young lady. How about yourself?" The old man said staring at her like a piece of meat.

"I'm fine."

"What can I help you with?" The old man asked.

"Um yes, do you know the young lady that stays in that house with the yellow tape around it?"

"No I didn't know her." He answered.

When he said, "He didn't know her." Candi's heart sunk.

"But her little girl was outside crying early this morning and someone called the police. When the police came and knocked on the door and didn't get an answer they got suspicious, I guess because the young lady's car was still parked in the driveway. The police got the landlord to come unlock the door, and 15 minutes later a ambulance, fire truck, news team and police were out here tapping the house off."

"What the fuck you mean an ambulance and news team?" Candi said with tears filling her eyes.

"When the paramedics came back out they had two body bags on stretchers, they said it was the lady that stayed there and her boyfriend."

"Noooo! You don't know what the fuck you talking about, with your old ass!" Candi said.

"Are you ok, miss? Did you know her I'm sorry." The old man said trying to hug her.

"Don't put your fucking hands on me!" She slapped his hands away, then stormed to her car.

"What's wrong?" Beautiful said about to cry, hugging Candi when she got in the car.

"Candi please tell me what's wrong!" Beautiful said.

"H-he s-said she's dead."

Now they we're both crying hysterically holding each other. After 15 minutes of sobbing they pulled off.

"I know this can't be true. I'm about to go to her mother's house and see what's really going on, my girl not dead." Candi said.

Twenty minutes later they were pulling up in front of Coco's mother's house, to see at least 25 cars parked outside. They both knew what was about to be said but still didn't want to believe it as they got out the car and headed for the front door.

Knock, knock, knock...

Ms. Judy opened the door with red eyes and a handkerchief in her hand letting them in the crowded house.

"Hi Ms. Judy we heard some bad news please tell me Carmin is ok? Please say what I heard is not true!?"

Ms. Judy couldn't even talk she just hugged Candi crying. They cried on each other shoulders with Beautiful joining them.

"W-what happened? Carmin ain't never hurt nobody. Why would somebody kill my friend?" Candi asked.

"I don't know hunny I don't understand either." Ms. Judy said wiping her tears.

"The police didn't give me much of nothing when I asked them, after going to pick Alexis from the police precinct, they just said someone broke in and murdered her and her boyfriend, and it was under investigation. I've almost had 2 nervous breakdowns today." Ms. Judy said.

"This is so messed up Ms. Judy, I can't believe Carmin is really gone." Beautiful said.

Ring, ring, ring,...

"H-hello?" Beautiful said sobbing picking up the phone.

"Bitch you took money out my pants when I was sleep!?" Reese yelled.

"Boy ain't nobody take no money out your pants!"

"So why the fuck am I missing $800 dollars out my shit!? Nobody else was here but me and you bitch!" Reese yelled through the receiver.

"I don't know what the fu-" She stopped herself before she went off knowing this was the wrong time and place.

"Look my friend just got killed last night and I'm with her family, I'll talk to you later."

"Bitch if you do-"

"Click." Beautiful hung up the phone and turned it off.

They walked into the living room full of people. They were all conversating about what they thought happened and how it happened while waiting for the 5 o'clock news to come on. Beautiful went and nosily joined the gossip conversation, while Candi sat on the couch in a daze listening to all the conversations and how surreal it was.

"I heard her boyfriend caught her cheating and killed her, the nigga, and hisself. You know she was a stripper." One person said.

"For real?" A person responded.

"Hell yea!" Someone said back.

"I heard that they was selling dope and got robbed, then the robber shot both of them!" Another person said.

"Somebody told me Chuck had owed somebody from the East side some money when he went to prison and when he got out he told his plug he wasn't paying shit. So they came and took him and Carmin out." Somebody else said.

"Damn that's fucked up!" A person responded back.

While everybody gossiped and came up with their own versions of what they think happened, time seemed to fly by.

When the news came on everybody got quiet with their eyes glued to the TV.

"This is the live news at 5." The local news played. Then the words Crime Stoppers flashed across the screen.

"Earlier today the body of Devin Harris was found in an apartment where his girlfriend stayed. We have a new lead, this man Reese Harris is said to be in connection to his murder and is armed and dangerous. If you have any information as to his where about call 911 immediately." A picture of Reese popped on the screen.

Beautiful almost pissed on herself when she saw Reese's face on the screen.

"This just in." They had a news anchor at Coco's house, going over what they thought might happened.

"In the early morning hours a call was made to authorities, due to an abandoned child crying outside. When the police arrived on the scene no one answered the house door, the officers entered this house, to find the body of Carmin Parker and Chuck Long murdered inside the house this morning which are the young girl's parents. The police believe the intruder came in through this window which is the daughter's bedroom window and murdered Ms. Parker and Mr. Long. Then placing the young child outside the house. Other than that, we have no other leads at the moment. If you have any information on this crime, please call 911. Back to you Lisa."

"Thanks Shaun." The anchor lady said to her coworker.

The room erupted with conversation. Candi couldn't take it anymore, she went to get Beautiful so she could go home and mourn in peace.

"Come on, Beautiful let's go."

Beautiful looked like she had seen a ghost. Candi thought it was because of what the news said about Coco.

When they got in the car Beautiful started shaking and crying.

"Are you okay?" Candi asked.

"N-no."

"You'll be ok we all will, God will punish who did this to her. I promise. She is in a better place now." Candi said.

"It's not that, d-did you see the m-man that killed the dude at that apartment." Beautiful asked.

"Yea what about him?" Candi asked.

"You d-don't remember him from Jay's p-party they w-were both there throwing money with Jay."

"No shit! That's crazy what the fuck is going on in the world. That shit crazy."

"That's not it...I'm fucking him and a-and he at my house." Beautiful said.

"What!? What you mean he at your house!?"

"He came over a couple of days ago. I didn't know what he had did that." Beautiful said crying.

"Girl you always getting caught up in some crazy shit, what the fuck!"

"What should I do Candi?" She asked behind tears.

"Girl you better call the police before they think you had something to do with it. What you mean what should you do? You got a murderer in your house, you harboring a fugitive."

"Ok you're right."

"We going back to my house, I'm not losing two friends. I heard you arguing with somebody about taking some money out their pocket. Was that him?" Candi asked.

"Yes." She said sobbing.

"Girl you staying with me for a little while. This shit is too much." Candi said.

"O-ok thanks Candi."

"Damn girl, I'm just glad we didn't go back to your spot before watching the news. That nigga could have killed us both."

They pulled off and headed to Candi's house to call the police.

CHAPTER 32

*J*ay had just finished watching the news to see what they had on the murder he had done, as tears rolled down his face. He had just found out the only nigga he fucked with, was killed by a fuck nigga, his own blood.

"Damn shit fucked up out here. How the fuck you let that pussy nigga kill you D? That's why that nigga ain't have no work like that. Fuuuck! I promise if them folks don't lock his ass up before I get to him, I'm a murk his ass! On my mama big brah!" Jay said to hisself.

He called Erica and told her what happened.

"What, how did this happen!? That is so sad, I had just met him and I saw the friendship you had with him. Y'all were like brothers." Erica said.

"Yea, I know bae that was my big homie for real, I fucked with that nigga hard." Jay said.

"Have you talked to Nikki yet?"

"I tried calling her but she didn't pick up the phone."

"I want to see you. Can you come to Beaufort today?" She asked.

"Nawl bae I can't drive right now this shit got me fucked up. Why you can't come down here."

"I can't come down there I have class early in the morning."

"Oh, ok then." Jay said not giving a fuck about her classes at the moment.

They sat silent on the phone for 3 minutes, Jay was mad that she could talk about fuckin school at a time like this. His brother was just killed.

"I'll talk to you later bae I'm about to take a nap."

"Ok, I love you Jay."

"Yea, love you too."

When he hung up he called D's sister she was mourning like everybody else was.

"Have you talked to Nikki at all?" Jay asked her.

"No I haven't heard from her and she's not answering anybody's calls I hope she's ok." Tina said.

"Ok well just keep me posted on the funeral and what I can do to help out."

"Ok."

Jay took a nap and as he was sleeping he dreamed about killing Reese. As he was about to pull the trigger, he was woke up by his phone ringing. It was Candi.

"Hello?"

"Hi Jay, how are you doing?"

"I'm straight. What's up with you?"

"Nothing I'm sorry to be calling you."

"Nawl you good. What's up?"

"Coco is dead Jay. She was murdered last night and I'm sorry to hear about your friend too. I don't know what's going on out here." She said crying.

"Wait what you mean, you sure?" He said acting surprised about Cocos murder.

"Yea it's all over the news. Can I meet you somewhere so we can talk in person?"

"Umm yea just come to my house, I'm home." Jay said.

20 minutes later she was knocking on his door, with Beautiful on her side.

"What's up y'all ok?" Jay said, giving them both a hug.

"Yea we good we just can't believe that our girl is actually gone."

"This is some crazy shit. Who would want to hurt Coco she didn't fuck with nobody." Jay said.

"It probably had something to do with her boyfriend, that nigga stay in some bullshit." Coco stated.

"But we have something else to tell you Jay." Beautiful said.

"What?" Jay asked confused.

"The two dudes that were at your party with you um, Reese and D?"

"Yea what about them?" Jay asked.

"Well Devin was found murdered at his girlfriend's apartment right and the police think it was his cousin Reese who did it."

"Yea I heard about that shit. I hope they find his ass." He lied, knowing he wanted to iron Reese ass up before the police got to him.

"That's not all." Candi said.

Now Jay really was surprised.

"What's the rest this shit can't get no worst." Jay said.

"That dude Reese. Beautiful has been sleeping with him and he at her house right now. We called the police and told them he was there." Candi said.

"What!? What you mean he at her house!? Why y'all didn't tell me this over the phone! I'm bout to- ooh!" He stopped before he let a females know his business.

"Because we were scared he might try to kill me, so we called the police and told them where he was. They told me I had to come to the precinct and make a statement and get questioned. Then we came straight over here." Beautiful said.

Beautiful and Candi were crying hard.

Jay sat down feeling defeated because he wasn't going to get to put his hands on Reese before the police did.

Candi thought he was morning for his friend and sat beside him. But he was really mad that he couldn't get to Reese.

"It'll be okay Jay." Candi said hugging him then kissing him softly on the cheek.

Jay had missed Candi and her soft lips reminded him how he missed her touch.

"Jay I know I have a man and you have a girl, but I miss you and being around you."

"I missed you too lil mama." He said wiping the tears from her eyes.

"What happened to Coco made me realize life is too short to lose a friend." Candi said.

"Yea you right I feel the same way." Jay said.

"So will you continue to be my friend regardless of what's going on in our lives?" She asked.

"Yea lil mama I can do that. I never wanted to stop being your friend it was just how things went down, but that didn't stop me from thinking about you."

"I'm happy to know that because I've felt the same way." Candi said and gave his a soft kiss on the lips then getting up to leave.

"Come on Beautiful, I'm tired let's go."

"I'm not going back to my house right? The police said they would let me know if and when they caught him." Beautiful said scared.

"Girl bring your scary ass on. I told you, you can stay to my house."

"If you knew you was sleeping with a killer you would be scared too so don't front."

"You ain't lying." Candi said shivering at the thought.

Jay walked them to the door and let them out.

"Y'all keep me posted on everything." Jay said to them.

"Ok bye Jay."

"Bye Jay we love you." Beautiful said.

"Love y'all too."

"Damn that fuck nigga slipped right through my fingers." Jay thought to hisself as he closed the door.

He tried calling to check on Nikki again but didn't get an answer.

CHAPTER 33

Reese was mad as hell, but chopped the $800 up as a lost. The only thing on his mind was getting the fuck out of Georgia.

He parked his car in Yamacraw apartments and walked to the bus station from there, not wanting to take a bigger chance driving and risk getting pulled over. He had called Beautiful 15 times and it went straight to voicemail each time. It wasn't enough time in the day to wait on her to come back home the way things were going each and every second counted since he had killed D. Reese wasn't dumb he watched first 48 and knew technology was a motherfucker. He had got in a fight with his cousin so he knew his DNA would be found somewhere on his body, and they would be able to see D had been fighting before he was killed. So he figured by bus would be the safest way to travel, even though it would take a couple of days to get back up North it was safer.

"Hi may I help you sir?"

"Yes can I get a ticket from Savannah to New York?" Reese asked.

"Round Trip?" She said keying in the information.

"No one way please."

"And your name?" The cashier asked.

"Jason Craft." Reese said lying.

"Ok the total will be $105.93."

He reached in his pocket and pulled out a $100 dollar bill and a $10. She took the money and gave him his change.

"Thank you ma'am." Reese said grabbing the change.

He walked to the bathroom pulling out a bag of coke and creasing a dollar bill down the middle, digging in the bag placing a bump to his nose.

"I hope this shit last me on this long ass fucking ride. Suuuf, suuuf. All these fuckin lay overs about to blow the fuck out a nigga already, and I ain't even get on the bus yet. Fuck it 2 more hours and I'm out though fuck it. Suuuf." He said talking to hisself in the mirror...

It had been almost week since Nikki found D dead on the bathroom floor and she still hadn't had any contact with the outside world only her immediate family. She really didn't want to talk to anybody. She had given birth to a baby boy that came two weeks earlier than planned due to stress. Nikki named him Devin Harris Jr., but was unable to look at him for long periods of time giving him back to the nurse every time they would bring him to her because he looked too much like his father and it was hurting her more. She had left her phone turned off and was in a very bad state of depression.

"How could you do this to your own blood Reese? D loved you he would have given you anything!" She said crying herself to sleep like she did every day...

Jay was on the highway driving past the digital billboard, looking at Reese's mug shot as "Wanted for murder" flashed across the screen. They still hadn't found him and Jay knew he had went back up North were he felt comfortable.

"I'ma get yo ass pussy nigga." Jay thought to hisself.

He had just figured out were Nikki was and him and Erica were on their way to visit her.

When he entered the hospital he walked past the check in desk and straight to the elevator. Nikki's cousin had told him the floor and room number she was in.

When he got to the room 312 he knocked twice then pushed the door open and there she was sleeping peacefully.

"Hey you still sleep it's 3 o'clock in the afternoon." Jay said waking her up.

Nikki looked up at Jay with tired eyes.

"Jay?" Nikki said still half sleep.

"Yea it's me big sis, the one and only. The sexiest man on earth."

"Boy please." Erica said.

Erica and Nikki busted out laughing.

"Oh y'all think that's funny huh?" Jay said smiling.

"How did you know I was here Jay? I mean I don't mind, but nobody was supposed to be able to know what room I was in but my mom, dad and a hand full of other people."

"Well your cousin Free told me after I told her about how close me and D were and how you were like a sister to me." Jay told her.

"I'm a kick her ass when I get out, giving out my whereabouts to strangers. You could have been a contracted killer or some shit, she ain't know." Nikki said a little pissed.

"Yea right. Pretty boy Floyd scared to bend his nails in the wrong direction, who going to think he a killer?" Erica said laughing.

"You ain't lying about that." Nikki said joining in.

"Whatever y'all both know I don't play no games, but I see you lost the extra weight, where my nephew at?"

Nikki's smile faded when she thought about little Devin.

"The nurses have him in the baby room."

"Well tell them to bring him in, I want to see him. Who does he look like, you or D?" Erica asked.

"Me? Please, he look exactly like D. That's why I can't have him around me for long periods of time, because all I do is cry and think about D." She said with a tears rolling down her cheeks.

"But I have to shake this and stop being so selfish because my son needs me." Nikki said wiping them away.

Erica started crying too, helping Nikki wipe the tears from her face. Buzzzz.

"Yes Ms. Harris, how can I help you?" The nurse asked.

"Could you bring me my baby to me please?" Nikki asked.

"Yes I'll let one of the nurse on that side know to bring him to you right now."

"Thank you."

7 minutes later a nurse came in carrying little Devin in her arms.

"Here you go Ms. Harris here's your little angel, I bet he missed you." The nurse said passing her Devin.

"Thank you." Nikki said smiling taking her son out the nurse's arms.

"How is mama's boy doing? Those ladies been spoiling you down there?" Nikki said smiling at him.

"Dang sis you ain't lying. He look just like D. He don't look nothing like you." Jay said.

Erica sucked her teeth and slapped Jay's shoulder.

"What?" Jay asked.

"It's ok, I know he looks like his daddy. Now you can see why I get so depressed every time he's around me." Nikki said.

Lil D was staring at Jay with his eyes wide open.

"My nigga reincarnated, I knew you couldn't leave like that big brah." Jay thought to hisself.

"Let me hold him sis." Jay said.

"Be careful, and make sure you hold his head up." Nikki said protectively as she passed Lil D to Jay.

"Ok. Aww man, you a handsome lil fella, what's up little man?" Jay said talking to Lil D.

After they all held and played with little D, Jay left his cell number with Nikki and told her to call him when she left the hospital so he could buy Lil D some clothes. Then him and Erica left and headed back to his house.

"Bae I got something I want to tell you, but I don't want you to get mad at me." Erica said.

"Well if you think it's going to make me made, why ask me?" Jay asked.

"Because it's important that's why." Erica said with a slight attitude.

"Ok what is it then Bae?"

"I want you to stop selling drugs, I don't want to end up like Nikki."

"What, what you mean by that? Ain't nothing about to happen to me girl." Jay said frowning.

"How much longer do you think you'll be able to sell drugs, before you eventually get caught or worst killed? I want you to be real with yourself, you know there's no future in it. Why not stop while you're so far ahead? I mean you got money, so what's the problem?"

"I'll think about it." Jay said trying to brush it off.

"What is there to think about? I mean look what happened the other day with Coco for example, how you put your life in somebody else's hands so easy just by trying to look out. Every day you go out in the streets you're putting your life in somebody else's hands by selling that shit. Plus I ain't going to say you had something to do with Coco and her boyfriend's murder, but the shit just crazy. How she get you set up, and next thing you know she gets killed a couple of days later?" Erica said stressing.

"Girl shut the fuck up and don't let me ever hear you say some shit like that out your mouth again!" Jay yelled at Erica louder than he ever did, losing his cool.

Erica sat back in her seat scared, he had never talked to her in the voice he was using before.

"Well I'm pregnant so I guess we not having it. I'll just get a abortion." She said with tears rolling down her face.

"You what?"

"I said I'm pregnant and I guess I'm not keeping it! I refuse to tell my child their dad is in jail for the rest of his life or was killed selling drugs fuck that!" Erica said emotionally.

"Damn bae, why you just telling me this?" Jay said softening up.

"Because I just found out a couple of days ago and wanted to surprise you. I was thinking you would be happy and would want to change your life and start a family with me but I was wrong." Erica said.

Jay pulled over.

"Girl are you crazy? I'm fuckin in love with you and I am going to change. I know I can't sell drugs forever bae I'm not stupid. But I just can't up and quit right now I don't have a career as of today, but with you telling me you carrying my seed changes everything though I promise you that. I'ma do what I need to do to make a transition as soon as possible."

"Don't lie to me Jay." Erica said seriously.

"Bae I don't want to lie to you and wouldn't lie to you. Give me a couple of months to tie some ends up and I'm done with the streets no lie. That's me keeping it 100 with you."

"You promise." She asked.

"I promise bae." He said.

Jay drove back to his house happier than the day he had been released from prison…………………………………………..

The next morning Jay woke and forced Erica out the bed to get ready.

"Where we going bae?" She said as she brushed her teeth.

"I'm taking you and my mom out to eat breakfast, and I'ma give her the good news."

She gargled and spit.

"What? Bae I'm not ready to tell your mom yet, you know she going to be mad at me. She wanted me to finish school and start on my carrier before we had any kids and plus you know she think she too young to be getting called grandma."

They both started laughing.

"You're right but she'll be ok bae."

"Whatever." Erica said.

They finished getting ready and headed out the door to go pick up Ms. Brenda.

When they pulled up to Ms. Brenda's house, they got out the car and went in.

"Hi big brother." Courtney said giving him a hug.

"What's up big head? You doing good in school still?"

"Yes, I made all A's on my report card." Courtney said.

"You did?"

"Yes so may I please have some money to get the new Kevin Durant's? Mama said they cost too much."

"Well you did make all A's, so you worked for them right?" Jay asked.

"Yea." She said smiling knowing her brother would give her the $150 for the shoes.

Jay reached in his pocket and pulled out a hundred and fifty dollars. He was in an extra good mood. Courtney's eyes were wide and glowing from the two big bills.

"Thank you big brother I love you so much." She said hugging him tight.

"Yea, yea, yea, you better keep them grades up or your cash flow going to get cut off. Where Kayla at?" He asked.

"I don't know she out with some boy, ever since she graduated she think she grown. Mama said she will be out in ten minutes to."

"I know that means 30 minutes. Why women take so long to get ready bae?" He asked Erica.

"Perfection takes time that's why." Erica said.

"Whatever." He said turning on the TV.

40 minutes later his mom came out the room.

"Hi mama." Erica said hugging her.

"Hi y'all ready? I'm sorry I took so long. If Jay would have told me we were going out to breakfast yesterday, I would have been ready when y'all got here. He know I don't like surprises."

"Well I like giving you surprises. Now my two favorite ladies, can we leave before we miss breakfast? I'm hungry." Jay said holding out his arms to walk them both to the car.

They left the house and went to a local I-Hop. As they ordered their food and waited for the waitress to return Ms. Brenda felt there was more to it than a surprise breakfast.

"Ok I know there is more to this breakfast, so spit it out." Brenda said.

"Mama what you talking about?" Jay said.

"Boy I changed your shit, so I know when you holding some shit. So let's get it over with."

Erica squeezed his leg under the table nervously.

"Ok but it's nothing bad though." Jay said.

"All right. So tell me."

"Erica is pregnant!" He said excited.

"Um umm, well congratulations." Brenda said flatly.

"You don't sound like your congratulating us mama." Jay said.

"Because I just hope you kids know what you are doing. Bringing another life in this world is not easy and it takes time and effort from you both. And I know you still selling that shit?" Brenda said.

"Come on mama you know I don't sell nothing, I work every day." Jay said.

"Yea whatever, I'm just letting you know them police got all kinds of technology these days and undercovers working for them. So if you won't stop for me or Erica, you need to do it for your child. With that being said as much as I don't want to be a grandmother at 37 congratulations, I'm happy for y'all." Brenda said, this time smiling and giving them both hugs.

"Thank you ma, I love you so much!" Erica yelled getting up to give her a bigger hug, smiling from ear to ear.

Jay was happy he got his mom's half consent. When their food came she gave them both some parenting pointers as they enjoyed their breakfast.

CHAPTER 34

It had been three weeks and Candi was sick of Beautiful staying at her house. The police still hadn't found Reese. So her and Beautiful would take trips back and forth going to get clothes from her house, because she was scared to stay at her own house.

But bringing another woman in her house around her man started to dawn on Candi and bother her thoughts. Because even though Beautiful was her home girl she was a bona fide freak and everybody knew that, but she also knew she couldn't just put her friend out. If something happened to her she would never forgive herself. She had already lost Coco.

On Monday morning Candi woke up early and motivated to help her friend out, by finding her a new place to stay.

"Beautiful, Beautiful? Wake your butt up." Candi said pulling the blanket off of her.

"Ummm, what? It's 8:00 in the morning." Beautiful said looking at her phone.

"Let's go look for you a new place. This is ridiculous, we can just move your stuff into a new place. You can't live your life running from this nigga every day, you have to start over. Now get your butt up."

"Candi I'm tired, can we do this later?"

"Girl you lazy as hell. I'm about to go and get started and pick up a couple of applications for you. So when I come back you need to be ready." Candi said.

"Ok you the best girl." She said pulling the blanket back over her head.

"Whatever, I'll be back at 1 o'clock, yo ass better be ready bitch." Candi said leaving.

She stopped at Burger King to get breakfast, then started on her search for Beautiful a new place.

192

STREET MONEY

She stopped at five different apartment complexes, in high hopes but only one would accept Beautiful's straight cash, without a check stub.

"I told that bitch to get one of them tax forms and report her fucking income. So she wouldn't have a problem with shit like this, now look. Damn its 11:05 a.m. already I'm about to go get some lunch and I might as well get my man and bestie something to eat too before I head back.

She went to a Zaxby's and ordered three wings and things with tea then headed home...

Beautiful was in a deep sleep when she felt the blanket sliding down her body again.

"Girl I'm still tired give me 30 more minutes." She mumbled with her eyes still shut putting the pillow over her head.

"Damn I finally got a chance to be alone with yo pretty ass. I gotta get some of this pussy." He said to hisself.

John was standing over Beautiful naked with only his sox on, pulling on his dick admiring her pretty face. Then guiding his eyes down her slender body. Then to her fat juice box that that poked out through her thong.

He moved slowly inching his face and hands towards her juice box, readying hisself to eat her pussy even if she wanted him to stop. But he felt she wouldn't want him to, because he was hungry and was going to eat her out like he was.

As soon as his hand touched the side of her thong he pulled it to the side revealing a pussy so fat, that it looked like it didn't belong on her body.

"Damn lil mama."

Placing the thong over one booty cheek, he licked on both of her pussy lips and sucked on her clit, eating her out from the back sending electricity through her body causing her eyes to shoot open.

"Ssss, what the f-fuck!" She said locking her ass cheeks on his face.

"W-what you d-doing? Ssss oooh shit!"

John continued to lick and suck on her love box, using extra saliva making her fat pussy sloppy wet.

"Oooh, sssss s-shit." Beautiful kind of wanted to stop him, but her body wouldn't let her.

"D-damn, oooh sssss fuck ummm!" She moaned.

193

"Huuu!" She exhaled as he stuck his finger in her hole and touched her g-spot, moving his finger back and forth while still sucking on her clit.

"Sssss, I-I'm bout to c-cum!" She said loosening her legs rotating her ass on his face.

"Damn Candi was right, this nigga do give the best head." Beautiful thought still gyrating from the hard orgasm.

John opened the one condom he had saved for a moment like this, sliding it down the shaft of his dick.

Beautiful was still hot from the head he gave her plus she hadn't had sex in three weeks and that was unlike her. Her pussy was thumping for more.

John leaned his body over hers as she pulled open one of her cheeks for him to enter her, looking back at him biting her bottom lip. As he slid the head of his shaft up and down between her pussy lips, he pushed her other cheek up causing her lips to open around the head of his shaft as he slid in her wet juice box.

"Ssss ummm, that feel good!" Beautiful moaned.

"It feels good to me too baby." John said leaning over and kissing her on the neck as he took slow pumps inside of her, trying not to cum.

Beautiful wanted to fuck hard so she bounced back on him greedily, causing him to pump inside of her faster with force.

"Sluuup, puuump, sluuup, puuump. Sssss fuck!" Her box was making noises as she bit down on her bottom lip, cumming on his dick.

"Damn this some good pussy, shit!" John said out loud.

Booom!

"What the fuck, you fucking my man bitch!?" Candi said as she slung the hot food at them.

"Baby, baby it's not what you think!" John said with his hands up, revealing his wet condom.

"It's not what motherfucker!" She said charging at him with her keys in between her fingers as she swung at him, cutting him across the chest.

"Auuugh fuck girl!" John said trying to block the blows getting cut on his arms.

Beautiful was scared as shit from the ass wiping Candi was putting on him. She knew she was next if she didn't get the fuck out of dodge. So she tried to get out of the bed and put some clothes on fast as she could as Candi attacked John, but Candi caught a glimpse of her out the corner of her eye.

"Bitch where you think you going!?" She yelled charging for her.

"I'm sorry Candi I didn't mean too. It was him!"

"Wap!" She punched her in the eye.

"Auuugh!" Beautiful tried to run for the door, but could barely see and was dazed from the blow.

Candi grabbed a hand full of her hair and yanked her off her feet, then got on top of her punching her in the face, leaving her head with nowhere to go but to the other fist.

"Bitch I trusted yo ass, let you come in my house and you fuck my man!" Candi said punching her again and again, until John pulled her off of her.

"Get off me! Get the fuck of off me!" Candi was kicking and screaming trying to break loose from his grip.

"Baby calm down you going to kill her!" He said.

"That's what the fuck I'm trying to do, you dog motherfucker! Get the fuck off of me!" Candi yelled at him.

Beautiful was still dazed but clearly heard what she said about killing her and knew this was her opportunity to get the fuck out of there.

Beautiful grabbed her cell phone, pants and shirt and shot for the door as fast as she could. When she got outside she darted into the woods and put on her clothes.

"Get the fuck off me, uga!" Candi grabbed his balls squeezing the life out of John causing him to let go.

"Auuugh fuck!" He yelled falling to the floor holding his nuts.

Candi picked up her keys off the floor and ran out the door to find her murder charge. She rode around for three hours looking for Beautiful. She checked her old house and all her hang out spots trying to find her, as John blew her up calling and sending her multiple text of how sorry he was.

"Fuck you John you are sorry, a sorry motherfucker!" She said looking down at her phone.

She drove to La Quinta Inn on Hwy. 204 and rented a room for the night. When she got in the room she sat on the bed crying about the past events.

Her best friend had been killed and the other one was fucking her man. Candi felt horrible and felt she needed to talk to someone about this so she picked up her phone and called Jay.

CHAPTER 35

Jay had been trying to find a new plug for the last month. It was coke in the hood but the quality wasn't good. After Erica had told him about the baby he checked his stash box and he had saved up $30,000 since he had been home.

"Man this ain't enough money to raise no baby he said looking at the rubber banded money. Man I shouldn't have thrown that party and blew all that money in the club on my birthday. Then I don't got my same plug on the work, niggas selling me this stepped on shit causing me to have to let this shit go for cheap. This shit fucked up I'm about to have to find another hustle to go along with this shit, to make it add up. This some bull shit, damn I miss you my nigga."

Jay was stressed out from thinking about the baby and how he was going to go broke once the baby was born. He rolled a blunt and put it behind his ear and headed out the door, getting on the road heading towards Georgetown to take his white homeboy Mike a ounce of Loud.

"Ding, ding, ding." The gas light went off.

"Damn this bitch be drinking gas." He said as he pulled into a Parker's gas station.

He walked into the store to pay for his gas, grabbing a bottle of sprite before walking to the cash register.

He saw a muscle head white boy staring at him out the corner of his eye. When he turned his head and looked at the dude, the white boy put two fingers to his lips making a smoking signal then pointing at Jay.

Jay pointed at hisself, then shook his head no.

"I don't sale weed." He mouthed to the dude.

The white boy did the smoke signal again, but touched his ear.

Jay started frowning but touched his ear causing the blunt to fall and hit the floor.

"Oh shit!" He swiped the blunt up off the floor swiftly and put it in his pocket hoping a police officer wasn't in the store.

"Appreciate it homey." Jay said.

"No problem man, I figured you didn't know you came in here like that."

"Hell nawl, that ain't even my style brah brah. I was slipping just now."

"Word my name Tiger."

"Fasho, my name Jay." He said dapping him up.

"Shit you got some more of that though? Now I'm asking." Tiger said.

They both started laughing.

"Yea just holla at me when you come outside." Jay said.

Jay paid for the gas and soda then went to pump his gas. He grabbed a 3 grams of Loud out his car and waited for Tiger to come out the store.

When Tiger came out he looked around and spotted Jay. As he walked to his truck he waved with his hand, for Jay to come to his truck. He was pushing a Ford 250.

Jay walked over and hoped in with him.

"What you got for me homie?" Tiger said trying to act black.

"Shit all I fuck with is the Loud." Jay opened his hand letting him see the budded up exotic weed.

Tiger smelled it.

"Damn that shit smell good." Tiger said.

"It smoke good too. What you was trying to grab?" Jay asked.

"I don't smoke that much just let me get $10 worth."

"$10?" Jay was disappointed but wasn't bout to pass up on the cash even though it was petty. He broke the bud in half and gave it to him.

"Damn this all I get for $10?"

"Hell yea this ain't that Reggie shit, that's Loud brah brah. The quality is way better than that bullshit you probably been smoking on." Jay explained to him.

Tiger started laughing.

"I respect that, but check this out you know anybody that fuck with the Roxy's or Oxycontin 80's?"

"What the fuck is a Roxy or Oxy?" Jay asked.

They're prescription drugs man bros, but you can make a killing off of them." Tiger said laughing but serious, reaching in his pocket pulling out a Altoids case.

It was filled with blue and green pills.

"Shit how much they be going for?" Jay asked.

"The little blue ones go for $25-$30 a pill, and the big green ones go for $70-$80 a pill."

"These little ass pills go for that much family? Man you bull shitting me." Jay said.

"No I'm not bros, this is what I do. I sell the Roxy's for $12 apiece and the oxy for $35 a piece." Tiger said.

Jay sat thinking about the profit he could make, if what Tiger was saying was true. Shit if the pills was legit, he was about to expanded his hustle into something else.

"I tell you what give me 5 g's of that weed and I'll give you 4 Roxy's, so you can see what you can do with them. If you can't get off of 'em, I'll buy them back from you."

"Fasho that's a deal." Jay gave him the weed for the pills then went to the car and got him two more g's.

They exchanged numbers and went their separate ways to handle their business.

Jay went to take the white boy Mike his weed.

"What's up Mike?" He said dapping him up.

"Ain't shit homie what took you so long? I'm so ready to burn brah, I'm feeling like a fucking junky." Mike said.

They both started laughing.

"My bad brah, I had to stop and get some gas, but check this out. You ever heard of some pain pills called Roxy's?"

"Fuck yea! Why you know where some at?" Mike said getting excited.

Jay was surprised at his reaction but didn't change his demeanor.

"Yea I be having them." He said coolly.

"How much you be wanting for them $20 a piece?" Mike said trying to get them for the low.

"Come on Mike you know they go for $25-$30 a pill."

"$25-30 dollars, man when I was in Pittsburgh I used to get them for $20 a piece and if I got 3 or more $15 a piece." Mike said lying.

"Well we in Georgia and these motherfuckers hard to come by, so what you trying to do brah? I got like 4 left."

"Man let me see 'em." Mike said looking the pills over.

"Man shit, let me get three of 'em." Mike said pulling out his money.

He gave Jay the money for the weed and pills paying $25 a piece. When he got in the car to leave he got a call from Candi.

"Hello?" He answered.

"H-hey Jay." She said crying.

"Candi what's wrong with you, you ok?"

"Y-yes I can't believe this shit though. Ugh I hate that bitch!"

"Who?" Jay asked.

"Beautiful! I caught her and John fucking!" She yelled.

"What, when all this happened?"

"Yesterday, I can't believe she did this to me! I should have never let that bitch in my house, when I knew she was a hoe!"

"Where you at now?"

"I'm at the La Quinta Inn on Hwy 204. Jay I need somebody to talk to before I go crazy. Could you please come out here?" Candi asked.

"Yea I'm on my way. What room number you in?"

"I'm in room 163."

"Ok, I'm on my way."

20 minutes later Jay pulled up to the hotel, going to the room Candi was in knocking on the door. Candi opened the door with red eyes hugging Jay letting him in.

"Hi Jay."

"What's up lil mama you ok?" He said giving her a hug.

"No I feel so stupid for not seeing this coming." She said wiping her face.

"It's not your fault this happened it's your niggas fault, just as well as Beautiful's fault. They both grown and knew what they were doing." Jay explained to her.

"You don't need to be stressing yourself out over spilled milk, you didn't even spill."

"You right, it just hurts. Everything that's been going on from Coco to this, it's just too much for me."

Jay leaned over and wiped her tears from her eyes.

"If that nigga don't see he has the best thing that ever happened in his life and wants to cheat with a slut he a fool. Look at how beautiful you are, you can have any man you want." Jay said trying to console her and make her feel better.

"Thank you Jay, you always know the right things to say that's why I called you."

"You good lil mama, but it's the truth and you're my friend."

He leaned and kissed her on her forehead causing a shock to run through her body and her nipples to get hard.

When Jay looked in her eyes, they looked full of want, need and desire. Jay stared in her eyes for a second. Then leaned in and kissed her lips. Then he tongue kisses her.

Candi kissed him back, but then placed her hand on his chest and pushed him back.

"No Jay we can't do this."

"Why baby I missed you and I know you missed me."

"Yea but you have a girl and Jay you know this ain't right."

"This is right you need me right now, I can tell by the way your body responding to my touches." He said then he leaned in and kissed her on her neck.

"Ssss, n-nooo s-stop Jay." She moaned.

Jay didn't stop because he knew she really wanted to say no don't stop.

"It's ok lil mama. Just let go and let me take care of you. You're stressed out just relax." He whispered in her ear.

Candi closed her eyes letting go of the past events, causing tears to roll down her face while Jay continued to kiss on her neck. He lifted her shirt over her head and laid her on the bed, getting on the top of her and putting his knee between her legs. He then pulled her breast out of her bra putting one in his mouth and squeezing on the other, while moving his knee back and forth between her legs.

"Ssss ummm, w-why you doing this to me?" She said moaning.

"You want me to stop?"

"No please don't."

"Ok lil mama."

He continued to suck on her nipples and rub his knee between her legs until she started to rotate her hips on his leg, he knew she was wet now.

He slid down and placed kisses on her belly and unbuttoned the skin tight jeans she had on, pulling them from under her plump ass and sliding them down her legs.

Candi's eyes were still closed when he looked at her face.

When he separated her legs her thong had a wet spot in the middle from grinding on his knee. Jay took off his shirt and pants and slid her thong to the side.

Candi thought he was about to eat her as he placed his hand on her clit, but when she felt him enter her sliding his whole dick inside her. Her eyes shot open with shock, pain and pleasure all in one.

Jay knew what she needed and that was to be fucked good.

"Huuu, oh my g-god, sssss ummm!" She moaned loudly.

"Damn baby your pussy always tight." He said taking three long strokes then lifting her legs in the air, speeding up his pace, but continuing to go deep as he could.

"Ssss oooh, auuugh f-fuck I'm about to cu- sssss! She came hard on his dick.

Jay had to pull out, because he was about to come with her and he wasn't about to go out like that. It hadn't even been 5 minutes yet.

"Turn over." He said helping her up.

Candi was too drained to lift her butt in the air, so she laid on her stomach. He entered her from the back grinding in her hard admiring her ass as it clapped on his dick.

"Plop, plop, plop."

He then separated her cheeks holding them as he watched hisself enter in and out of her.

"Damn baby you feel good." Jay said.

He took his thumb and rubbed it over her booty hole as he fucked her hard, holding her cheeks making her booty hole wet too.

"Sssss ooh shit!" She moaned as he slid his thumb in her other hole, entering her faster and harder.

Candi squeezed her eyes tight, as tears of pleasure rolled down her face as she creamed from both holes.

"Ummm yes daddy!" She moaned as she came again shaking.

"Fuck!" Jay yelled.

He couldn't hold back anymore as her juices rolled down his shaft he tried to pull out fast as he could, nutting on her butt and back.

He had fucked her pain away for the moment, causing her to pass out in the position she was in.

Jay went and wet a rag wiping her off then laid beside her.

When Candi woke up, she kissed him waking him up.

"What's up lil mama you ok?"

"I'm ok but I was thinking while you was sleeping."

"About what?"

"About us."

"Man I know she ain't falling in love off a good nut?" He thought to hisself.

"I mean I know we can't be together right now but we got history and we been fucking around a lot. I feel if I wasn't fucking with that lame ass nigga we would be together."

"Fasho, but what you saying lil mama?" Jay asked.

"What, I'm saying is I will always be there for you like you've always been there for me Jay. We have something special between us and I'm not going to let it go. It doesn't matter if you're with somebody right now. You've always kept it real with me and I love you Jay'sean. You will always have a place in my heart forever." Candi said.

"Damn, I love you too lil mama. We won't ever grow apart as long as we keep it 100 with each other." He lied knowing he only loved Erica and if she found out he was fucking her he would leave her ass alone forever...

For the next month Jay had been running the streets harder than he ever had. Going against his judgement and hustling from sunup to sundown making all ends meet. Trying to balance out spending time with Erica and fucking Candi.

He had been getting less than 3 hours of sleep a day trying to balance everything out between the streets and two women. It wasn't easy. Candi was still renting out a hotel room not even wanting to see or deal with John at all, she had made up in her mind she was done.

CHAPTER 36

*J*ohn had been getting on the job training for the last 5 weeks, by officer Ricks. He was showing him the ins and outs of being an officer of the law. They had started building a friendship and getting comfortable with each other on and off the job.

"We have a shoplifting suspect at the BP gas station on Mohawk St., the suspect is a white male in his late fifties, white t-shirt and blue jeans." The dispatch said over the radio.

"This is squad car 12, I'm in route to the location 10-4 over." Rick said over the radio.

"You ready to make your first arrest rookie?" Officer Ricks asked.

"I've been waiting for this day since I was born. I'm ready as I can be." John said.

Ricks mashed the gas speeding towards the scene arriving at the gas station in less than 5 minutes.

When they pulled up there was an old white man arguing with a lady at the register with a white shirt on.

Ricks and John entered the store with precaution.

"You take the lead John." Ricks said walking behind him.

"Excuse me sir could you please step over here." John asked the man.

"He stole a beer and some chips and tried to walk out the store and I locked his ass in!" The young girl yelled, behind the glass.

"Ok we got it ma'am. Please step over here sir." John said again.

The old man continued cursing the cashier out, not listening to John.

"Sir, I said step over here!" He said grabbing the old man by the arm.

"Get your fucking hands off me!" The old man said swinging his arm.

John grabbed the old man with force and pushed him against the wall.

"Auuugh!"

"Put your hands behind your back now!" John yelled.

"Fuck you!" The old man said bucking.

John grabbed one of the man's arms bending it up behind his back, placing the hand cuffs tight on his wrist while reading him his rights.

"Ouch, man that's too tight!"

"You should have cooperated sir." When he grabbed the man's other arm, the beer can and chips fell out of his coat.

"You have the right to remain silent anything you say or do will be used against you in a court of law."

"La, la la, la, la fuck you pussy!" The old man yelled as John tried to continue to read him his rights.

After John read him his rights, he patted him down pulling a crack pipe out of his coat. He walked the old man to the car and placed him in the back seat.

"I'm going to sue you motherfuckers for beating me and dislocating my arm!"

"Yea, yea." John said.

"Wow I'm impressed. My first time trying to make an arrest, the suspect ran on foot and I didn't get to arrest him." Officer Ricks said.

"Why is that?" John asked.

"Because he was too fast that's, why."

They both busted out laughing.

"I'm glad I didn't have to chase nobody today, but if he would have ran he wouldn't have got far, but look what I got off him though." He said holding up the crack pipe up.

"Good job rookie now for the hard part."

"What's that, I thought the hard part was over?"

"The police report, bullshit paperwork, from beginning to end and you also have to go back in the store and get a report from the store clerk."

"Damn well we might as well get started."

"We? That's your job. You made the arrest. Your arrest, your report."

"Ain't that some shit." John said.

They both started laughing.

John walked back in the store and questioned the cashier, getting a full story of what happened from the beginning until time they arrived, while Rick's sat in the car with the petty crack smoker. After he finished he walked back to the car and hopped in the passenger side.

"You ready." Rick's said putting the car in drive.

"Yea I'm ready." John said going over his report.

They drove to the precinct and logged the crack pipe into evidence, filled out the rest of the report and placed the old man in the patty wagon to get dropped off to the county jail. They pulled off from the precinct and got back on the streets to patrol, looking for any criminal activity they could find.

Officer Ricks decided to spark up a conversation on something that he had been wanting to ask John about.

"So what happened with you and the situation from downtown?"

John was shocked Ricks mentioned the night he got his ass beat and put in the hospital, but didn't know how he knew about it.

"What situation?"

"Come on man the situation that left you in the hospital. I'm a cop. I don't forget a face."

"Oh that crazy shit that happened with me and my girl?"

"Yea that night and don't give me the watered down version because I saw the tape from the hotel. You were there not downtown that night. Another male and your girlfriend helped carry your bloody ass out of the hotel to the car. What happened man?" Officer Ricks asked.

"How did you know about the situation at the hotel?" John asked surprised.

"I was the officer called to the scene and after questioning some people at the hotel and looking at the tape, I went to the hospital on a report of a possible assault.

After questioning your rude ass girlfriend and looking over the tape again the next day, I put two and two together on what happened. So what's the whole story?"

"Alright man you got it Matlock, damn you know everything!"

They both started laughing.

"I haven't been doing this for the past 9 years for no reason." Officer Ricks said.

"True, but man I caught my girlfriend fucking another dude. Me and her ended up getting into a big fight and when I went after the dude he hit me with a gun catching me off guard. If he wouldn't have had the gun I would have fucked him up." John said lying.

"Damn he pistol whipped you and was fucking your girl? Now that's fucked up."

"Yea but I got her ass back." John said.

"Man what you could you possibly do to get even with her after that? That's a far stretch my man."

"I fucked her best friend."

"Nooo, you dirty fucking cop! She doesn't know, does she?"

"Man get this shit, this little piece of ass is so beautiful, her name is Beautiful. She had been staying at our house for a couple of weeks and one day my girl left us alone giving me a chance to get my shot at the ass. When she came home I was still swimming deep in the pussy!"

"What? I know she flipped out!" Officer Ricks Said laughing.

"Man I haven't even heard from her in the last month. She probably back fucking that drug dealing motherfucker." John said with a little hate in his voice.

"You think so?"

"It's no telling. She not fucking me, so I wouldn't put it past her."

"Damn that's fucked up. You miss her?"

"Hell yea. I'm not going to front, I call her every day and text her how my day went, but she never responds back."

"Damn you got it bad my man, well I know what our next job is."

"What you got planned for us now?" John said ready to police some shit.

"Getting another scumbag off the streets, so you can get your girl back. What's his name so I can pull up his address? I've been to his house once before for questioning, on that hotel situation. I could tell he was a drug dealer by the way he was answering my questions but I can't remember exactly where he stays anymore. Trust me we going to get his ass off the streets, because I'm going to also put under his car's license plate number, "Possibly armed, narcotics dealer." Officer Ricks said.

"It's that easy?"

"Hell yea, we're the police. Now what's his name again?"

"Jay'sean Moss." John said excited.

After about 3 minutes of typing in some key notes, into his computer it was done.

"And there we go." Ricks said clicking enter.

Any time Jay's tag would be ran by an officer they would pull his car over with the quickness so they could search him.

CHAPTER 37

Jay had just finished dropping off the last 6 Oxycontin 80 mg pills he had. He had been grabbing so many Tiger had dropped an extra $5 off the Oxycontin, and $2 off the Roxy 25 mg pills. Even though the money was coming in Jay wasn't getting any sleep. He was really tired of running the streets and wanted to switch his hustle up on some legit shit. He had even started selling clothes and music out his trunk just to see what it was like to sell something other than drugs. To his surprise he kind of liked the shit and all his plays on the drugs was fucking with him. Plus all the females was fucking with him because he had that dope boy swag along with a hustler's conversation to go along with his sales pitch. He was selling MK, Louis Vuitton and Gucci purses and sandals to the woman and designer belts and watches to the men taking money out of everybody's pockets and into his hands.

Shit was going good, he was a one stop shop. He was starting to feel he had mastered his street hustle and was smart enough to know once that happened, it was time to cash out.

"Hi baby?" Erica said with a big smile and pregnant glow.

"What's up baby?" He said smiling giving her a kiss then kissing her belly.

"How my two little women doing today? What did y'all eat?" He asked.

"We are doing fine and we just had steak and potatoes for lunch."

"Oh y'all did?"

"Yep."

"Well were mine at? You ain't tell me we was having steak for lunch."

"I did, you know you don't be answering the phone smart ass. Pick up the phone and you would know."

"Whatever." Jay said brushing her off.

"Your plate is in the microwave Jay, you know I wouldn't fix myself anything to eat without fixing you some too."

"Oh ok."

"Don't run the fuck out!" She said frowning at him.

Jay walked to his room and opened his safe to count his stash before he made his last flip. He had made up his mind he was done with illegal money making. He vowed once he made the transition he would never forget where he came from. He was going to take 75% of his stash and open a business and live off the rest until his legal clientele picked up. He knew he couldn't just go open a business with no paper trail, so he was going to put everything in Erica's name.

Through all his life experiences he knew God had blessed him and preserved him to make it through it all.

When he finished counting up he had $63,220 all profit. A tear rolled down his face because he knew in order for him just to get to $63,220, a lot of people had been hurt, killed and became broke because of this money. He took 6 rubber banded stacks out of his safe and went to enjoy his meal with his girl.

Jay left the house and met up with Tiger and also calling his weed and coke plug re-uping one last time, making his normal runs afterwards.

Jay had been booming as usual and feeling good about making a change in his hustle. He knew anything he touched he could turn into money.

Jay had just dropped off the last ounce of weed he had been riding with, he had fronted the other pound and a half of coke to his young niggas on the East and West side earlier.

He only had 23 Roxy pills left on him and the customer he was supposed to take them to was waiting on her stockbroker husband to come home with the money.

"Man why you gotta wait on him to come home?" Jay asked ready to get rid of the pills.

"Because he took all the cards, he doesn't want me getting high without him." The lady texted back.

"Damn, I tell you what I know you going to pay me my money. I've never had any problems out of y'all and I don't like riding around like this, so I'm a just drop 'em off to you and y'all can call pay me th-"

STACKS

Whoop! Whoop!

The sirens made him stop his text.

"What the fuck?" Jay said looking in his rearview mirror.

He had been blue lighted. He pulled over to the side, the young white cop got out of his car and walked to his car. With his hand on his pistol.

"How you doing today, sir?"

"How you doing? Licenses and registration please?"

"Yes sir. May I ask why you pulled me over?"

"Yes you didn't come to a complete stop at the stop sign two blocks down."

"Ok sir." Jay said calmly.

"I'll be right back, hold tight."

When the officer ran Jay'sean's information, "Possibly armed, narcotics dealer" flashed across the screen, so he called for backup..................
....

"I have a black male pulled over on West Chester Street, Jay'sean Moss. He is possibly armed so I'm calling for backup." He said over the radio.

"Yes this is Officer Ricks responding to the back up call, over." Officer Ricks responded to the call before anybody else picked up.

"Yes, this is Officer Neil. I'm requesting backup for a possible armed suspect."

"Yes sir. Me and my partner will be there to assist you shortly." Officer Ricks said over the radio.

"10-4." Officer Neil responded back.

Officer Ricks and John were on the Southside patrolling, so they weren't even supposed to respond to the call on the Westside, but they couldn't pass up on this kind of action especially after they had put in the work.

After Officer Rick's wrote the young girl a ticket for speeding, he turned on his lights and did the dashboard all the way to the Westside.

When he pulled up Officer Neil was pissed.

"What took you guys so long man? I could have called somebody else?" He said to Officer Ricks.

"We had to stop and get gas." Officer Ricks lied, knowing they just came from the other side of town and wasn't even supposed to be on his side of town today."

"You can leave me and my partner can handle it from here." Ricks told the less superior officer.

Officer Neil turned redder by the second, but knowing not to say anything out the way to his superior.

"Yes sir is there anything you would like me to assist you guys with?" Officer Neil asked.

"No you my leave. I said me and my partner will handle it from here get back on patrol officer." Officer Ricks said with authority.

"Yes sir." Officer Neil got back in his car pulling off fast, but not fast enough to piss Officer Ricks off.

CHAPTER 38

*J*ay was nervous as hell. He had been sitting in the same spot for the last 20 minutes, with all the pain pills in the glove compartment box and a now unloaded .380 under the passenger seat. On top of all this, another cop car was pulling up.

Jay looked in his rearview and watched as the cop that pulled him over give the other cop his information and leave. He watched as the other cop walked up to his door with his hand on his gun, while his partner stayed in the car.

"Put your fucking hands where I can see them and step out of the fucking car!" Officer Ricks yelled pulling his gun out of the holster pointing it in Jays face. Then yanking Jay's door open.

"Ok you got it sir. Please don't shoot. What did I do?" Jay said with his hands up trying his best to get out of the car with his hands up.

"Shut the fuck up, Officer John come cuff this motherfucker!" Officer Ricks yelled.

"Officer John?" The name played around in Jays head as everything was happening by the second.

John jumped out the car, running to his partner's aid, pushing Jay against the car with force reaching for his hand cuffs.

Officer Ricks felt John had the situation with Jay under control, so he started to search Jay's car looking under the front seat.

When Jay looked back and saw John's face he busted out laughing about the situation he was now in, as John fumbled to pull the cuffs out because of how mad he was.

"Man that's what all this about, me fucking your bitch, ain't this some shit!" Jay was laughing so hard, he had forgot about even going to jail for the drugs and the gun.

"So you made it to be a broke ass co-"

"Whop!" John's gun came crashing down on the top of Jay's head.

At first Jay was dazed, then his survival instincts kicked in. Even though he was dealing with officers of the law, he felt threatened and that his life was in danger.

Jay swung around with a viscous elbow, catching John in the jaw knocking out two of his teeth.

John dropped the gun holding his jaw in pain, tripping over Officer Ricks' legs, while he was searching the car.

Ricks popped up on guard, gun aimed shooting at Jay causing him to duck and dodge. As he was ducking, he picked up John's gun off the ground.

John regained some consciousness, charging at Jay with anger not caring about the gun.

"Mother fucker!" John yelled running towards Jay, on the other side of the car.

"Boom!" Jay fired a single shot, hitting John in the forehead. He was dead before he hit the ground.

Ricks had seen when Jay picked up the gun so he was already ducking and on guard behind the door waiting for the moment he could fire. This was not his first time in a shootout situation. He knew John had made a big mistake, by letting his guard down like that.

"Come out with your hands up!" Officer Ricks yelled.

"Fuck you! So you can kill me!? You got me fucked up!" Jay yelled back.

"If you don't come out with your hands up, I will kill you!"

"Fuck it kill me. I'm holding court it the streets today. Y'all motherfuckers wrong. I ain't do shit!"

Jay could hear multiple sirens wailing, he knew the officer had called for backup ever since he had put one in John's head.

Officer Ricks inched his way around the car and peeked around just enough to see an opening sprinting towards Jay firing.

"Boom! Boom! Boom!"

Jay ran trying to make it to the other side of the car before a bullet touched him. He dived sliding to the other side of the car breathing uncontrollably.

He couldn't feel his fingers on his left hand. When he looked at his arm it was blood everywhere.

"Augh fuck!" Jay grimaced.

"I told you to give up, now I have to kill another nigger! I mean I don't have a problem with black people, just the niggers! The ones that sale drugs, don't graduate high school, sag their pants and shit! You know niggers just like you, those the ones I don't like!" Officer Ricks said laughing.

Jay could feel hisself losing blood and energy with every breath and the sirens were getting closer. He knew the officer wasn't going to let him live to talk about this.

"M-motherfucker you know why my people a-act the way they do?" Jay asked.

"No tell me why before I kill you nigger, then I'll know the reason!"

"Because people like you oppressed us for so long. Y'all broke us down. Not white people, nawl people like you. Y'all oppressed us causing us to make our own ways to live life motherfucker! That's why we do what we want to do, join gangs, sag and shit like that, because we're different. You think we want to look like people like you or act like you after what y'all did to us!? Ha, ha, ha, motherfucker you crazy!? I know why y'all always hated us, because we got big dicks!"

"Fuck you! Boom, Boom!" Ricks said firing and missing.

"Yea I know the only reason bitches like you get government power jobs like this is because you're racist and you need it to protect you from people like me. That racist shit don't really mean nothing to niggas like me. So I guess that's the problem we having today. I'm dealing with the devil! But the devil can't fuck with God!"

"Yea whatever nigger, just bring you ass out and we can get this over with real quick!"

Jay opened and closed the front door of the car causing Officer Rick's to get confused and wonder.

"What the fuck is this dumb ass nigger doing?" Officer Ricks thought to hisself peeking his head up.

By the time his eyes made it to the car window across from the other side of the car, Jay had already centered his aim in the middle of his head. He just wanted him to look him in the eyes before he flat lined his ass.

"Boom!" Jay fired off.

STREET MONEY

The bullet penetrated through both glass widows and into Officer Rick's head. He didn't even fall to the ground after the bullet hit his skull. He died kneeling with his head leaning on the car door with blood leaking from the hole in his head.

Jay felt weaker by the second, like his soul was being lifted out his body. He laid on the ground as his body stiffened up and went to sleep.

CHAPTER 39

"**W**hat you doing here nigga?"

"What you mean what I'm doing here? Man look at this shit, we can see everything from up here." Jay said.

"Yea but it ain't your time son. You just dreaming right now."

"D what the fuck you talking about nigga this shit real." Jay said.

"Nawl fam. You dreaming, but these are my real thoughts and visions. This is my spirit in your mind." D said.

"Damn that's deep big brah."

"Yea, but you about to wake up soon B."

"Why? Man a nigga want to chill with you up here for a little while longer."

"Because this shit fucking with you too hard. Look at you, you about to start crying and shit. Yo soft ass."

"Fuck you nigga!

They both started laughing.

"Take care of my family for me. The Man said He ain't done with you yet. He got big plans for you fam."

"What? A, aaa!?"

Jay jumped up with his wrist handcuffed to the hospital bed and two F.B.I officers in front of him.

"So, you've finally woke up Mr. Moss? Well of course you know why we're here right?" One of the officers asked.

"And why is that?" Jay said hoarse.

The other officer laughed.

"Ok you want to act like a little bitch. We can use grease or we can go in raw dog. Now start talking."

"Man what the fuck you mean? All I remember is being shot by somebody and then waking up in here. When I woke up, I thought I might see my lawyer or my family. Shit maybe even wake up with my dick in your bitch mouth. But I didn't think I would see you two ugly mother fuckers here though."

"That was cute but guess what, your little state lawyer not going to be able to help you on this one. You killed two police officers motherfucker. You going to hell, not jail motherfucker! The judge going to give your ass the chair! You going to the F.E.D's dumb ass!"

"So since you don't want to talk, see you in court no grease motherfucker." The other officer said giving his partner five as they left.

"Fuck Ya'll!" Jay yelled as they left.

The only thing Jay could think about was his unborn child and how he could get out of his situation and get back to his family...

At first Jay's lawyer didn't believe he was being 100% honest with him, but after he watched the tape of Officer Ricks dash camera that was in the squad car, what Jay had told him was adding up. Even though you couldn't hear clearly what was said on the tape, it spoke for itself. He knew it had to be a reason also for the tape not being released until 2 weeks later.

fter doing some more investigating he made some calls to a few of his good federal lawyer friends, so that Jay would have a better chance when he went to trial. It was no way in the hell he wasn't going to have to go to trial after killing two police officers, along with having an unlicensed gun and pain pills, "Which are considered a controlled substance, without a prescribed bottle," that are both felonies that were all found in his car. Jay still kept hope in his heart.

PART TWO COMING SOON

ABOUT THE AUTHOR

I'm a "True Hustler" and regardless of if I was using my "Talents" in a legal way or not, I would go out and do what I had to do to provide for my family. I didn't care if what I was hustling was wrong or right, or even what people might say or think of me. I was thinking, "F$$$ what they thought I had to get it." I've always had the "Ambition" to go out and get done what was needed and accomplished, but I would go to jail along the way. So, I started to wonder, why me? That's when I knew it was something I could've been doing different by using my creativity and talents in a completely different way, that's when I gave my life to God. I made the decision to go completely legal and educate the "Streets" with knowledge so that people don't have to go through the same things I had to or make the same mistakes I made in life.

No one person, government official, police officer, or even the president can stop a "True Hustler". I don't understand why people so worried about the president, f$$$ him and do better for your family and community. The devil affects people in different ways, but it's up to you if you let him affect your own ways, STAY WOKE. Even though I switched up my grind, everything I do is for the Streets and the type of environments that I grew up in.

Printed in the United States
By Bookmasters